STAR-CROSSED

THOMAS JAMES TAYLOR

Star-Crossed By Thomas James Taylor

Book Review by Michael Radon (U.S Review of Books)

"You're in love, you idiot,' he said, stepping out of the water. 'You can say good-bye to rational thought."

After growing up in Port Moreton, Amber Powell knew she was destined for greater things. After going off to college, she finds herself estranged from small-town life and the subject of nasty rumors and animosity. Soon those rumors start to take on an ugly reality, and while Amber finds opportunities to make use of her business acumen, she remains a target among men nearby. Daniel Gilmour is a young man returning to the area where he grew up, boarding with Amber's parents in their guest house. A dark secret from his recent past clings to him, though nobody around him seems the wiser. These two young adults gravitate towards each other romantically in a world they both feel lost in and amidst a local Aboriginal legend and a series of horrific murders that seem to involve them somehow.

Thick with personal drama and tragic backstory, this is a book about the kind of melo-drama that often accompanies the emotions of young love. In the case of this book, though, the stakes and circumstances surrounding Amber and Daniel are high enough to match their heightened emotional states. The incorporation of a native tale about a young member of a tribe who is destined to be alone forever ties neatly into the story-telling without being oppressively blunt. There is a fair amount of suspense that bubbles to the surface as the police, primarily a detective, work their way into the cast, and that rising action working in tandem with a budding romance gives this story great accelera-tion and intensity. Readers will find themselves hoping for a happy ending in what seems like a hopeless situation, becoming fully invested in this well-spun tale.

Contents

Prologue

Small children frolic delightedly in the shallows as a languid shore-break washes the white sands with an incoming tide. Parents and other adults stand, cooling themselves in the deeper water, or sit beneath brightly coloured beach umbrellas staring out across the blue-green gulfwaters, occasionally marking the progress of a power boat speeding across the sparkling surface like a skipping stone; the slap of water against its hull and the resonating drone of twin outboards following, time-lagged and out of sync.

Others seek shelter from the sun beneath the jetty, and there between the wooden pylons resembling some ancient, weathered colonnade, laze contentedly in its shadow. Some engaged in idle conversation, perhaps of a domestic nature, a tidbit of gossip or news of an upcoming social event, or repeat, listlessly, the rhetorical question so many others had asked during the past two weeks. How much longer can this heat last?

Midway along the jetty where a set of wooden steps descend steeply to the waterline, many of the area's young people gather the herding instinct strong, drawing them here to see and to be seen, to exhibit their maturing bodies to members of the opposite sex, to admire and to be admired, and to demonstrate their feats of skill and daring in diving from the rails, or in the case of those driven to a more theatrical display, in leaping from the lamp-posts which stand at regular intervals along the structure's length.

At the end of the jetty a vertical steel ladder affords white knuckled access to the reef below; a launching place for the many scuba divers and snorkellers who come here to explore the aquatic reserve beneath the shimmering surface.

Looking shore-ward reveals a picture post-card scene which is in fact dis-played on numerous picture post-cards for sale within the town.

To the left of the jetty the coastline thrusts steeply up to form a bluff. It is layered in limestone and clay of varying colours, rising to almost eighty metres before fall-ing back again to sea-level and another sandy beach on its opposite side. Perched along the top of the bluff are the expensive residences, most two-story with tinted windows, landscaped yards and broad balconies adorned with potted palms and elaborate out-door furniture from which to admire nature's handiwork.

To the left of the jetty (south) is a large building comprising a terrace, a kiosk, surf life-saving clubhouse and a seaside restaurant, all constructed of the same dun-coloured bricks. And just south of this, separated by a car-park and an adjacent avenue, stands the most striking building of the area. A white perimeter wall, six metres high and notably resembling the defensive wall of a fortified palace encircles a stone mansion sit-ting atop a natural hillock, its architecture reminiscent of the German feudal manor of twelfth Century Europe, with its prominent twin turrets, narrow embrasures and crenel-lated walls surrounding the roof-top. Were it not for the fact that it was painted all white, subtly blending with the white sands of the beach it overlooked, it would certainly pres-ent a much more looming landmark than it does.

Southward extends the beach and verging dunes before abruptly terminating at the mouth of the Wunjunjurra, beneath the brow of a limestone cliff. A river old even by geological standards, the Wunjunjurra held special significance to the Aboriginal people who once inhabited this region. It was storeyed to be the route taken by a petulant boy who, one night, angrily left the tribal campsite after being told he was not yet old enough to be included in the hunt which was to take place the following day. His resentment took him far into the night before he realised he had lost his way, but rather than being frightened, his hostility only increased.

In his rage he flailed at the countryside, kicking up the ground with his feet and beating everything down before him with his spear, not realising that until he calmed himself and thought to look up to the stars for guidance, would he ever find his way home. Anger was all the boy knew, and it raged in him for a long long time.

At last he arrived at the coast, very old and embittered, and the people he had expected to discover there were nowhere to be found. Grief returned. Anger once again overtook him so that he blamed the spirits for his plight, cursing their names, insisting that they guide him home. But he could not return to his kind, they each agreed. As the one alone he had been allowed a glimpse of things unknowable. A mistake, the spirits realised, born out of misplaced pity. He was the one alone and must remain so, always.

The ocean, who until this time had been silently watching on, began to roll and churn about. In long, low whispers now it spoke to him. Beneath the waves he was in-vited to rest after so long a journey. Here was a comfortable bed, and when he woke he might then return to his tribe, having dreamt away the sacred knowledge which now excluded him.

Deciding that this was his best choice, and admitting that he was greatly wea-ried by his journey, he agreed. Into the beckoning ocean he walked, and thereby to his death, quite unaware that behind him, having followed the course of his destructiveness and the trail gouged by his dragging spear, flowed his mother's tears.

And so, as generations of spellbound children were once told beside the lam-bent glow of camp-fires—by generations of grave-faced mothers, struggling to conceal their mirth—the reef which lies out in the bay beneath those treacherous waters, is in fact the transmuted form of Wunjunu, the errant child. . . the one alone.

Behind where the children play in the shallows lies the town of Port Moreton, the private residences for the most part built upon the hill which plunges sheer at the coastline in the form of Winton Bluff. The Esplanade, the road which follows along and down its scalloped edge, at its foot turns back inland and from here is known as Fleet Street. After a short distance, through which it dips substantially, it divides Y-shaped around an old two-storeyed building with a timber balcony facing the sea. For many of the town's residents this is the hub of social life. . . the Port Moreton Hotel.

To the right leads out of town, running past a chemist, a doctor's surgery, a petrol station, a C.F.S. depot and a motel before traversing a concrete bridge across the Wunjunjurra, then on to a string of other coastal towns.

The left fork sweeps around the northern wall of the hotel where it is met by the road which runs directly over the hill (Winton Road), past the brush fence enclosed beer garden at the rear of the hotel, and in its remaining length serves as the town's main street, as its name Main Street implies.

It is here that a few small commercial ventures struggle to survive: A curio shop, a second-hand store, a hair salon, hardware, butcher and pottery shop. Not so the town's only supermarket—secure in its monopoly—or the well-positioned deli which carries everything from bobby pins to fish bait, or the posh new restaurant situated across the road from the hotel, which nets its fair share of the tourist trade, particularly in the eve-nings when weary holiday-makers, sunburnt and sore-eyed, retreat from the scorching sands with empty bellies and appetites sharpened by their activities in the fresh, salty air.

It is Saturday, mid-afternoon and very hot. There is little movement on Main Street, although the hotel car-park is almost full. A woman in a brightly printed cotton dress pauses for a moment in front of the display in the pottery shop window. She moves on to the hair salon, parts the coloured plastic beads strung across the doorway and enters. On the opposite side of the street a woman exits the supermarket, pushing a stroller with a plastic shopping bag swinging from one handle. The infant lies in an exhausted sleep beneath the visor.

From beyond the bend at the top of the street, the rumble of a diesel motor dis-turbs the air, announcing the arrival of the afternoon bus from the rail terminus at Mar-ion, some twenty kilometres to the north-east. The dilapidated vehicle lists heavily as it negotiates the bend at inordinate speed, the driver indicating her intention of pulling up at the stop just short of the Port Moreton institute—an intention seemingly ambitious judging the scant few metres remaining in which to complete the manoeuvre. But in apparent contradiction to at least one physical law, and with the stridency of tortured brakes resounding from every solid surface up and down the street, the unwieldy vehicle succumbs to the driver's will as it lumbers to a halt at the designated spot.

A single passenger alights, stepping down onto the verge to be immediately engulfed by a swirling cloud of dust the bus has whipped up from the roadside. He is dressed in jeans and dusty, once-white sneakers, a light-blue denim shirt, and he wears his brown hair tied back into a short pony-tail. Of fair complexion, it is evident he has recently caught a little too much sun. His face, clean shaven, at first glance youthful but with signs of weari-ness about the alert, hazel-coloured eyes. His left hand grips a duffel bag which he swings up to his shoulder while offering a friendly wave to the driver as she guns the bus away much noise and smoke ensuing. He stands, watching after it, the light of amusement dancing in his eyes as it lurches precariously upon turning left to bypass the town's centre, that way to meet with Fleet Street, then out across the bridge to destinations farther south.

From his shirt pocket he withdraws a piece of paper on which a crude map is pencilled. He glances twice from it to the roof-tops along the hillside before appearing to recognize a specific landmark. Satisfied, he returns the paper to his pocket and purposefully sets off across the street.

There is one building which catches a searching eye. It perches against the hillside looking almost to be a natural part of the landscape; large, old and rambling, with white stucco walls and a roof of grey slate tiles. H-shaped, comprised of three steep gables. It is two-storied the slope of the block it occupies such that the upper floor sits at below street-level on the uphill side. On the downhill side, overlooking the township and the Wunjunjurra flood plain beyond, a broad balcony furnished with a mismatched collection of tables and chairs is supported from beneath by tall, wooden stanchions.

The lower level is partially below ground—the hillside having necessarily been excavated to facilitate construction of so large building—so that the side walls disappear into the slope, giving the impression that a landslide had once buried a portion of the house's base and no one had bothered to clear it away, leaving it to become over grown.

From the street the house seems to crouch behind a neglected garden of flowering shrubs and rose-bushes fronted by a dilapidated picket fence. An uneven pathway of slate pieces set in cement leads down to the front verandah stretched between two prominent gables.

Over the porch a wooden signboard, black Gothic on olive back-ground, reads "Powell's Guest-house."

One

Theodore Powell's shirt clung uncomfortably about his corpulent torso, the result of pushing the old Victa back and forth across the slope, cutting swathe after swathe into the dry, almost waist-high grass which had claimed the yard since he had last applied himself to the task six months ago. His face was flushed with the exertion of impelling the mower through the thick growth. With each thrust the under-powered mower laboured and threatened to stall, coughing out balls of mulched grass which lay in neat, parallel rows over the mown surface. The blades regularly met with rocks or occasionally some long-lost artefact such as a shifting spanner or even a grass-entangled deck-chair, which would stop the engine dead each time, evoking a heartfelt oath from the puffing and irritated Ted, resulting in the further aggravation of having to restart the antiquated and unwilling machine.

But for that "Damned snoopy council inspector" he wouldn't be bothering with this. The council had already condemned the house as unsafe for habitation on grounds of structural weakness. With no way to raise the money to finance the considerable renovations outlined in the inspector's report, they would be denied renewal of the lease which terminated in just six weeks time. As a final insult, the inspector had demanded he cut and remove the tall grass from his yard. "An unacceptable fire risk," he had cited; and if the work wasn't done within a week the council would do it for him. . . at a cost of two hun-dred dollars.

Out of obstinacy, and out of an inveterate resentment of authoritarianism, he resolutely set his mind to defying the orders of this "Jumped-up, self-important bureau-crat". It wasn't enough that they had condemned his home—and they were actually talking demolition here but he had been instructed to mow his grass, as if he were nothing more than a forelock-tugging tenant receiving orders from the feudal lord, and it rankled like an open wound. Five days he brooded.

Elizabeth, his wife of forty years, knew just how to handle the situation. She was an uncomplicated, no-nonsense kind of woman who possessed the uncanny ability to read people. . . best of all her Ted. "Just do it and have done," was her one comment on the subject, and she left it at that, quite sure in the knowledge that after his initial show of playing the innocent victim he would succumb to reason, or at least to the additional insult of paying the council two hundred dollars to mow the grass.

This morning when Ted had come to the breakfast table, he was greeted with a bright "Good morning" and a lavish serving of bacon and eggs, prepared by his smiling Beth. Ted loved bacon and eggs. With his cholesterol level, however, his doctor had warned him away from such indulgences, and his wife had assiduously maintained vigil over his diet ever since. To his questioning look she had replied: "A man should eat a hearty breakfast. Just put your plate in the sink when you finish, dear. I'll wash up when I get back from the church."

He knew something was up, but chose not to reply, lest he be manoeuvred into whatever it was she was planning to spring on him when he asked what was up. It wasn't until he had washed down the last of the tasty morsels with hot coffee and went to the sink with the plate, that the plot was revealed to him. Down there in the yard someone had wheeled out the Victa.

Ted chuckled to himself as he forced the protesting machine into an especially troublesome tussock. He had been out here in the sun for hours now, and still he was only half-way done. Picturing the face of that "jumped-up bureaucrat", there in the tus-sock, he went in for a second, then a third assault, sweat and dust stinging his eyes.

I'm gonna die, he thought self-mockingly. The ol' ticker could give out at any moment. I could keel over and croak right here with one leg stuck in the air. And who'd pay for the funeral? Not the flamin' council, that's for sure. I could be here for hours before anyone thought to wonder where the old man was.

He pictured the image of his wife climbing into their bed at the end of the day, content but with a vague feeling that something was not quite as it should be ... some-thing missing ... and him out here, alone and in the dark, leg in the air and providing sustenance for the ants.

He chuckled again, amused with the conjured image and pushed the mower into a concealed chunk of lime-stone, stalling the motor yet again.

"Blast," he hissed, and in a sudden eruption of anger born out of heat, frustration and fatigue, he slammed a steeltoed boot into the side of the lawn-mower. Unexpectedly, the fuel tank tore free, spilling petrol over the searing engine and surrounding grass.

"Christ!" . . . .Ted's heart leapt to his throat as he stared in horror at a potential catastrophe; and not even a garden hose, should it ignite. Then like a transcendental experience a wondrous calm descended over him. As if an obscuring veil had suddenly been lifted, his mind became totally clear. . . precisely focussed. In the bottom drawer of his desk—and he saw it now with absolute clarity— the full cover house insurance policy Beth had insisted on. Tentatively, reverently, he sent up a silent prayer.

Despite her sixty-two years and in defiance of the increasing discomfort suffered due to swelling and stiffening joints, Elizabeth Powell was still a vital and energetic woman. Her morning had been spent behind a food stall at the local church; a fundraiser for underprivileged children, where her cakes and pastries had sold exceedingly well, fetching the tidy sum of thirty six dollars and fifty cents.

Her appearance reflected her chosen station in life as her rubber gloved hands worked dexterously in the sink water, scrubbing potatoes. Beneath a fringe of auburn hair her still handsome features held a slightly harried look, though her brown eyes calm-ly contradicted this perception,suggesting that this, for her, was a natural, even com-fortable state of being. As for her black cotton slacks and white blouse, protected by a crisply starched apron, house guests and family, alike, had affectionately come to know her attire as "the uniform".

Since returning from the church stalls her energies had been directed to preparing an evening meal for six. From the oven came the aroma and sizzle of three roasting chickens which were to be served cold, accompanied by salad. Tomatoes, lettuce, coleslaw and rice with capsicum, corn and peas already sat in glass bowls sealed with plastic wrap, cooling on the refrigerator shelves, and preparation of the last dish was now under way her own very special recipe for potato salad.

With Beth in the kitchen was Amber, her twenty-three-year-old daughter, a strikingly attractive young woman dressed down in jeans and a sloppy Joe, with shoul-der-length hair the colour of. . . well, Amber—the result of a failed attempt at blonding her natural strawberry colour. She sat at a Laminex-topped table, pouring over the pages of a lifestyle cum fashion magazine, her deep-violet eyes enviously soaking up the implied chic and opulence portrayed on each glossy page, imagining how wonderful it must feel to be one of those girls, so slim and so elegant-looking, surrounded by wealth and luxury and handsome, sophisticated men—men who weren't fishermen, bricklayers or footballers but movie actors, corporate executives or formula-one racing drivers. This was mere fantasy, she knew; even sad and pathetic she imagined, but somehow it helped ease her constant anxiety.

Amber seemed to have a very low opinion of herself, apparently oblivious to the fact that she was attractive; denying it in fact. She secretly harboured the self-image of being just the opposite, which tended to sap her self-confidence. Her mother vaguely suspected she was deliberately trying to conceal her femininity, but the notion seemed not to make sense. What possible reason could a girl have for hiding her looks? Every girl wanted to be beautiful. . . ipso facto, the idea was erroneous. Although, when Beth had expressed honest criticism about the colour-change of her daughter's hair, Amber had unexpectedly raged: "It beats the hell out of looking like a god-damned Welsh doxy!"—a comment which hadn't gone down so well, considering her mother's view on blasphemy, and especially in view of the fact they were a Welsh family, and damned proud of it, if Beth had a say! But had she been less offended and swift in reproach, she may have recognised the clue.

Amber hadn't always been this way. Not as quiet and unassuming as she now was. After doing very well at high school she had ambitions of entering the business world, eager to succeed in what she saw as still being mainly regarded a male domain. Succeeding in this was important, though the underlying motivation for it was never perfectly clear. For her the challenge itself was inspiration enough. To climb high on the ladder of success and be somebody in this world, not just a small town girl.

Ted and Beth were proud of their daughter's ambition, even if they didn't quite understand what she meant by success, or so strong a desire for it. They were uncompli-cated people, hard-working and content to live quietly on the modest income generated by the guesthouse, accepting life's challenges in typically stoic fashion and tackling their problems one at a time as they arose.

In their daughter they saw something special, a spark of something which ought not be allowed to stifle through want of opportunity. They loved Amber very much—Loved her enough to send her away to a business college at Malvern where they paid for her schooling and accommodation from the money they had squirreled away for their retirement. She had been happy there, an A-student no less, working hard through each term, making new friends and returning home to stay with the family at each opportunity.

With each visit she sought to maintain contact with her old school friends, each time be-ing confronted with change as her once high spirited girl-friends seemed to conform and fade into the general community of Port Moreton. Already, three had fallen pregnant.

Had been coerced into having an abortion and had surreptitiously moved to another town. Another had married and was totally committed to making a home for her hus-band who worked on the council, and their as yet unborn child. Of the third, Maureen Baxter, for whom she had always felt a special affection, she found her living alone in a tiny weather-board bungalow near the beach. A single mother living on a meagre in-come while her family had all but disowned her.

As time went on these friendships became increas-ingly strained. More and more were marrying, becoming housewives and mothers; and much to her distress and dismay, she noticed a growing animosity being directed towards her.

To them, Amber had come to represent something they could never be. She was beautiful, bright and steadily working towards a career. She would, of course, be a big success, and they couldn't help but resent her for it. Even worse than that, each time Amber arrived back from her "posh college" and her "snooty friends" in Malvern, their husbands and boy-friends would act like over-sexed ado-lescents, vying for her attention, ogling her whenever they thought they weren't being observed by the missus, and gathering in small, murmuring groups, trading lascivious remarks and generally airing their carnal desires. It was hardly surprising then, that spiteful rumours began to circulate, initiated by disgruntled wives and girlfriends whose jealousy demanded they destroy their rival; if not physically then certainly by reputation. But exasperatingly, the stories portraying her as a bed-hopping slut served only to make her all the more desirable to their unwor-thy partners.

Amber's first year at college had been a hard slog, being primarily concerned with general business practices and taxation, but she had worked assiduously, happy in the pursuit of her dream.

With Investment Management and Stock-market, the featured subjects of the second year, she found greater reward, which translated into excellent grades through the first half of the year, leaving only six more months before she graduated with a certificate graded high enough to maybe get her a start with one of the big corporations. Already she had encouraging replies from the prospective employers she had canvassed, and each had urged her to contact them when her results came through.

The final break of that year, Amber was as happy as she thought anyone could be. There was one thing, though, but it wasn't really a problem. . . not really. And it didn't bother her that much anyway. There had been two boy-friends. Both were pleas-ant enough, in their way. They had taken her to dinner, the cinema and that sort of thing, but she had never. . . They had tried, of course. "All men do." But they just weren't. . .right. Then again, no, perhaps she wasn't being totally honest with herself.

It was really quite difficult to know how she felt about it, and it was becoming a mild source of embarrassment for her, what with the way her female college friends were all so open about such things. They had all had sex, and weren't a bit afraid to talk about it. Inevitably they had gotten around to Amber, where she sat on the lawn with the girls, eating canteen sandwiches and cakes while titillating one another with stories drawn, seemingly, from a wealth of erotic experience. To her own chagrin and complete amazement, she heard herself perpetrate a fleshy fabrication which, at best, could only be rated as plausible. . .possibly even bizarre. But how could she admit to being a twenty-threey-ear-old virgin? They all said she was the best looking. They all expected to hear. . .something!

It was in the spring break that Amber tentatively accepted an invitation to a drive-in movie with a young man named Barry Curino, a tall, tanned and rather handsome individual who worked locally as a carpenter and occasionally as a deck-hand on the fishing boats when things were slow. They had mutual friends, he pointed out. Funny how they hadn't crossed paths before this. Hard not to in a town this size. Malvern? Oh, well that explained it.

She thought him a charming and personable fellow, perhaps even a bit of a hunk. No, she had nothing planned for this evening and, Yes, all right, she would go with him to the Picton drive-in theatre to watch Overlord. There was just time enough for her to change her clothes while he went for beer and ice to put in the cooler, then off into the evening they drove in his shiny black panel van.

He paid for the tickets at the gate and drove to a position "away from the rowdies" which put them well back from the screen in a rather secluded spot. He bought her potato chips and a soft drink from the kiosk when she declined his offer of a beer, and they chatted for a while about movies they had seen, scoring them out of ten. He asked her about college and about what it was like living away from home, to which she replied glibly, though she was pleased that he should be interested enough to ask.

He talked about work, carpentry and fishing boats, telling stories of gnarly old sea dogs and stormy weather out at sea. She listened and smiled, even laughed at the appropriate moments, doing her best not to let show in her face that her interest was beginning to wane.

Each time he paused to reach behind the seat for a beer, Amber seized the opportunity to steer the conversation towards something which might be of mutual interest. And beer after beer, he would interrupt, remembering the V-8 Chevy he used to own, the cruel jokes he had played on the "wops" or "reffos," people he considered to be "fair game," or some other equally ill-bred pursuit.

Amber realised she had made a terrible mistake. She desperately wanted to go home, but the movie had been running for only forty minutes and she was worried he might be offended. By asking questions about what was happening on the screen she discovered she was able distract him, enough to get him interested in the film, and for a while, at least, they both settled back to enjoy the movie.

A couple of times he tried to persuade her to have a beer, but she managed, politely, to resist, confessing that beer tended to put her to sleep.

Several times in the next half-hour Amber was aware of being vaguely uncomfortable. The feeling persisted, increasing steadily in intensity until it became a palpable presence in the air. At the periphery of her vision she discovered that he wasn't watching the movie at all, he was watching her. The atmosphere in the car was suddenly oppressive. Her cheeks began to flush she could feel them glowing. She could feel his eyes surveying her, sizing her up. Instinct told her for what.

"I think I'd like to go home now," she managed tremulously, her throat constricting.

"You think you're clever, don't you." He replied, ignoring her obvious plea.

She was unable to move. Fear gripped her with icy fingers which seemed to be crushing the breath out of her. She wanted to say something, anything to break the terrible spell, but her throat was so dry. All she could do was sit like something wooden and stupid, staring out at the confusion of movement on the distant screen: Spence! Spence! Don't worry buddy, we're coming out to get you. Just hang on. You can do it. Think of all those women waiting for you back on Orion Four.

"You're very desirable," he said in a voice he might use in discussing the weather. Then sardonically, "But you know that already, don't you."

His touch made her wince. "It's easy to see why you're such a popular girl."

The knot in her throat choked her startled cry, turning it into a whimper.

"Yes, you like it. I've heard."

With his hand gripping her thigh, he dragged her across the vinyl seat towards him. Paralysing fear overwhelmed her—her ability to reason, sapped. Her breath came in short, hard fought for gasps as his hand pushed searchingly up under her skirt. In a sudden paroxysm she arched rigidly back into the seat, her flesh fighting his gross violations. Ineffectually, she slapped down at his arm, tried to scream NO! but it only emerged as a long, ragged squeal.

"Oh yes-s-s," he hissed. "You sure do like it all right." Her mind reeled. Why couldn't she make him stop!!

Fear changed to terror when she felt her panties being torn from her. She lashed out with fingers curled, nails catching him across the face in a raking motion and drawing blood instantly. He hit her so hard that bursts of white light exploded inside her head.

"Come on, you slut," he growled." You know you want it." Then suddenly and viciously he twisted her arm up behind her back, and terror turned into unbridled horror. With a choice of even greater pain or compliance, she was forced into a kneeling position up on the seat. He twisted her painfully until she faced away from him, and with brutish force bent her until her face was pressed against the upholstery.

How long he used her, she didn't know. Her memory would later refuse to supply the details, though the shame and humiliation would remain. The drive home was nothing more than a daze, with vaguely recognisable landmarks passing by.

He had driven her home, said good night as if nothing had happened, then driven away leaving her stunned and confused at the front gate of the guest-house, with a pair of torn panties clenched in her hand.

At the end of the break she returned to Malvern and the college, feeling so degraded and ashamed that she was unable to admit to anybody what had happened to her. Perhaps, she reasoned, it was her fault it happened. . . some defect in her character. Why, after all, hadn't she made him stop? It wasn't really rape; she had let him do those horrible things to her. Didn't that make her something dirty?

While she struggled for passable grades, unable to maintain concentration in the classroom and feeling strangely cut off from the other girls, the nights alone in her tiny apartment were more than she could endure. She didn't know what was happening to her, and considered the possibility she was losing her mind. For the first time in her young and, until now, happy life, suicide presented itself as an option; lambently entic-ing amid the gathering murk in that room.

The Port Moreton rumour mill gained sudden momentum, grist supplied by Amber's rapist himself. Proud of his conquest, he had taken to boasting about his night at the drive-in; his drinking companions only too willing to lend their attention to his sordid account.

His telling of the night made him an instant celebrity, even won him a few beers from his admiring audience. He was asked over and over to tell it, and each time there was some new detail remembered, a little something extra to delight his avid listeners; the description of Amber's performance being limited only by the baseness of his imagination.

Predictably there were other, similar stories put into circulation, the creations of intensely envious young men who impetuously claimed also to have been " fucked by her;" and by vindictive women whose out-rage bordered on distraction, the most bizarre stories were concocted. They had yet to learn that every sex-hungry man in town be-came increasingly fascinated the more lurid the tale.

Amber's spirit had been crushed. Her dreams of success were broken and scattered, the whole world was obscured by a fog of uncertainty and self-doubt. By the time she arrived home on the bus, late one Friday afternoon, just two weeks before her final exams, there was only a superficial resemblance to the vibrant young woman of just those few months ago.

Her parents were greatly concerned. She looked so ill—so pale. And something about her eyes. . . their lustre was gone. A doctor was called to the house despite Amber's weak protestations. Nervous exhaustion was diagnosed, plenty of bed-rest and home cooking pre-scribed. . . with never a mention of how near she had come to her goal. They loved their daughter and they were justifiably proud of the effort she had put into her studies. There would be no expressions of regret, and there would be no probing questions about what had laid her so low. With the benefits of what only a loving family could provide, Amber's condition began to improve; slowly but steadily over the following weeks of the Christmas season, she hastened towards a full recovery.

With a terrific effort she banished the memory of her greatest failure to the nether regions of her mind. Sometimes, though, and then only deep in the night, would the torment rise up like a scorpion's tail to sting her from sleep.

Early in the new year a friend of her mother, Mrs Grieves, who owned the second-hand shop on Main Street, called to say she was looking for someone to lend a hand in the shop. Amber detected the conspiracy immediately, and accepted the position anyway, glad to have something to alleviate her growing restlessness and Mrs Grieves had hired herself a very capable assistant.

Amber totally immersed herself in the work and was somewhat surprised in discovering how much pleasure she derived from it. Just an old shop job, was the way she had seen it but there was a little more to it than that.

Mrs Grieves held a pawnbroker's licence, which meant the ability to estimate the value of goods was important. Items of jewellery were always the trickiest, and certainly anything with strong sentimental value. Having to tell a woman that her precious ring was no more than zircon and gold plate was not an enjoyable task.

With her bookkeeping skills Amber Mrs Grieves' laborious system, which wasn't so much a system as an inefficient routine which had been devoutly practiced for almost twenty-six years. Items were numbered and logged; every taxation allowance was taken advantage of; useless stock was liquidated in an End-of-Summer Sale to make room for goods more in demand; and on her suggestion money was spent on building new shelves for better presentation of stock, providing the added benefit of reclaiming valuable floor space. Her innovations proved themselves successful in the ledger book, with a thirty seven percent net increase over any previous six-month peri-od. "You're a treasure," Mrs Grieves was fond of saying to her. "And a fine catch for any young man."

Late one autumn evening, a telephone call to the guest-house summoned Amber to Mrs Grieves' bedside. She was dying, that much was evident by her pallor and dark-lidded eyes. The doctor was with her, no one else. . . she was a childless widow. And as Amber entered her bed-room she was resting quietly with her eyes closed.

She came up beside the bed, sat down gently on the edge and took the old lady's hands in her own. Mrs Grieves opened her eyes, and seeing Amber there offered a fey smile. "Dear girl," she whispered. "Thank-you for coming," and in that moment slipped peacefully away.

Before she left, the doctor handed Amber an envelope with her name on it, written in Mrs Grieves' bold hand, saying: "For you, Miss Powell. She thought the world of you, you know."

With no surviving family and because of Amber's dedication and friendship, Mrs Grieves had bequeathed the shop to her. Saddened though she was by the old lady's passing, she saw the positiveness of it—saw that life had offered her a second chance. Dear Mrs Grieves, thought Amber with great affection. You planned this all along.

There was a curio shop on the corner of Main and Clarke Street. A shop she occasionally called into when business was slow, just to chat with the proprietor, Mr Edwards. He was barely making a living, he confided. The population was too small and people just were not interested in the "odds and ends" like he had to sell. She could have made some suggestions for improving the business, but she resisted the urge.

The shop itself was a curiosity. She liked the way it curved around the corner, the yellow tiles with red borders and the large display windows under the raking verandah. There was opportunity here. Some of the stock was quite valuable, too. The books, for instance, which were stacked untidily at the back of the shop. This illustrated to her his ineptness for the business. Particularly, he had done nothing to capture the tourists' interest, whom, she felt sure, would be delighted to browse through such a quaint little shop, had they known of its existence. It had good earning potential, her instinct told her so; and when she made him a conservative purchase offer, he agreed, relieved that someone would unburden him of it.

The talk started up again, maybe because of her good fortune in being left old lady Grieves' business. It was even suggested she may have done the old girl in—"You wouldn't know with a bitch like that" though nobody really believed it. Whatever the reason, like a favourite toy rediscovered it was picked up and played with again.

At the post office one day she noticed two men leering at her. She stood her ground and was about to voice protest when one of the men made a disgusting gesture. Her cheeks burned with suddenly remembered shame. They knew! She wanted to run but couldn't. She was paralysed again, like she had been that night. She could only stand and tremble until the clerk caught her attention. In jerky, barely controlled movements, she reached for the door and escaped to the street.

This was one more titillating story for the barroom. A good one too. She had exhibited embarrassment, confirming beyond doubt that the stories about her were all true.

The experience had shaken her to the core. Did they know or didn't they? Or maybe it was just guilt and paranoia. The way they looked at her, like she was meat in a butcher shop window. And that thing he did with his thumb. They knew, and if they knew. . . God! how many others? And it dawned on her, then, that her shameful secret might be common knowledge throughout the town.

It was just two days later when a second affront took place. Four teenage boys came into her store and began browsing, concentrating mainly on the CD and cassette-players. She was behind the glass-top counter, cleaning some pieces of jewellery, taking care not to be overtly watchful of them, because there had been some small items go missing over the past few weeks, and she was hopeful of catching the culprits in the act.

After a few minutes they had browsed their way to the end of a shelf, and were now standing quite near. . . not especially interested in the kitchen utensils displayed there.

"Can I help you with something?" she asked, which produced a round of chuckles from the boys.

After a moment's hesitation one stepped forward, approaching the counter.

From his pocket he withdrew a fifty-dollar note and placed it before her.

Mystified, she looked from it to his wide-eyed, young face. "What is it you want? You want to buy something?"

Again chuckles, and a lurking suspicion now growing in Amber's mind.

"Go on," prompted one of the rearguard.

"Is fifty enough?" he said, and pretended to chew gum during the subsequent silence.

Amber had a hunch what was coming, but there was always the chance of being wrong. "I'm not a mind-reader," she said, losing her patience.

The boy lifted the fifty from the glass and waved it in the air between them. "Do the four of us for fifty? My brother says you give the meanest head in the state."

She struck him without knowing she had reacted. A slap so hard it resounded around the walls, and in a flurry of movement the four boys were gone, their hoots of laughter carrying along the street.

Amber remained at the counter, tears welling in her eyes. She was frightened. There was no doubting this manifestation of her worst fear. But now anger was part of the equation too. She had to concentrate on that anger, her only source of strength—or else fail, and failure was something she would never endure again.

Towards her goal of buying the curio shop Amber approached the local bank for assistance, and on the afternoon of her appointment she was ushered through to a private office where Lester Bishop, Branch Manager, rose from behind his oak desk in greeting.

Lester Bishop was a big man, barrel-chested, with short greying hair and a ruddy complexion. At forty-five he prided himself on his fitness, achieved through many years active membership with the Port Moreton Surf Life-saving Club. A handful of trophies, prominent on the shelf behind him, attested to his achievements as a steersman in the surf boat competitions.

After the cursory formalities and an offer of refreshment, Amber got down to her simple proposal: an eighteen thousand dollar loan, with her shop as collateral, for the purchase of Mr Edwards' property. She did not want to mortgage her shop—she would not relinquish ownership out of respect for Mrs Grieves—but she would sign a standard loan agreement, agreeing to settle from the sale of the shop should she be unable to meet the contract schedule. She had brought her deed to the property, proving ownership; she brought the ledger with her, proving there was a healthy income, and she carefully explained her plans for the curio shop, how she would transform it into a healthy and viable business.

Lester Bishop was having some difficulty focusing his attention. It was a fair proposal and she was putting forward an adequate case for herself. She would have her loan. Head office would approve it on his recommendation. But there, sitting right across from him was the Port Moreton sex nymph. . . the infamous Amber. Nothing else much mattered just then.

Her face was that of a temptress, fresh, clear, belying the burning passions which simmered in those wonderful eyes. He watched as she spoke, those crimson lips, upturned ever so slightly at the edges, tauntingly. The stories of what those lips were capable of. . . He repositioned himself in his chair. It was time to respond.

He explained that her decision not to mortgage posed a slight problem. He believed in her business instincts, but it was up to head office to approve a loan under the conditions she had asked for. He allowed time for uncertainty and a trace of disappointment to reg-ister on her face. "But if I speak to the right person, we might inspire a special degree of consideration in your case." Already he had formulated a crude plan to quench his carnal desire.

In maintaining the charade he was obliged to delay things for the appropriate length of time, providing the semblance of ordinary, workaday routine. What his staff perceived as a certain preoccupation duringthis period, was, in fact, the effect of mounting anxiety, and the piquancy of his expectation of implementing the final act of his pro-duction. Every rumour he had ever heard came to mind as he sat in the quiet of his private office; unbidden, at first, then willed from his memoryto be savoured with frantic scenarios of his own lurid design.

He telephoned her at work, late on the second day, informing her that his per-sonal support had won the day; after initial resistance the pragmatic official had relented and acceded to the terms she had requested.

Amber's response came over the line just the way he had hoped spirited ex-pressions of relief and excitement, and heartfelt gratitude for his personal involvement. She couldn't thank him enough, while he assumed the role of the modest bank Manager whose job it was to encourage local businesses—especially initiatives taken by intelligent and productive young ladies like herself. If she liked, she could drop by the bank, after hours, by which time he would have the necessary documents drawn up and ready for her signature. If she rang the bell at the rear door, around seven, he would be there to let her in.

She agreed without hesitation, elated in the knowledge that soon the curio shop would be hers; an acquisition demanded by her deep and abiding need to be someone.

Her enthusiasm brought her to the bank's rear door nearly ten minutes early. She pressed the button marked "a.h." and stood back from the doorway making quick, final adjustments to her clothing, recognising the fact that she was, perhaps, just the tiniest bit nervous.

After a short wait, Lester Bishop appeared behind the glass. He fumbled with the keys, then had trouble with the lock, but, finally, swung open the door. "Right on time," he grinned, gesturing for her to cross over the threshold. And once she was in, he relocked the door.

"Damned weather, eh?" he said, leading the way. "How was business today?"

"Good. It's been steady all week." It felt strange being in the bank with no one around. . . at night!

On Lester Bishops desk was an expensive-looking lamp, his executive pen set, and placed squarely in the centre, the document.

"That's it," he said, turning to Amber to observe her expression, and was rewarded with a look of delight. "Sit and read it through before you sign. I'll pour us a drink, shall I?"

Amber watched as a sliding wood panel revealed a small fridge and a mini bar.

From the fridge Bishop brought out a stout, green bottle.

"Champagne?" she simpered, affecting mild enthusiasm, though normally she was averse to the drink.

She sat down at the desk to begin inspection of the contract, but as soon as the glasses were filled, Bishop interrupted her by placing her glass on the page. "There you go, Amber. You don't mind if I call you Amber, do you?"

"No, Mr Bishop," she replied, lifting the glass from the paper. "Please, call me Lester. Well, here's cheers," he said, hastening to clink glasses before she placed it aside, and she followed his lead in taking a swallow.

"After all, we're almost partners in this, in a sense. Aren't we?" "Partners?" Amber repeated. "Oh, yes, you've been marvellous

Mister. . . ah, Lester." "Bottoms up," he prompted.

"Yes, er . . .bottoms up." And she drained her glass, which he promptly refilled.

She returned her attention to the document while Bishop moved off to one side where his interest was seemingly divided between the furniture and fixtures of the room, and the proximity of the tantalising young woman alone in his office with him.

Amber was thorough in her perusal, taking care to look for anything ambiguous, or even bold departures from the requirements she had articulated. Her excitement of the moment was tempered with a cool business acumen; unless everything was in accord with her wishes, the document would go unsigned until the proper adjustments were made.

Bishop's nerve wavered. It was the silence that did it. And although the air-conditioning maintained a steady twenty-three degrees, beads of sweat gathered on his brow and above his top lip. After the second glass of champagne, he poured himself another, dabbed at his brow with his handkerchief and took a steadying breath.

"You're not drinking," he intoned jovially. "Don't you enjoy expensive champagne?"

Amber looked up at last, folded closed the pages and turned to look at him. "I don't usually, but. . ." She lifted the glass and took a swallow.

"Are you happy with the terms, Amber?" "Yes," she nodded. "Good—good. I'm glad. Let's make a toast to your success then."

He grabbed the bottle off the bar and came over to refill her glass. "I'm sure you're going to do very well in your new venture. You're a very clever young lady."

Amber was about to tell him that she didn't really want any more to drink, that she wasn't used to it. But instead, she found herself saying: "Thank-you. It's kind of you to say so, but without dear Mrs Grieves generosity I shouldn't be doing half so well."

"Nonsense," he chided. "You have talent, young lady. Edna saw it in you. If not her, then someone else would have recognised it, and beenmad not to put you on their payroll."

Bishop saw the opening and raised his glass. "A hearty toast to dear Edna Grieves, eh? Bottoms up."

For some reason "Bottoms up" made her want to giggle. She checked the urge and, in memory of Mrs Grieves, took a good swallow of champagne.

She was feeling good. She realised she was really happy for the first time in so long. Before her was a document which would broaden her business interests; and she was actually sipping bubbly, after hours, with a bank manager. It made her feel spe-cial.

"Let me use one of your lovely pens?" she said, indicating the executive pen set on his desk.

"Eh? Yes, of course," he chuckled. "Use my lovely pen, by all means."

She was suddenly very appealing to him extremely appealing. She was grateful, as he knew she would be. The drink had loosened her up. He let his eyes feast on her feminine form as she stretched herself across the desk to reach for the pen, her firm young breasts pressing against the delicate material of her blouse. She was magnificent, and he ached to have her, there, then.

She signed the contract. "Now you," she said, handing him the pen. He moved up beside her, and the proximity, the smell of her sent blood surging to every part of his anatomy. As she handed him the pen, their hands touched for the briefest of moments. It was overpoweringly intoxicating.

"There," he said, finishing his signature with a flourish. "Signed, sealed and delivered."

Now he was nervous again, so nervous he could feel himself beginning to tremble. Or was it excitement? He couldn't tell the difference just then. "We must have another toast, now that it's official."

"I don't know if I should," Amber demurred. She gave her face a tiny slap. "I think I might be getting drunk," she giggled.

"Nonsense. Refreshing after a hard day's work. A hard-working woman like you should allow herself a little luxury. Especially on a day like this. A successful business-woman with expanding horizons?" The allusion drove to her deepest need. Amber was totally defenceless against such flattery. To be respected by someone in Mr Bishop's position was the realisation of a long-held dream. A dream which, at one time in her life—one terrible time—looked to be hopelessly out ofreach. "Okay," she agreed blithely. "To what?"

Bishop sat himself on the desk so that he was looking down at her. Her face was tilted up to the light, showing off her lovely features to best effect, framed by pale red-golden hair as lustrous as silk. Her eyes flashed violet under the fluorescent lights. She was smiling up at him, and it occurred to him then that what he was feeling for her might just be wrong.

"To beauty," he said awkwardly.

"No, that's not good enough," she said, waving her hand dismissively; and becoming pensive, she took to tapping a finger against her pursed lips, searching the ceiling as though the answer might be there.

"I know!" she beamed, finger upraised and looking him squarely in the eyes.

"To happiness. How about that?" she asked, smiling. "To happiness," he repeated. "Bottoms up."

She drank half the glass before she began to laugh. The champagne went down the wrong way and, with a splutter, it spilled down her chin and over her blouse. While she coughed and spluttered and continued to laugh, Bishop produced his handkerchief and moved to dab at herblouse.

"No, it's all right," Amber said huskily, struggling to regain composure.

"Mr Bishop, really. . . no need to fuss."

Bishop's last vestige of self-control was in tatters. The handker-chief he let fall, his hands were firmly on her breasts, squeezing and pushing upwards. A salacious, almost malign expression contorted his features.

Long-buried fear rushed up from the depths. "Mister Bish..! Mist-aah!" Her breath came in ragged bursts as she slapped in frenzied effort to dislodge his hands.

"Oh come now, Amber. No need for all this," and he bent to kiss her, finding it necessary to hold her head firmly between his hands.

She struggled but could not resist his surprising strength, as an old horror crawled out from a dark place to seize hold of her senses.

He felt her yielding, mistook her ragged breath for sexual arousal. When he withdrew just a fraction she found room to push up out of the chair, propelling him backwards. "Nooooooo," she pleaded, and it emerged from her throat like the creaking of a rusty hinge as she stood with her arms crossed and pressed against her breast. Her eyes were fully dilated, full of fear and virtually unseeing.

Bishop stood staring at her, seeing only what he wanted to see and as randy as hell. She was vulnerable, beautiful, and the hottest little bitch he had ever laid eyes on.

"I mean to have you," he almost whispered. "Damned if I don't." But her fear had already claimed her ability to comprehend.

"You've screwed every man Jack in these parts. What about me? You too good for me? You can't just turn it on and off when it suits, youlittle harlot."

He made a grab for her arm, caught it and dragged her staggering to him. In a desperate manoeuvre he had her going backwards over the desktop. Frenzied now, his own breath rasping, he worked hurriedly to divest her of strategic articles of clothing, thrilled by her lack of resistance. She wanted it after all. He knew it. She was the town whore and she loved it.

Catalepsy rendered her powerless while he let loose his obsession on her flesh, her weak protestations being interpreted as expressions of pleasure and serving only to increase his fervour. "You're beautiful," he found himself gasping. "You're so fucking beautiful" as though she might appreciate these words. And he remembered, he had actually been intimidated by that beauty. Her loveliness had almost shamed him. . . him! But now he was in control, and he would show this wanton creature just what sort of retribution a man like him could exact from a pretentious little whore.

Reality ceased to exist, it had been usurped by a terrible nightmare. The despicable things he did to her were viewed both with repugnance and detachment, as though she were disembodied. And horror had its limit, she discovered. When fear invaded the brain with such force, the senses became overloaded, no longer able to register the devastating violence of the assault. Nightmare it was, but her mind had found a place to take refuge from the maelstrom which had swallowed her world, and very nearly her sanity.

From somewhere deep within, a quiet, reasoning voice spoke to her. "Your mind is your own," it told her. "Remember. No one can take that away."

She was on her feet again. Had she dressed herself? Her clothes were dishevelled, her stockings were twisted all around. She hurt where he had been.

Bishop's face was up close to her own. He was saying something. ". . . with you?" He was shaking her roughly." . . .sakes girl . . .yourself together." He looked worried, even frightened. ". . .anyone about this. . ." He propelled her through the rooms and up to the back door ". . .or I'll tear up the contract. You hear me? Everyone knows what you are anyway. Who'd believe you? Be a good girl and I'll see about your loan." The door locked behind her and shewas alone in the night.

Amber was at work the next day. She was resilient, determined. She had learned from her first experience of rape, things can be locked away. Keep it locked, tight, lest it tears you down. To fail again simply could not be endured.

She was at work again on the following day. To her customers there were no outward signs to betray her torment, but by her family she was pressed to admit to "feel-ing a bit out of sorts" when they questioned her sullen disposition. She was at work on the third day, holding her own, and now there was even an air of purpose about her.

On Monday the news was all over town. Lester Bishop had been found dead in his home. His house-cleaner had let herself in and found him tied to the bed-posts, *"stakers, and slit from gullet to gonads"*.

On Tuesday the bank contacted Amber. They had discovered her loan contract, apologised for the delay and invited her to come in and pick up the cheque.

"Amber? . . .Amber," called her mother from the kitchen sink. Will you put down that magazine, dear, and go ring the fire brigade. You father has set light to the back garden."

Two

The source of the smoke became apparent as he reached the top of the rise on the hillside. Two fire units were parked on the road while men in khaki overalls unfurled hoses and hurried down the slope to the rear of the house. Drawing level with the open side gate, he halted, watched them work with practiced efficiency, smoke billowing sky-wards as the flames ceased their creeping advance under a cross-fire of high pressure water sprays. Satisfied that all was well, he heaved the duffel bag to his opposite shoulder and continued on to the front gate, down the pathway and onto the porch.

The first knock went unanswered. No doubt they were out back watching the action. He tried once more.

This time, movement seen distorted through the frosted glass panes in the door. The door swung open to reveal a young woman with yellow-orange hair, wearing jeans and a raggedy grey wind cheater several sizes too large.

"Hi. My name's Daniel Gilmour," he said, smiling. "I telephoned two days ago. . . about accommodation?" he added, not sure what to make of the expressionless face before him.

Amber looked at the man standing on the porch. His face was sunburnt. He needed a shave, and there was something unsettling about men with pony-tails. "Just a minute."

The girl went back inside, leaving him standing with a slightly bemused expres-sion on his face. The rose-bushes beside the porch were beginning to wilt, he noticed. A gecko emerged from a large crack in the wall, scampered up into the shadows beneath the eaves. Footsteps approaching. . .

A buxom woman wearing a navy-blue apron arrived at the door-way. "Hello," she smiled. "Daniel? I'm sorry to keep you waiting. I told my daughter, yesterday, we were expecting our new guest today. I'm Mrs Powell, I talked to you on the phone. But call me Beth. Do come in from the heat."

"Thank-you." He stepped by her while she held back the door, into the coolness of the old stone build-ing. His eyes were slow in adjusting from the brilliance of outside, but slowly, through the relative gloom, the interior became discernible. A large room full of furni-ture. A long table beside well stocked book shelves, an old-style radiogram, television set, two old sofas and two armchairs with a tall reading-lamp positioned behind one. The atmosphere felt immediately inviting and com-fortable, he thought.

"This is the guest's room," said Beth, pleased by what she read in his face. "The front room. And behind that partition," she pointed to where hinged wood panels blocked a wide entrance," is the dining room. Dinner is at six o'clock. Breakfast, usually juice, toast, bacon and eggs or cereal, is served between six-thirty and eight-thirty. Lunch is left for the guests to provide for themselves.

But if you're working I'll prepare sand-wiches if the sup-plies are paid for at the end of each week."

"Yes, that's fine," he affirmed.

"Off of the dining room, back there," she said, indicating behind the blank wall to the left of the dining room entrance "is our private quarters mine and Ted's, my husband. That's out of bounds, unless it's important. All right?"

Daniel nodded.

"The kitchen," she pointed to the restaurant-type serving door in the central wall. "My sacred domain," she smiled. "Even Ted knows not to get in my way when I'm preparing the meals. Now. . ."

She moved off towards a passageway to the left of the kitchen, at the end of which a door opened to a the broad balcony at the back of the house.

"Out here," she said, leading him up to the rail, "is a nice place to sit and look out at the view. Plenty of chairs and tables, as you see." Daniel looked down at the charred yard. A small gathering watched as a fireman searched for anything smouldering. The girl who had opened the door to him was one. The others he would meet later, he expected.

"My husband's way of not mowing the grass," Beth intoned dryly.

"Effective anyway."

"If somewhat extreme," she added, permitting a trace of humour in her tone.

"Down here on the left," she pointed and moved towards the east wing, "is your shower and bathroom facility. Downstairs guests have their own," and she indicated the wooden stairway descending against the rear wall. "And through here are the rooms."

Beside the extending wall of the eastern wing a low doorway gave access to a cool, dark passage, thH floor covered with blue carpet. To the left, only one door, presumably leading back into the front room. To the right, and one at the far end of the passage, were five doors.

"Number five," said Beth, pushing open the door nearest. "I hope you'll like it. It's nearest the facilities and balcony."

Daniel stepped inside. It wasn't bad. Not big, but not as small as many rooms he had stayed in for double the price. Dressing table and drawers, wardrobe, single bed and bedside table, and a writing desk under the window. The fly-screen was clogged with dust but. . .

"This is just fine, thank-you." He tossed his bag on the bed in gesture. Beth was not quite ready to leave however. Her innate curiosity had yet to be appeased. Over the telephone he had sounded a much older man. If a voice could be said to be weighted, and with what she didn't know. . . well, weighted was the impression she got. But he was a young man, early thirties, she judged. And his eyes suggested the presence of a natural interest and thoughtfulness which Beth—a trifle surprised at herself for doing so—found herself hoping were the discernible signs of an eligible bachelor.

"What do you do, Daniel? My son works in the building trade. He could ask around for you, if you need work."

"Thanks, but I've put a bit aside from my last stint. I intend taking it easy." He reached into his back pocket. "Twelve months straight will do me for a while. Now, if

I pay you for eight days," he said, flipping open a dilapidated wallet. "That'll see me through 'til um. . .cripes. Is it Saturday or Sunday today? I've been on the road so long." "Saturday," Beth obliged. "But you don't have to-"

"Two hundred, right?"

"Yes, thank-you." Beth accepted the money extended to her.

"Were you working in Perth?"

"No. I just called from there when I came down from the Kimberlies. Exploration work for the mining companies."

"Oh." said Beth, wanting to ask more questions but realising it was time to allow her new guest some privacy. "Well, I'll leave you to relax after your long journey. Make yourself at home now, won't you. The front room is for everybody. Television, books, radio. The balcony is a nice place to sit and meditate, and dinner is at six o'clock. Oh, and there's a clean towel here behind your door, in case you want to freshen up. Okay?"

"Thank-you Mrs Powell. I might just do exactly that."

"And one last thing, Daniel," she said, halting by the door and affecting mock displeasure. "If you persist in calling me Mrs Powell, you leave no choice but to address you as Mr Gilmour. So what's it going to be?"

Daniel's face split with a broad smile. "Thank-you, Beth."

Beth replied with a crooked smile of her own. "That's more like it young fellow." And she quietly pulled the door closed as she departed.

The smile gradually diminished as the effects of fatigue irresistibly began to unravel the fabric of the long,

long day. Lowering himself to sit on the corner of the bed, he caught sight of his image reflected back at him from the dressingtable mirror.

"You look like you feel," he said to himself, grimly. He peered at his wrist-watch, his eyes focussing with difficulty. "Ten to three," and reached across to drag the duffel bag towards him. He unzipped it enough to root out a small travelling alarm clock, set it for five o'clock and placed it on the bedside table. After a thoughtful pause he pulled the zipper further along, exposing two calico bags crammed full with something lumpy. He patted them, "Happy days," he said, without enthusiasm, and after a moment's further contemplation he zipped the bag closed again and consigned it to the floor of the ward-robe.

As though unable to remain in his feet a moment longer, he let himself fall backwards onto the bed, a sigh of exhaustion escaping him. His eyes were closed with the weight of forty hours sleeplessness, but his mind was maddeningly alive with pieces of random information dancing a chaotic mazurka the afterimage of the long road still rushing in towards him, as thought projected onto the back of his eyelids in vivid surreal-scope. "Snafu," he said to the silence, and before long he fell into an uneasy sleep.

~

Ted looked over the blackened yard with some satisfaction. It would be a good while before he had to mow this again. Of course he may need to have the mower seen to. It lay, overturned, in a puddle of black muck.

A long-haired man emerged from one of the down-stairs rooms, climbed up the three steps to yard-level and propped, hands on hips, surveying the damage. His pale face, the result of spending so little time out of doors, was impassive. The pale-blue eyes and broad face beneath stringy hair always seemed to remind people of Janis Joplin, a comparison he never minded, since Janice was an all-time favourite artist of his, even something of a heroine. He hooked a long strand of hair behind an ear. "Good job, Ted."

Ted turned half around. "Gordon. Hope we didn't disturb your siesta?"

"No worries. Best excitement we've had for a long time. See old Horrie come out? I was scared he was gonna get too close to the flames and combust. Hey Horrie!" he shouted to the ground-level window next along the wall.

"Get stuffed," came the hoarse reply. "Only jokin', Horrie. You're all right, mate."

"Well," said Ted, dusting his hands off against his trousers. "My work here is done. Coming up for a beer, son?"

"Absolutely, my man. I'll be along in a jiffy," he said, ducking back to his room.

Ted climbed the stairs, stiffly, an effect he hoped wouldn't go unnoticed by Beth from the kitchen window. She still hadn't commented on the fire, and hopefully it would stay that way.

He had barely set foot in the kitchen when. . . "Theodore! Don't you dare come in here with those boots," he was forestalled.

He looked down at the offending boot, lifted it back out the door.

"What are you after?"

"I was just going to get us a beer and a couple of glasses."

"All right, dear. You go out and sit down. You look tired. I'll bring it out to you."

He was greatly relieved. "Thanks pet. And make it snappy, eh? We men got a powerful thirst," he chanced in withdrawing.

Amber looked up from her magazine, laughing at her mother's feigned scorn.

"It's all right for you to laugh. He's not your husband."

"Come off it, mum. The old man's a gem, you have to admit. You

wouldn't trade him for quids."

Beth hurrumphed, apparently reserving her view. "You take the beer out, will you? You've been sat on your backside all afternoon, reading that silly nonsense. Make yourself useful."

When Amber appeared on the balcony with the tray, Gordon looked up from talking with Ted to announce: "When I get my own place, I'm gonna get me my own serving wench, just like this one."

"Yeah? When you get your own place as if we'll get National Geographic in to photograph your empty room. Evidence that troglodytes aren't extinct."

"Oooo," he teased, while assisting with unloading the tray. "That was devastating. Ted, your daughter is merely denying her attraction to my irresistible good looks and animal magnetism."

Amber banged him on the head with the tray. "You've got the animal part right, anyway." And she walked off towards the kitchen.

Gordon watched her departure with a wistful expression on his face. "How much do you want for your daughter, Ted?"

Ted finished pouring the first glass and handed it over to his companion.

"More money than you've got, boy. No offence."

Gordon chuckled. "How long have I been here now, two..?" "Three," Ted corrected. "Three years at the end of the month." "No shit? Damn, and I was only gonna stay a couple of months,too. That room is like a time machine or something. Yeah. .? Three years, and in that time I've never once seen her go out with a guy. I mean, what's the story?"

Ted shrugged. "You tell me. But I figure there's plenty of time for fellahs. She's concentrating on her business. . . gives it all her attention. I reckon she's got her priorities exactly right. Anyway, if you're so interested, why don't you ask her?"

"Are you kidding? She'd tear strips off me, tell me to mind my business."

Ted raised his glass. "Well, there you are then."

"That'd be right," came a rich, baritone voice. They turned to see Ted's son standing in filthy overalls by the door. "A bloke's been bustin' his guts pushing concrete all day while you guys are sipping beer and taking it easy."

"Hello, son." Ted greeted.

Gary stood just over six feet tall in work boots. Red-brown hair, droopy moustache, brown eyes and a handsome face.

"Hi, Gary," said Gordon. "Bring yourself out a glass."

"No you don't!" Beth called out from the kitchen. "I'll kill you if you come traipsing through here in your mucky boots. I'll bring one out."

"Thanks, ma." Gary came over to join them at the table. "So what's...hey! What happened to the yard?"

Ted looked up casually. "What does it look like, you great goose?" With Gary, it was necessary to explain the event in full and in great detail. Especially detail. At the end of a ten-minute account he was sipping his beer, saying, "I can't believe it. The fire brigade and everything? I wish I'd been here."

Ted moved to side-track him. "So how was work today, son?" "Murder," he expressed animatedly. He let his mouth fall open, rolled his eyes back in his head and let his head fall forward, nodding. He sat up again. "This heat. Sweated my guts out, I did. My back's killing me." He arched his back and applied a hand to the offending area, grimac-ing.

"Cash in hand, wasn't it?" Gordon queried.

"A hundred and eighty smackers," he replied with an exaggerated grin, and eye-brows bobbing. "I'm going to ring Annette and see if she'll come out with me tonight."

"That's right, son. Work hard for your money and then go out and blow it on your floozies. You make me wonder sometimes, boy." "They're not floozies, dad. They're just. . . very friendly. Say, what's the new boarder like?"

Ted looked to Gordon and drew a blank, then back to Gary. "Haven't seen him. Is he here?"

"Yeah, mum gave him number five, next to the Colonel. She says he's just come down from the North-West. A miner or something. He's in his room, now."

Daniel woke by degrees, beginning with a growing sense of being, and of being supported by something firm yet yielding to his form. Phantom thoughts and images re-treated. Awareness was slow in coming. He was content to drift awhile longer in a com-fortable grey limbo where existential concerns could not penetrate to unsettle the mind with inextricable limitations of logic and physicality.

Silence. . . rare silence. There was no noise! His mind seized hold of the fact. Silence on a round-the-clock drilling site meant trouble. . . maybe an accident!

He opened his eyes with a sense of alarm, expecting to see the inside of a camp transportable. What he saw instead made his mind swim. A strange room. He had no idea where he was and had to fight the discomfiture of disorientation while coaxing his thoughts into order. The bus ride. . . Yes, he remembered. Things fell into place now. Moreton Bay, the guesthouse. How long had he been asleep? He turned his head to look at the little clock beside him. Twenty minutes to seven. "Damn thing," he cursed, regarding it accusingly.

He reached over and tested the mechanism and found the alarm fully wound down. It had gone off at the right time. He had slept through it, was all.

"Well, I've missed dinner," he grumbled, and swung his feet to the floor. He pulled off his boots with a groan and made a face as he peeled off each of the sticky socks. "Phew, that's disgusting," he laughed, and realised he was feeling pretty good for only three and a half hours sleep. Too good, perhaps. He sensed there was something wrong about the light. He turned to look out the window, climbed over the bed to get a better look. There was some cloud over the hills in the east, then emerging between one cluster and the next, the sun blazed out, low over the ridge-line. "Cripes, I've slept for"—he counted—"over fifteen hours!" He went to the wardrobe and pulled a clean T-shirt and jeans from his bag, shaving kit and shampoo, lifted the towel from the rail on the back of the door and headed for the bathroom.

It was a glorious morning, he decided, pausing awhile on the balcony to take in the view of the town, the coast, the river and the hills stretching southwards until they turned mauve and faded from sight.

A retching noise issued from the bathroom; the unmistakable sound of someone jettisoning the contents of their stomach, and it didn't sound as though there was much left but the stomach itself. He had been through that, himself, on one or two occa-sions; and he mused for a moment on why it was that the condition was usually viewed with amusement, except, of course, by the poor sod suffering it.

He considered going back to his room until the coast was clear, but he was keen to get on with the day. He walked on in and looked around for the shower. The wash ba-sins were straight ahead, two toilet cubicles to the right, and further on were two shower nozzles pro-truding from the wall over a concrete wet area.

He ran the water from one nozzle and began strip-ping off, just as the cistern was flushed in the closed cubicle, and the latch released with click. Gary emerged wearing only pyjama-pants tied with a cord, and looking decidedly seedy.

"G'day," said Daniel, smiling. "Rough night on the turps?" Gary used the back of his hands to wipe the tears from his eyes, swayed a little and grabbed hold of the cubicle, chuckling. "I'll say. It was the pizza at three o'clock this morning that was the mistake though. Anchovies. . .

yuk. I didn't taste 'em last night, but I can now." He wiped his hand on his pyjamas before extending it. "I'm Gary, anyway."

Daniel noted the strong grip. "Daniel. Pleased to meet you." "We missed you at dinner last night, Dan. I guess you were a bit knackered from the trip."

"Totally. I'm sorry I missed the meal. I was looking forward to meeting the other guests."

"Not many of the guests eat in the dining room any-way, Dan. Gordon, he's downstairs. He eats take-aways in his room mostly. And old Horrie, he's downstairs too. The only time he comes out of his room is to go down the street for a couple of litres of red ned. Then there's the Colonel. He's a good old stick. And the phantom, he appears and disappears like an apparition. His name's Jack, an Aboriginal guy. So it's usually only me, mum, dad, my sister and sometimes Gordon and the Colonel who eat in the dining room. But you'll catch up with everyone eventually."

"Yeah, I suppose I will."

"Hey, Dan, do you play pool?"

"Some," he answered guardedly.

"A few of us are going over to the football club for a few beers and to play in the pool comp' this arvo. You want to come along?"

"I was planning on just having a quiet look around today, Gary.

Thanks for the offer, but maybe next time?"

Sure. No probs." Gary's hand went to his stomach, and he rolled his eyes back to signal annoyance. "Bloody anchovies," he managed to say in the midst of a convul-sive heave, and he rushed back into the cubicle. , shaved, shampooed, once again in clean clothes and having replaced his boots for a pair of comfortable thongs, Daniel set off down the hill towards Main Street. It was absolutely still up and down the street when he arrived, the only detectable movement being a gentle warm breeze lapping at his freshly shaven face. He walked on around to the foreshore and stood, looking out over the bay. A few boats were still moored, but most, even though it was Sunday, had already gone out for a morning's work.

He walked out along the jetty where some early morning anglers leaned against the rails, twitching at suspected nibbles. The day was warming up fast now and it prom-ised to be a scorcher. He mentioned this prognosis to one elderly angler who had spent the whole night out on the jetty with his Jack Russel terrier and transistor radio for company, and received the laconic reply of "El Nino" which presumably was intended to an-swer the whole question of the weather.

He walked to the end of the jetty to watch the waves breaking across the reef, watched as their force was spent on the impervious coral and the white surf as it washed over to where the water was deep and tranquil on the sheltered side. "Wunjunu," he said softly.

He thought of how long it must have been since he stood here last. Perhaps as few as fourteen. . . no, it was almost seventeen years ago, he remembered. Eighteen years old and ready to take on anything. Huh.

Where was that confident youth now, the spirited young man who had left home all those years ago to discover the world? Yes, a voyage of discovery and adventure; a maiden voyage full of wonder, and how suddenly it had turned into grief and abandonment with the loss of his family.

Wunjunu. He remembered the story, how his grandmother told it as they sat on the river bank, late one magical autumn afternoon. He must have been four years old, but the story was never forgotten and this reef had been ever afterwards more than a thing, it had identity and there was always a mixed sense of melancholy and wonder whenever he came to it. And it was odd, he knew, but he felt that the little boy he once was resided here with the spirit of Wunjunu. After all, they deserved to be together; in a way they were the same.

He walked back along the jetty and descended the wooden stairs to the sand. He slipped off his thongs and went down to the shoreline to wet his feet in the cool wa-ter; absorbed the land, sea and sky until the tightness in his belly turned into pangs. He strolled back up to Main Street, feeling good about things and allowing himself an op-timistic thought for the future. Before getting some breakfast he decided to do a lap of the shopping area, out of curiosity.

The Place hadn't changed all that much. A few additions, but the old buildings were still intact. As he neared the second-hand shop he noticed a broken window. He came up close to it, being careful of the shards around his feet. Who would do such a thing? The method was obvious enough, a house brick lay in the display amongst an assortment of electrical goods. It didn't appear as though there was anything missing, which surprised him. Evidently the work of a moron with a brick. He shrugged, turned to cross the street and made for the delicatessen.

"Good morning," he said to the large women behind the counter, and received a cheerful "Good morning" in reply, her voice hinting of Sweden or perhaps Norway, Daniel thought.

He ordered a pie and a milk shake, and bought a Sunday paper to read while he ate at a table by the window. The newspaper made him nervous.

What he feared wasn't on the front page, but that didn't mean too much; a television personality's "Tears of Joy" occupied that position. Page three caused his heart to skip a beat with, "Bandit Bags Thousands, Bank". But the headline proved to be only a sham: an old lady had died and left instructions for her bank to administer her account on behalf of Bandit, her nine-year-old basset-hound.

Beyond the window a red Renault pulled up at the curb. The driver got out and walked around the front of the car, began counting coins in her hand as she crossed the footpath. Daniel looked up as the plastic ribbons over the doorway clattered together. He recognised the girl from the guest-house.

She went directly to the newspaper rack for the Sunday paper, and only on turn-ing did she notice him sitting there by the window.

"Hi," he said, flipping the page.

"Hello," she replied reflexively, on her way to the counter. "Just the paper this morning, thanks, Gretta. How's business?" "Plenty of cool drinks and ice-creams," she replied with a smile.

"How's the second-hand trade?"

"I sold the two air-conditioners that I've had for nearly a year, and three electric fans yesterday afternoon."

"That's very good," Gretta said, picking out a chocolate sweet from a box beside her. "Here, you win a prize."

Amber laughed in accepting it. "Yes, this weather does have its advantages.

Well, I'd better get a move on. Its almost eight o'clock." "Okay. I'll be seeing you later on," Gretta intoned with a very Scandinavian lilt.

Daniel swung around in his seat as she made for the exit. "Hey. You run that second-hand store over there?" He pointed along the street.

"I'm the proprietor, yes. What of it?" she said, halting and regarding him with some suspicion.

"Well, nothing, except some crud has lobbed a house brick through the window. Probably a-" But he was addressing her retreating back. Her eyes had sprung wide and her jaw had dropped. She hurried out to her car. He watched as she fumbled with the ignition key, started the engine and made a hasty U-turn back towards the shop.

Amber's heart sank as she neared the premises and pulled over out the front. The footpath glistened with broken glass, and a great, jagged hole gaped at the centre of the display window. When she turned the key in the lock and tried to push the door open, pieces of glass jammed under the frame so that she had to force it back a bit at a time, leavingdeep gouges in the linoleum. She hunted around trying to discover what was missing.

The jewellery cabinet was untouched. The display area was a mess, but it didn't appear anything was missing. Not that the stuff in the window was particularly valuable. It held mainly small electrical appliances, the sort people were sometimes wont to buy on a whim.

For the moment she wasn't sure what to do about the terrible disarray. Her assistant, who handled pick-up and deliveries, didn't work on weekends; and, anyway, she didn't need him. . . she could do this herself.

She went to the telephone book and searched for glass installers. She dialled the one number listed for the area and got a recorded message telling her that business hours were eight to six, Monday to Friday, and Saturdays until midday.

"Blast!" She slammed down the receiver in vexation.

"Can I be of help?" Daniel stood just inside the doorway; her distress was hot lost to him. "Don't worry, we'll have this cleaned up in no time."

Amber glared at him. She needed no one's help. He had startled her and she didn't much like it.

"Someone's ear must be buzzing." He stood with his hands pushed into his pockets and nodded towards the phone. "I've had that done to meonce or twiceand it doesn't half pop. The glazier?"

She relented a little. "Their answering machine. No go until tomorrow."

That's a blow. I bet there's a lot of this sort of thing happens on Saturday nights, too." He looked around at the wreckage. "Well, let's get this mess cleared upfirst, so it doesn't look quite so bad. We might be able to work something out, meanwhile." She was beginning to unwind a bit. The debris did have to be cleared away, and here was someone offering to help. "Thank's" she said, finally. "There's some shovels and brooms and such down near the back."

They worked at it steadily, being careful to avoid being cut on some of the nas-tier edges. With a wide broom Daniel knocked out the glass remaining wedged in the frame, lest it fall while they worked under it. He picked up the offending brick to show her, and saw the word bitch chalked along one side of it. He rubbed at it to erase the letters, but she had stopped to look at what he was doing he lamely let his hand fall until the brick was concealed behind his leg. "You never heard of the brick genie?"

She straightened herself and stretched out her hand. "Let me see." handed it over, saying, "Just dickhead kids, that's all."

Amber turned the brick over until the chalked letters caught her eye. Her lips thinned as she pressed them together. "Brick genie?" she said, tossing it into the wheel-barrow.

"Yeah, well. . ." He shrugged. "Maybe the genius who tossed it just likes to auto-graph his work? Then all we gotta do is find a dyslectic moron named Butch"

Amber began to giggle. It wasn't particularly funny. In fact it was rather stupid, but the anxiety which had been knotted tight in her solar plexus without her realising suddenly sought urgent release. She shook in effort to hold it in, but finally yielded to outright laughter.

Daniel joined in, though not with as much abandon. He was actually a little concerned; he knew nervous laughter when he saw it, and he was seeing it now. This chick is really uptight, he thought. Tight as a piano wire. It was his own personal observation, but he had seen people laugh with the look of fear in their eyes before, though never a woman, and he had seen them self-destruct in an assortment of shocking ways.

He felt something happening to him at that moment, and even though something inside told him there would be hell to pay, he could do nothing about it. He felt his heart going out to her.

Amber struggled for control. She found that if she sat on the floor, it helped, and she leaned back against the shelves, trying to relax. "Take a deep breath," Daniel suggested.

She did as he suggested, and it seemed to help. "Oh, shit." She took another breath. "What am I laughing about? Some arsehole has just cost me God-knows-how-much for a plate glass window." She stifled a giggle and took another breath.

"Aren't you insured?" he asked, surprised.

"Of course. . . Oh, yeah."

"See? It's only an inconvenience. No need to worry." Conversation dropped off when they resumed cleaning up, except for Amber's occasional cursing of vicious-minded people who went around smashing windows.

When the wheelbarrow was full enough, he wheeled it around to the back of the store where a hard waste skip stood by the wall, and realised he would never get it up to the lip of the bin by himself. He called Amber out, and together they struggled with the weight, but after some precarious moments they managed to tip it in.

They had almost completed the task when Daniel stopped what he was doing and turned to Amber. "I've been thinking," he said, in order to gain her attention. "I reckon vandals see society as something they feel cut off from."

Amber spotted another piece of glass under the door. "What?" "I said, I reckon vandals-"

"I know what you said," she said. "I mean, then why do they reject its values?"

"They don't, not in their own eyes anyway. Society rejects their values. Teenagers have their own value system, a system which is much more naive and trusting than their elders, who have become inured to the ravages of life. Youngsters see the possibility of a better world far more easily, while the establishment sees only the complexities and possible pitfalls. You know what I mean? A kid will say, 'Okay, so the world is a polluted, violent, rotten place. . . so let's fix it.' It's just that clear and I remember seeing it that way myself, how about you?"

Amber nodded. "Yes, I suppose I did, too."

"Right, and who listens to kids? They're trapped in a world which certainly is no Eden, they're denied a voice, any positive input, and rarely taken seriously. They're frus-trated at home, at school, on the streets, and sometimes it just boils over into a purely emotional act." He indicated the empty window frame. "It's right to say vandalism is a mindless act, technically, only because blind emotion has overridden the thought pro-cesses. Believe me, half the time these kids don't understand their own actions. I think it's really bloody sad, personally."

Amber was sweeping the last of the splinters into a pile. She stopped what she was doing and propped the broom handle under her chin, watching while he began stacking some of the displaced items to one side. "Are all miners usually so philosophi-cal?"

"I'm not a miner. I was only a well-trained menial with an exploration team. And the only conversation up there was about machinery, money, women or where you were going to spend your money on the next break."

"So how do you know so much about angry youth?"

"I was one of them. I wondered for years why I had been that way, why I failed to succeed when so many of my peers forged ahead with their lives. When I finally worked it out, I saw that my anger was justifiable, and I realised, also, that I wasn't what society had tried to tell me I was. In a sense, I had discovered my own truth, and it made all the difference."

Amber liked the way he talked. No stranger had ever talked so openly to her before. "Didn't you like your job?"

He stacked the last item and decided to sit for a while on the display ledge. "Not at all. Blokes doing a bloke's job in bloke country, eating, sleeping, drinking with blokes and talking about blokey stuff. The work was bloody hard and the country was, I suppose, ruggedly spectacular. But if I never see another work camp again, it'll be just hunky-dory with me."

Daniel looked at the way she was posed with her chin resting on the broom handle. She sure was pretty, now her crustiness had given way. He had never seen eyes like that before. "I know you're Beth's daughter, but I don't know your name yet. I'm-"

"Daniel, yes, I know. I'm Amber."

He gave a short laugh. "That'll be easy to remember." "Why?" she asked, uncomprehendingly.

"Well, ah," he gesticulated. "Your hair is . . . Amber is the colour of your hair, isn't it."

Her hand left the broom handle and drew a length of hair between fingers and thumb. "I never thought of that," she said with a trace of Welsh accent in her voice.

Daniel cocked an eyebrow. "You're not going to tell me no one has ever said that before, are you?"

"Never," she said, making an innocent face.

When he smiled at her, it was as if a switch had been thrown. She was being almost intimate with this man! Something cold stirred in her mind.

Daniel saw the change, a hint of something in her eyes. "Something wrong? he asked, concerned.

Nothing," she replied crustily.

"Okay," he responded, unconvinced, but if that's the way she wanted it. . ."Lis-ten, I might have a way of getting you your glass. Was that Cunningham's you tried?"

"Ah-ha," she confirmed.

"Good, I know the family. I went to school with their sons. Do you know where we can get a loan of a ute or a truck? If I drive out there I might be able to convince them to cut a sheet for us. We'll get your brother to give us a hand and fit it ourselves. All we need is some putty from the hardware shop."

"I've got a tray-top parked over behind the curio shop,"Amber said."I keep it there because it's got a look-up yard. But did you say you know the Cunninghams?"

"Yeah, many moons ago. I guess I forgot to mention, I grew up in the area. This is my old stomping-ground. But what do you say to my idea?"

Amber was in favour of anything that would put glass in her empty window before nightfall, and the plan went as smoothly as all plans do, which is to say not quite so smoothly as planned.

Gary agreed to lend a hand, and Daniel picked him up at the guesthouse to drive out to the Cunningham's place. He was still a touch seedy and was determined that they should pass through the drive-in bottle department at the hotel on the way, which in fact was in the opposite direction. It was a twelve mile drive out to Pedlar's Creek, tak-ing them through some picturesque countryside, with Gary insisting they stop and enjoy it. The stop lasted thirty minuteswhile he consumed four beers to Daniel's one, and the trip was resumed. At the Cunningham's property they found one brother on his own, the rest of the family having gone into Port Moreton for a day at the beach and a meal at the hotel.

Angus Cunningham was glad to see Daniel—so glad that they must come in-side and have a beer, to which Gary immediately agreed for them both. The traditional beer took an hour to drink before Angus laconically supposed he ought to do something about their glass. Measurements were given, diamond-tipped styles put into motion and the glass sheet was loaded aboard the truck. With fond farewells and a parting gift of a stubby each (for the road) they set off on the return journey, which had to be interrupted, twice, to water the eucalypts. By the time they arrived back at the shop with the glass it was twelve-thirty and Gary was something less than sober, though he proved capable of working in this condition, and within forty-five minutes the sheet was up and fixed firmly in place.

Daniel gave Amber the bill for $350-00, with "PAID" stamped across it.

"What!" she gasped, open-mouthed. "But-"

"Give that to your insurer," Daniel said. "You'll see it says supplied and installed. I gave him a hundred bucks. Old mates and all that."

"Thanks," she said, resentful of the fact that she had to be grateful to anyone.

I'll give you the money.

Daniel followed her inside where she retrieved her purse from under the count-er, and she handed him a hundred-dollar note. Then opening the till and withdrawing a fifty-dollar note, she held it out to him.

"What's this?" he said, taken aback.

"For your labour. Take it," she said, sounding irritated. It was bad enough having to be thankful to him. Now he was going to pull that "no, really oh, all right, if you insist" routine on her.

"For my labour? No, really. You're out of pocket a hundred bucks already today. It wasn't any inconvenience, I promise. I enjoyed myself."

Amber knew he was patronising her. "Take the damn money!" she exploded with greater force than she had intended.

Daniel was dumbfounded. He looked at the money in her hand, then to her eyes which shone with an unfathomable mixture of fear and anger.

"Keep your wretched money," he said in a quiet voice, turned and walked out of the shop.

Three

Besides having a room at the guest-house, which her parents kept vacant for her use on weekends, Amber also rented a single bedroom unit by the beach which she liked to use during the working week. Having her own accommodation was important to her, it proved her independence and it gave her the privacy she needed whenever her mood demanded solitude.

When Daniel had left it was already two hours past Sunday closing time, and so she had locked up for the day and climbed behind the wheel of her car. But instead of go-ing back to the guest-house, as she would do nor-mally, she had driven out of town, out across the bridge and along the coast road for several miles before deciding to retreat back to her flat. Upon entering, she slammed the door shut behind her, the resulting crash jolting her enough to bring her to examine what she was doing. Why had she driven along the coast road, and why had she come back here? she was forced to ask herself. It was odd behaviour but she didn't know where she wanted to be just now. But, yes, it was best to be alone, she knew. Her disposition would only attract unwanted comments at the house.

There was half a bottle of spumante in the refrig-erator, she remembered, left over from New Year's when she had allowed the woman from next door in. She went to the refrigerator and poured a glassful. It didn't taste good but she swallowed it anyway, took what remained to the couch.

"Why should I care?" she said to the walls. "I didn't ask for his damn help in thefirst place." And she remembered his face as he had walked out of the shop. It wasn't an angry face, why not? If someone had spoken to her the way she had spoken to him, she would be as mad as hell. But his face had been calm. It was his eyes she remembered now . . .penetrating, searching. She remembered how he had talked to her while they worked together. It was nice. All that stuff about angry young people and that stupid joke he made that had made her laugh so much. She found herself beginning to giggle again. She felt strange. Perhaps it was the wine. A tightness in her chest and midriff. It made her feel restless and she didn't like it.

Daniel returned to the guest-house with the intention of cleaning up and, per-haps, relaxing with a book or watching some television for a while. Amber's behaviour had worried him. He didn't understand why she had gotten so emotional over his refusal to accept her money. He disliked trying to work people out, but it was a habit he had gotten into in the work camps. There, it was often a matter of self-preservation to be able to judge people's character; such places had a tendency to attract some real crazies. What he had determined, with at least some measure of confidence, was that he had somehow represented a threat to her. It was the only assumption which stood up under examination of the events, but he tried not to dwell on it and decided to push it from his mind.

There was a blue Ford Transit Van and a maroon panel van parked out the front when Daniel arrived, and upon entering the front room he found an old gentle-man sit-ting in a wheelchair, reading beneath the lamp. His bony hands balanced a large volume across his knees while he hunched over, intent on the text.

"G'day," Daniel said, and the old fellow looked up, peering over top of his wire-rimmed glasses.

"So, you would be Daniel Gilmour," he said, his voice sounding as though it came from a severely constricted throat, and he cast an appraising eye over him.

Daniel found this a mite unsettling. "I'll take a guess and say you're the Colonel?"

"Right," said the old man, imparting a wisp of a smile. "I hope you're not desper-ate for work. There's not too much available in these parts."

"It suits me for the moment," replied Daniel. "I'm due for a rest." "Well don't let yourself get too self-satis-fied. There are enough loafers around as it is. Too much time on your hands and before you know it you'll start to lose motivation. No good."

"I suppose that's true, but I need some time to get a plan together. I'm afraid I left my last job on the spur of the moment, without any real idea of what I was going to do next."

"Oh? Bad move that."

"Yeah, I know. But I'd had a gutful and just had to get out." "You have people around here?"

Daniel wasn't sure how to answer, but went with "No. They're dead, actually."

"That's too bad," the Colonel said, consolingly. Then, having digested the answer: "What, you don't mean all of them? There must be relatives."

Daniel thought for a moment. "Well, if dad's brother, my uncle Joe, is still alive, then he is my only living relative. Apart from that," he smiled. . . "me last of Mohecans."

"Then you ought to start procreating like blazes and regenerate the tribe," the Colonel replied, joining in the joke. "If you're making plans for yourself, young man, think about a wife a home and a family before your drifting becomes a habit you can't break. Eh? You think about that."

Daniel was touched by the old man's sincerity. He had been given little enough advice by his father when he was alive, and no one since had taken the interest this old man was showing. It felt good.

"Yes," he said. "I will."

Talking with the Colonel had set his mind to thinking. He had managed for months now not to think about his situation. It was a trick of the mind to switch off what-ever brought discomfort, but again came that gnawing in the pit of his stomach, and it had a name, he knew. It was called loneliness; something a man ought never admit to.

He found Mrs Powell in the kitchen, stirring a huge pot on top of the stove.

"Hello," she beamed, almost singing the word. "Are you feeling better after your rest, love?"

"Much better, thank-you. I'm sorry I missed dinner."

"That's all right, Daniel. You'll be here tonight, will you? We're having spaghetti bolognaise."

"Absolutely my favourite," he grinned. "Count me in. I was wondering if there's a laundromat anywhere around?"

"There's a laundry downstairs, didn't I tell you? It's practically beneath your room. If you've got some washing, leave it by your door in the morning. I wash every Monday. Two dollars, flat rate."

"Well. . . I was thinking of doing it myself. I've only got one change of clothes and I'm wearing them."

"That's okay, dear. You go right ahead. The powder is in the cupboard."

"Thanks," he said, withdrawing.

While his clothes went through the cycle, he took another quick shower to wash off the sweat. He had imagined he would be coming to a cooler part of the country when he left the North-West, but this was extraordinary. It couldn't be far off forty degrees outside.

There was a distorted image of someone through the shower curtain.

"That you, Dan?" came Gary's baritone voice.

"Yeah, mate. You've got your pool comp on this afternoon, haven't you?"

"Not any more." He stepped under the neighbouring nozzle and turned on the taps. "I rang and told 'em I wasn't coming. Sod it. I can't play for nuts, anyway. And I should rest up a bit before tomorrow. If I kick the gong again, I'll be knackered for work."

"Yeah, right. Good thinking." He stepped out of the shower and began towel-ling off. "In the camps there's no such thing as a sickie. Well, not unless you're dying. I tied one on real bad one night, and I was so lay-down-and-die sick the next morning, you wouldn't believe. There was no way I was getting out of bed. No way, right? I just wanted to lay there and not move until the artillery stopped exploding in my head."

Gary turned off his shower and stepped out for his towel. "Yeah. Been there."

"Yeah, but then this pounding starts up on my cabin door, and when I don't answer in bounds the flamin' foreman, and he's going off his nut like some crazy drill ser-geant. Like, get out of bed you goddamn gold-brick and all of that shit. It turns out the road train has arrived with eighty drums of diesel to unload and the first drum has broken some poor bugger's leg, which left only me to replace him. I even tried to quit on the spot, but he wouldn't have it. He wouldn't leave my room until I was up and dressed and on my way. He was a big bugger, too, and I was in no condition to argue with him. I was as sick as a dog and I worked like a mule for bloody hours on an empty stomach, because I'd missed breakfast. I dead set thought I was going to die."

Gary chortled appreciatively. "Yeah, I bet. Sounds a lot like my boss, that one. A real slave-driver."

Sadist, more like," said Daniel, tossing his towel over one shoulder and moving to leave.

"Hey, Dan," Gary called, halting his departure. "What you doing now?"

"What... now now or workwise now?" "Now now. This minute."

"Nothing much, I suppose. I've got some clothes washing in the machine."

"Come down to Gordon's room with me. I'll introduce you." When he noticed Daniel hesitating, he added, "The guy's amazing.

He used to be a professional musician. You should see all the stuff he's got down there."

"Yeah, okay then. I'll just go and hang out my gear."

When he had pegged out his clothes Gary led him under the balcony towards Gordon's door. On the way past a neighbouring room, where a small window was set in the wall about half a metre above the ground, Gary called, "How's it going Horrie?" and received an instant reply of, "Get stuffed!"

Gary chuckled. "Just checking, Horrie."

Daniel followed Gary down the three steps to a beaten-up door with flaking brown paint. He banged hard on the door and turned to Daniel. "If he's got his head-phones on, he wouldn't hear otherwise." The door was opened and Gordon's shaggy head appeared around the corner. "You've got a knock like a copper, Gary. I nearly went to flush my dope down the toilet, 'til I realised I don't have a toilet." He looked up to regard Daniel standing up a step behind Gary.

"G'day Dan."

He backed up to open the door further, and knocked something over. "Shit, there go my flowers."

They stepped through the doorway and descended two more steps, squeezed around where Gordon knelt to pick up a collection of long-stemmed roses, replacing them in a flagon of water, some of which was pooled on the carpet squares.

"Find somewhere to sit, guys," he told them while working on the arrangement.

Easier said than done; the room was small to begin with, but the stuff he had stowed away in there took care of most of what little space there was. Daniel saw three guitars and two cases, an electric piano, a reel to reel recorder and a mixing desk stood on edge against the back wall. The floor was strewn with records, many of them out of their sleeves. A compact stereo unit sat up on a shelf above the bed, with head-phones dangling down, and a small amplifier sat against the outer wall. There was one chair.

"Just scrape some of that stuff off the bed," he said, meaning a pile of sheet music and Melody Maker magazines.

Gary shoved it all across into a pile, making a space for himself. "All right if I sit on this?" Daniel asked, pointing to the amplifier. "Yeah, yeah, no sweat. You won't hurt that thing, it's got a steel frame. It fell out of a truck once, didn't hardly scratch it."

"You've been picking mum's roses again, Gordon. She'll kill you.

She treats those flowers like her own children."

"Bullshit, Gary. If I didn't water them and prune them myself, there wouldn't be any roses."

"Oh, well. I suppose it's okay then."

Gordon finished arranging the flowers and stood up to face his guests. "I was just going to clean up, but now I can't, can I." He grinned. "All the time, interruptions. I told my manager no interviews and no calls. Oh well. . . what would you gentlemen like to drink, warm beer or warm Sauterne?"

I'll have a Sauterne, thanks Gordon," said Gary.

"Dan?"

"Warm beer's okay with me, thanks. You've sure got a lot of stuff in here."

"Yeah, and I couldn't bare to part with any of it. There's a bit of a story attached to how I came to be here with all this, actually," he said in passing Daniel his warm beer.

"Tell him, Gordon," Gary urged.

"Nah. Dan doesn't want to hear my boring old story, do you Dan?" "I have to admit to being curious. But if you'd rather not..?" Gordon took a quick sip of his drink. "No, I don't mind, and I guess the story isn't as boring as all that. You see, I came to this shit-hole of a town almost three years ago, to do a gig at the hotel, right? Me and the band. My band! So we do the gig on the Friday night and everything's just peachy, and they want us to stay over and do one extra show, 'cause we like doubled their trade and they reckoned by the time word passed around, Saturday would be even better. Okay, that's sweet, and we all agree to do it. And the pub's like layin' it on for us... good food, cheap drinks and we're happy, right?

"Saturday night, eight o'clock. Five hundred people rock up, man, and it's nuts. The room is big enough for what, two, two fifty, Gary? Yeah. So we're playing away, and there's all these people tryin' to get in and they can see everybody inside having a good time and they're getting pissed off and drunker and more pissed off until, bang! All these redneck country guys lose their cool, and I mean completely.

"They tore the fuckin' back fence down, man, and all this violence started happening. Windows got busted and all that shit, like a teevee western or something, you know? Anyway, the show is obviously over. It's a disaster area. The lads and I piss off upstairs while about four coppers are trying to sort out the shit below. And we're drink-ing in the private bar and starting to unwind because we were pretty freaked, and Harry the drummer says to me how him and the others wanted to toss it in and head back to Melbourne. Like we were halfway to W.A. where we intended to go for the high-paying summer gigs, and they wanted to throw in the towel? Unbelievable! I don't know who was pouring the drinks that night, or what they were putting in them, but I went off the deep end a bit.

"We ended up having this huge argument, with me sayin' shit like they weren't musicians, they were only poseurs making a living out of my talent and they could all go to hell because I wasn't getting anywhere with a bunch of hacks like them. I guess I was just pissed off with the way the night had gone, but the cretins took it all to heart! They left me high and dry.

"By the time I got up the following morning, the van had gone and my stuff was stacked in a heap downstairs. If I hadn't met this big ox in the front bar, where I was sit-ting, drowning my sorrows, I wouldn't be sitting here." He frowned at Gary in mock displeasure. "Hey, yeah, that's right. So it's your fault I'm here, you miserable sod."

"You love it here, Gordon. You know you do," Gary countered. "Here in your her-mit cave."

"Horrie's the hermit. Not me. Have you met Horrie yet, Dan?"

"No."

"I'd have been surprised if you said yes. Horrible Horrie doesn't come out much, except maybe for Halloween."

"What's his problem?"

Gary made a display of taking a drink. "This," he explained, pointing to his glass.

"Yeah? Bad is he?"

"Something chronic," Gary answered, shaking his head. Daniel sipped from his stubby and thought for a moment. "At the risk of touching on a sore spot, Gordon, you must still have a yearning for the business."

Gordon shrugged. "I'm glad you said business, because that's the crux of the matter, right there. The music business sucks. But the music? Man, I could never give it up. It's like the air I breathe."

"Why don't you play something for us?" Gary suggested. Gordon surveyed his instruments, his eye coming to rest on atwelve-string guitar. "Only if you freeloaders sing along. I'm not doing all the work myself. What about it, do you sing, Dan?"

"I suppose I could give it a go," he answered genially. "Good man. Pass me over that axe there."

His fingers worked quickly over the strings, testing the tuning and adjusting tensions. He struck a bright-sounding chord. "Okay. We'll start with something everybody knows."

Daniel recognised the song immediately he started into it... Pink Floyd's "Wish You Were Here."

When the verse started, he was on it, and to his surprise their three voices combined in the small room to create good harmony. Gary's baritone voice had changed to that of a tenor, and it overrode his and Gordon's during the choruses as he stood in an animated production of his best effort.

A Welshman in full song, Daniel thought. Something to behold. Gordon brought the song to its gentle completion, and there were looksof approval all round. He sipped his wine and replaced the glass beside his feet. "You know guys, that was almost pass-able," he said with an air of gravity. "All right, let's see how you go on this one," and he played the lead-in to Led Zeppelin's "Gallows Pole".

Daniel spent most of the afternoon down there in the small room. Gordon played them some of the material he had overdubbed with the sixteen-track recorder, using bass, electric and acoustic guitars, and the electric piano, together with miscellaneous wooden and metal objects which he used as percussion instruments. Although he knew he was no expert when it came to music, Daniel was aware he was listening to skilfully crafted composi-tions, and it was with some effort he refrained from ask-ing Gordon what he was doing in this hole-in-the-wall, when he ought to be practicing his art in mainstream society.

He left Gary and Gordon listening to old John Mayall records, sipping wine and arguing over who wrote or recorded what song, while he headed back towards his room. As he climbed the stairs to the balcony, he heard Amber's voice issue from the kitchen, and at the sound felt a twinge in his solar plexus.

Don't be a fool, he thought in rebuke. You've been out in the desert too long.

The first pretty girl you see and you go soft in the head. She was trouble, he just knew it.

As he entered his room, however, thought of Amber was lost to the ineffable presence inside the wardrobe. It was no good trying to ignore it, its existence would not be denied, and sometime soon, he knew, he would have to confront it. He had promised himself never to drink again, and already he had gone back on that. Another blackout like the last one and. . . He let the thought end there. It was still too difficult to think about without becoming perturbed. He lay back on the bed and signed. There was time for a nap before dinner.

Amber assisted her mother with setting the dining room table. For the first time since moving into her flat the solitude had seemed to close in around her. Solitude, the very thing she had sought out in renting the premises. She fought to counter her distress by engaging in routine things. She read a few pages of her book but found the words weren't making any sense. The television proved only to be an annoying distraction. She watered her pot plants and mopped the kitchen floor, and when she had done that there was nothing else to do, so she had filled the bathtub, undressed and immersed herself in the tepid water in hope of easing her feverishness. It helped.

The environs were quiet and she let her mind focus on the regular dripping from the tap. It plonked steadily, echoing in the confined space of the bathroom, drawing her attention in and calming her mind. She lay like that for an hour, not quite napping and not quite awake, a wonderful serenity and merciful release from the distressing anxiety. She emerged feeling refreshed, the soft texture of her bath towel against her was unusually pleasant, almost stimulating. Then once again the restlessness stirred, and a strange, tingling urgency inside of her. It had made her come here, wearing her white-belted summer dress, bare at the shoulders. And now she felt foolish for having come dressed like this, and she felt that peculiar tightness again as she wondered where Daniel might be.

"Since when do the forks go on the right?" her mother asked, snapping her out of her reverie. "What's the matter with you this afternoon? Too much of those airy-fairy magazine stories, I shouldn't wonder?"

"No. I just feel a bit. . . funny," Amber struggled to explain while rearranging the knives and forks.

"Funny?" Beth looked closely at her daughter. "You do look a shade off colour, come to think of it. Did you remember to eat today?"

"Only breakfast, but that's usual."

"It might be the heat," Beth said. "Better not push yourself too much." She remained silent for a few seconds while she distributed the plates. "That's a pretty dress, dear. Is it new?"

"This thing? No. I've had it for ages. It's not much."

"It's lovely," Beth expressed with a knowing smile. "Very fetching."

Amber stamped her foot in frustration. "I knew I shouldn't have worn this silly thing," she said bitterly, and abandoning what she was doing, stormed off.

"Where are you going." Beth called after her. "I'm going home to change!"

When dinner was served at six, Amber still had not returned. Daniel and Gary sat on one side of the table while the Colonel and Beth sat on the other, with Amber's empty chair between them. Ted sat at the head of the table and appeared to take great pleasure in presiding over the conversation. As this was the first opportunity he had had to meet the new guest, Daniel was pressed to tell something of himself.

"Nothing of great interest to tell, I'm afraid," he began. "I suppose I've travelled around a lot, trying my hand at different kinds of work. Worked in every state of the coun-try, and one territory barring Canberra. Mostly physical work. Offsiding, roustabouting and that sort of thing. Some fruit picking and the like, early on, but I soon learned there was no future in that. I found that the mining companies paid the best, and they usually look after their men better too, with one or two exceptions."

"So what brought you to Port Moreton?" Ted asked, and shovelled in a mouthful of spaghetti and meat sauce.

"I was raised not too far from here and I haven't been back for

nearly seventeen years. I figured it was about time I came back for a look."

"Yeah, no kidding?" said Gary. "Your folks around here?" "Dead, mate. Though the property is still there. I've been keeping up payments on the rates while I moved around."

"You own property?" Beth emphasised, her inter-est piqued. Daniel nodded as he chewed. "Ah-ha. Sole surviving family. Tenacres overlooking Gum Gully. The house must be a shambles by now, but the land it oc-cu-pies is productive and really pretty. I've yet to go up and take a look though."

"Gum Gully," said Gary, making a quizzical face.

The Colonel, who had been listening closely, answered for Daniel. "It's just back in the foothills, here. Twelve miles or so inland. It's beautiful country all right."

"You know it?" Daniel asked.

"I have a lady friend lives up that way. Up on the ridge road."

"You sly old dog," Gary teased. "You never mentioned her before." When the Colonel failed to reply, he said, "Hey, has anyone seen Jack in the past couple of days?"

Jack was the Aboriginal border, Daniel remembered.

"He'll turn up," Beth said. "Remember he was gone for three weeks, once."

"That's right," Gary recalled. "And he posted you his board money from Ceduna!"

"Perhaps he's worried the place might come down around his ears.

Skipped out before it did." Ted chuckled.

"Oh, Ted. Don't start, please," Beth crooned, her Welsh accent coming to the fore.

"Why not? It's about time we had a family meeting to discuss what we're going to do." He turned to Daniel. "If you're wondering what this is about, son, the council has given us six weeks to vacate."

"Why's that?"

"They reckon it's a bit shaky in the foundations, which is a load of-"

"Theodore!" Beth cut in. "Ted thinks they have a hidden motive for wanting us off the property. I don't know about that, but I don't think I agree that this house is unsafe. They say it has to be demolished." "Couldn't you get your own builder to come in and inspect it?

And even if it is out of shape, couldn't it be corrected?"

"We've been thinking along those lines ourselves, Dan," Ted replied. "Certainly we could have it renovated. You don't happen to know anybody with a bagful of money they don't want, do you?"

Daniel was in the act of swallowing his food as Ted said this. The comment had an inhibiting effect.

"Are you all right, dear?" Beth asked, rising from her chair. "I'll get you a glass of water."

After dinner Daniel went out to the balcony with Gary, Ted and Gordon, to sit with them while they talked over what Daniel assumed was their usual, evening beer. He politely declined the offer of a beer, himself, but joined in the conversation for a while, until he decided a walk along the coast might be conducive to a sound night's sleep.

The route he chose took him to the top of the bluff, where he sat for a few minutes on the railing, looking out over the bay. While he paused, his mind meandered back along the course of the day, inevitably to draw towards the moment she had tried to treat him like a hired lackey. And why hadn't she been at the dinner table? He had secretly anticipated seeing her there, wanting to resolve their quarrel, somehow, even if she was an uppity little bitch. But the more he thought about it, the more annoyed he became. He should have given her what for, instead of letting her think she had gotten away with something. His agitation set him in motion once more.

He followed along the edge of the bluff and down onto the beach, where he halted for a moment to take in the view at the waters edge before setting off along the sand towards the river mouth.

The mouth took twenty minutes to reach at an easy pace, and when he got there he sat in the sand at the base of a dune, watching the water flowing out into the bay. He thought about the family property and tried to ready himself for the moment he would see it again, after so long. There was no point in fooling himself, it would be in pretty bad condition, but with some work he could probably knock it back into shape. And then what? He couldn't stay up there alone. He would go crazy. And suddenly he didn't want to think about it any more; it was a responsibility he wasn't sure he wanted.

He had been crossing and recrossing the country for years, never staying anywhere for more than a year. How, then, could he settle in one place? ". . . before your drifting becomes a habit you can't break," the Colonel had said. He tried to remember what else the old man had said, but then Amber's face came suddenly and clearly to mind; her shining amber hair and the way she looked in those jeans and that snug-fitting top. A beautiful brat, he thought angrily, and stood to begin the walk home as the sun dipped from sight behind the waves.

Twilight deepened as he strolled over the sand, immersed in thought. The incoming tide had claimed a large portion of the beach and the piles of seaweed which had been dumped by a recent storm made navigation tricky in the failing light. As he passed in front of a row of beach-front units, he was startled by someone sitting in the sand just a few feet ahead.

Amber sat, hugging her knees to her chest, still waring the elegant summer dress she had gone home to change. The shadowy figure had given her a fright; she had been so intent on the changing hues over the horizon.

"Oops!" said Daniel, to the person he had almost stumbled into. "Sorry. I didn't see you there."

"Daniel?" Amber asked tentatively.

Her voice was unmistakable. It came to him as light and clear as singing crystal.

"Amber?"

There was a sudden tension in the air between them, a charged silence which even the waves seemed impelled to observe.

"What are you doing?" he said, finally.

This was what she wanted, her instincts told her so. But her emotions were con-fused, surging too power-fully, mixing old dreads with something entirely new and bewil-dering. She had wanted to see him at dinner, then found a way of not being there. There was an inexplicable urge to cry out for help. She wondered if he could see the new dress she had never worn before, how pretty it was. Help me, Daniel. Please.

"Watching the water," she replied in a quiet voice. "It helps me be calm."

"Good idea," he said, remembering her manner at the shop, and immediately wished he hadn't.

She hadn't noticed the sarcasm in his voice, there was too much turmoil inside her to notice. He moved, as though he were about to depart. "Daniel," she blurted out, not knowing what would come next.

"Yes?" He delivered the word with indifference.

Now he was being cruel to her, she knew. She had been unkind to him and this was his way of getting back. She wanted to invite him in for a coffee or something, so he would know she was sorryEut he was angry with her and she had to accept that.

"Nothing," she replied meekly.

"Well then, I think I'll head on back," he said dully. "See you around."

Amber didn't answer. She watched him walk off into the gathering darkness, where he was soon lost to view against the background of the cliffs.

She sat quietly for some minutes, feeling terribly let down. It was an ache which went to her very core. This kind of misery was hard for her to distinguish from another kind of misery she had experienced, not so very long ago. Pain didn't come in colours; were it so, she might have understood the difference, but she was confused, emotions coursed through her, the new and the old, until they mixed into the same, grey nonde-script beast which had tormented her to the limits of endurance on two previous occasions. It was a hell she could not endure again. She had found a way to make it stop, once. She would make it stop again. She had to.

Why had he done that? he rebuked himself. It wasn't like him to be callous. He had heard in her voice that she wanted to talk, but he had shut her out. Had she wounded his pride so much that he had to even the score like some damn fool adolescent? Even as he had stood there, feigning cool indifference, he had a strong urge to relent, to give her the opening to say what she wanted to say, but he had selfishly refused to allow her that. He had sensed her vulnerability and taken a perverse satisfaction in the knowledge. Now he was angry with himself. What he had done served no purpose—no purpose at all. Not even to satisfy his churlish pride. If anything, it only augmented an already uncomfort-able notion which he had been taking pains to ignore.

Some deep-rooted instinct had been awakened in him. It began, he realised, in that brief moment during the day, when he had looked into a young woman's eyes to recognise, unnervingly, her undisguised fear, perhaps even the ghosts of desperation, made all the more shocking because these things dwelt in the eyes of someone whose life appeared to be so in order, and, not least, because it seemed a travesty of nature for these things to reside in someone so lovely. And he saw that thiswas the reason he had acted the way he did. Fear and desperation had for too long been the major ingredients of his own life, had seen him in prisons, in weeks-long bouts of drinking, entering into drug addiction and all kinds of erratic, misguided journeys in search of that elusive something. That sort of behaviour, that brand of desperation frightened him now. It was a soul-destroying condition which few people could understand, and those who did could never explain. And he knew why he had been feeling the way he had and why he act-ed in a way which had shamed him in his own eyes. Amber was somehow at odds with herself. For whatever reason, he didn't know, but that was why he had tried to shut her out; he was irrationally fearful that it might be contagious, that it might unsettle his own precarious balance. But if Amber had that kind of trouble inside of her, who would she talk to? His own parents could never understand; only drunkards, junkies and outcasts ever really understood, and with them the issue barely warranted a mention, since it was stoically accepted as a life-long and irreversible curse. There was a tacit understanding among such people, and being among them during that time was the next nearest thing to having a real family. Together in a relentless, unhappy search for something he at last discovered was no more than illusion, but together nevertheless. And, yes, he knew that haunted look in Amber's eyes. She had somehow become One Alone, like Wunjunu, like himself, like so many other ill-fated people who had taken a shell-shocked sideways step out of the frame. What trouble could a girl like that have? he wondered. He would have to put his apprehensiveness and his petty indignities to the side, to either confirm or disprove his suspicion. He would have to talk to her, but after the way he had treated her back there, he knew that was going to be difficult.

~

In the dream, Amber stood balanced atop the railing at the edge of the bluff. A stiff sea breeze blew into her face, her hair lashing around behind her head. He saw himself walking up closer to see what she was doing, but when he came near she turned and regarded him with a look which stopped him short. She turned back to stare out to sea, where gathering storm-clouds darkened the horizon.

"Get down," he said, afraid for her safety, and he saw her lips curl to form a tiny smile. "You could fall," he said, sensing imminent danger.

Again she turned to look down on him, her lips parted to form a word.

"One," she said. "One man went to mow." "Amber, it's very dangerous!"

"Nine," she said. "Nine green bottles."

He tried to move closer, but the force of the wind held him back. "Fifteen. Fifteen men on a dead man's chest."

"You don't know how dangerous!"

Into the wind, so that her words barely carried to him, she said: "Your mother sends her love."

"What?" And instinct told him there was no more time. He fought to reach her as she leaned out over the precipice against the wind. "No. Amber, no!"

He woke, shaken, still breathing hard and soaked in sweat. The room was dark but the full moon outside his window bathed everything in a lambent silver light. The im-ages of the nightmare remained but were beginning to fade now. After a while he looked over to his clock, saw the phosphorescent hands indicating five minutes past three. He was thirsty, so he pulled on his jeans and headed for the kitchen.

When he entered the front room it was dimly lit by the reading lamp in the cor-ner. Only when the man by the front door moved, did he notice the presence.

Both remained motionless while they observed one another. He was Aboriginal, maybe thirty years old. Tall, fit-looking, wearing jeans and a dark-coloured sweater.

"Hi," said Daniel." You're Jack, I presume? I'm Daniel." "G'day," Jack responded with a smile.

Daniel went through to the kitchen and found a large tumbler to fill with water.

Re-entering the front room, Jack caught his attention.

"Hey, Daniel. Can you feel it?" His eyes seemed to be searching the ether.

"Feel what? I don't get you."

"It," said Jack, now moving his hands through the air in a mysterious fashion.

Daniel stilled himself, tried to feel. . . something. He was getting a dose of the creeps and gave a little shiver. "I don't know," he said.

"I think you do," Jack replied, standing stock still and engaging Daniel's eyes unwaver-ingly. "That old gadhaitcha man, he's walkin' about tonight. But don't worry, Daniel. He ain't after us. You're alright, and me too. But someone. . ."

Daniel gave a nervous laugh, trying to break the weird spell which seemed to have filled the room. "Well that's good news, anyway. You had me worried for a minute there. Good night, Jack."

"Good luck, Daniel."

He was at his bedroom door when the penny dropped. Good luck? He went back along the corridor and opened the door into the front room. It was pitch dark. "Hey, Jack," he called low, figuring this for some kind of silly prank. His hand found the light switch, and the room was empty.

Four

Daniel had fallen into a deep, dreamless sleep and woken at seven to the sound of a slamming door and Gary's stentorian greeting to the Colonel. He considered trying to sleep on a while longer but thought better of it; as the Colonel had remarked, it didn't do to take things too easy. Maybe he would go and take a look at the property today, he mused as he threw back the sheet. He felt good this morning, more confident and about ready to take things in hand. A volley of 'good morning's greeted him as he approached the dining table, where Ted, Gary and the Colonel sat waiting for their breakfast. Daniel took up his position alongside Gary, just as Beth entered, carrying their plates.

"Morning, Daniel. Sleep well?" she inquired cheerfully, moving briskly aroundhim.

"Yes, thank-you. Very well."

"Bacon, eggs and sausage this morning.Yes?" "Please," he replied. "Right-o." She placed Ted's plate of toast and baked beans before his disappointed face.

"Shaln't be a minute." She served the Colonel and hurried off towards the kitchen.

"What's the matter, pop?" Gary grinned at his father. "Not hungry this morning." He drove his fork into the sausage and lifted it from his plate. "Mmm, pork sausage. Deeelicious."

"Keep it up, boy, and I'll ram it -"

"Theodore!" Beth's voice issued from the kitchen. "And stop tormenting your father, Gary!"

"Up your nose," Ted finished, affecting a sheepish look. Daniel poured himself an orange juice from the jug on the table and sipped at it while the others tucked in, won-dering where he might hire a car to drive out to the property. My property: he liked the sound of that. Daniel Gilmour, esquire. . . landowner. But maybe I'll leave it for another day or two, he thought. It's been there this long, another couple of days won't make any difference.

"So what's happening today, da?" Gary asked.

"Well, son, I'm glad you asked me that. You won't be needing your car today, will you?"

Gary glanced at his watch. "Not if Kevin turns up on time." "Because I want to drive over to the council office and see what can be done about an extension, see?" "On the house?"

"On the bloody evacuation notice, you great wally."

"Oh, yeah. Yeah, that's okay. If you think you stand a chance." Beth came in with Daniel's breakfast and set it down in front of him. "There you are, Dan."

"That looks great. Thanks," he said enthusiastically.

When she had gone, Ted resumed. "I've got buck-leys, but I'm going to speak to the bloke in charge and see if I can't get another of those inspectors out here to take a look. Maybe he won't be such an arsehole."

"Maybe. It's worth a try, I suppose. Go for it."

"I agree," said Dan, seeing an opportunity to join in. "And what might help, if you reckon something suspicious is going on, tell them if you can't get another inspector out, you'll get a private bloke to come and take a look, out of your own pocket. It could be revealing if they have a change of heart. In fact, if they do agree to a second inspection after that, it might well point to something dodgy."

"That's clever," said the Colonel, putting down his fork. "I'll tell you what, Ted. If that's what happens, we'll get a private chap in any case. My shout. Agreed?"

Ted's mood was improving. "That's a generous offer, Colonel," he replied, hedging a little.

"Nonsense, Ted. This is my home too. I've been here for damn near eight years, and I'm not keen on moving, are you?"

"No, Colonel, I'm not at all happy about it. Beth and I have run this place for twenty six years. I don't think either of us could live any other way. I accept your offer."

"Good. It's settled," said the Colonel, taking up his cutlery again. A car horn sounded from the front of the house.

"There's Kevin," said Gary, rising and pushing the last piece of bacon into his mouth. "Car keys are on my dresser, da. See you all later."

When Gary had departed, the Colonel addressed Daniel. "What do you have planned for today, young man?"

Daniel shrugged. "Haven't decided yet."

"You want to come out with me today? Do you know how to hold a video camera?" He observed Daniel's bemusement with some humour. "That blue Transit van out there is mine," he said, hooking his thumb towards the road. "In it are three video cam-corders, mikes, sound recording equipment, an editing desk, video monitors and a bunch of other stuff. With it I record weddings, christenings, parties, make promos for businesses and sporting groups, you name it."

"What's today's job?" Daniel asked, still undecided.

"A hang-gliding club down at Ochre Beach want a short promo taped for Coast TV. They're keen to drum up new membership. Damn fool things if you ask me, though."

"How do you manage with. . ." Daniel gestured towards the Colonel's wheelchair.

"I manage well enough. I often get kids from the unemployment office to come along for the work experience. They need to have a driver's licence though. They drive, do most of the shooting, and I do the editing and take all the glory," he smiled. "Gary has been out with me on a number of occasions. He's damn good with a camera, but don't tell him that, eh?"

"Do you have someone else organised for today?"

"A young lass from over the hill. Gerda. But I could use your muscle to help me get around on the ground. Or do you have something important on, like body-surfing or beachcombing or something?"

Daniel laughed, more at the Colonel's presumption that he could be persuaded in this manner, than his sardonic manner. "You have a way of seeing things, don't you Colonel. What the hell. Yeah, okay. I guess it's more interesting than body-surfing and beachcombing." "Good decision," said the Colonel, grinning. "We'll be done by-lunch-time, I estimate."

"It'll be a good outing for you, son," Ted affirmed. "Gary enjoys it."

Ted's attention was diverted by something over Daniel's shoulder. "It's only sev-en-thirty," he said to Gordon, who was approaching through the front room. "You wet your bed or something?" he chuckled. . . but sobered quickly. "What's wrong, son?"

Gordon's face reflected concern. "Horrie's not answering, Ted. He's in his room. It's locked from the inside, but I can't get a peep." "It is only seven-thirty, Gordon."

Gordon dragged a length of limp hair behind his ear. "I think something is wrong."

"All right. Let's have a look," Ted acceded, rising.

Daniel felt a shiver run along his spine. "Can I help at all?" "No, son," Ted replied as he followed Gordon. "You stay here." "We have been expecting something like this for a while," the Colonel said when they were gone. "Probably just out of it from the booze, though."

Daniel and the Colonel sat quietly, not bothering to manufacture conversation. When Beth arrived with a pot of tea for the table, she inquired, "Where is everybody?"

"Gary has left for work. Ted has gone downstairs with Gordon to check on Horrie." the Colonel told her. "Might be trouble."

There was a vibration through the floor and the sound of Horrie's door being broken open. Beth put down the teapot and stayed still as the three of them waited in silence. After a minute, she said, "The poor man. He was a merchant sailor for forty-one years. He showed me some pictures from all over the world."

When Ted returned, his face was flushed from climbing the stairs. He answered their questioning faces with a small shake of his head. "I'll have to call the doctor for the medical certificate. He must have died in his sleep."

"Poor man," Beth repeated. "We must look after him properly and give him a funeral service."

"Yes, dear," Ted concurred. "We can do that."

The Colonel turned to Daniel. "I've got to get myself ready. That girl will be here at eight."

"Okay. I'll be ready."

Gerda turned up on time, and at the same time as the doctor and the ambu-lance arrived. She was a sturdy-looking girl; tall, with straight, blond hair and blue eyes set wide apart. Daniel guessed Scandinavian blood. Her strong limbs, apparent in a pair of khaki work shorts and navy tank top, and her overall bearing reminded him of sto-ry-book representations of Viking women.

"Hello, Gerda," he greeted her at the door. "We're just on our way. "Will my bicycle be safe?" she asked, indicating a rust contraption leaning against the front wall.

"I shouldn't think anyone would make off with it," he replied in all sincerity.

The Colonel's wheelchair bumped against the door as he entered from the guest's wing. "Ah, you're here! Good, let's be off."

When the Colonel's chair was firmly clamped down in the rear of the van, Daniel had assumed he would be taking the wheel, but Gerda knew who had priority here, and grabbed for the driver's side door-handle before him, with an adamant I'm driving look on her face.

"I'll ride shotgun, then, shall I?" he acquiesced.

By the time he had sauntered around to the passenger's side and climbed aboard, Gerda had the engine running and was ready to get under way. . . but why didn't she?"

"Seat-belt," she said to his vexed look of inquiry.

"Ah, yes, of course. Got it." And they pulled out from the curb. "Why is there the ambulance?" she asked, looking directly ahead. "Someone died."

Her countenance remained dead pan as she said, "Yes, you would be having the ambulance for that."

The Colonel spoke from behind Daniel's shoulder, where he had an unobstruct-ed view between them. "They're good people, Daniel. You won't find better folk than Ted and Elizabeth."

"I hope they can save their home, Colonel. It's a nice place, and there's no doubt that's where they belong."

"I have one or two connections. I'll be doing what I can." They crossed over the Wunjunjurra and sur-mounted a steep little hill, bringing them to the start of a residential district where modern brick homes clustered for a distance of a kilometre or so. From there the road stretched out, straight for several miles, into the coastal wheat-sheep district.

"This is work experience for you, is it, Gerda?" Daniel asked. "I'm going to be a journalist," she said. "I will be a journalist for television when I'm twenty-one, I wish."

"That's a fine ambition. You might be another Jana Wendt, if you work hard."

"Yes. I work hard already. Very."

"Gerda is a good kid," said the Colonel. "Damn fine worker and plenty of perseverance. You wouldn't pick her for a sixteen-year-old, would you?"

Daniel twisted around to get a look at the Colonel's face. He had to be joking, but his face betrayed nothing. He looked hard at the girl/ woman alongside him. "Are you sixteen, Gerda?"

As she answered she sat up tall, which had the effect of pushing out her well-developed bust. "I am a big girl for sixteen years old." "Gerda," said Daniel, his voice laced with suspicion. "You wouldn't be taking the mickey would you?"

"Daniel is your name?" she asked, taking a quick, sideways glance at him, and receiving a nod. "I am not taking the mickey. I know I am grown for my age, and I know people are making fun. I don't worry. Making fun is good. I like to laugh. But making cruelty is not so good."

"No, Gerda," he said, feeling somehow guilty but unsure of the charge. "Making cruelty is not a good thing. And I have a feeling you're going to achieve whatever you set your mind to."

"Thank-you," she said, a note of pleasure in her voice. "Gerda Wesson. . . famous reporter."

When Daniel broke into laughter, her serious demeanour gave way to a broad, white smile. "Yes," she said, turning the smile on him. "Now we are making fun."

The Colonel rode quietly along, smiling contentedly to himself. At seventy seven years-of-age nothing pleased him more than to be in the company of young people, and to be working in the company of young people was especially gratifying: not many his age could boast that. But Horrie's death had reminded him of his own temporality; not that he needed reminding, every ache and pain or occasional memory lapse was reminder enough of his inexorable advance towards what he preferred to think of as the unyielding enigma. He imagined there couldn't be a lot of time left for him, but it was that very fact which brought him a new appreciation of things others considered as mere commonplace and not worthy of contemplation. There was great advantage in age, he was thinking. Even sitting where he was, time's gallery stretched back behind him, down through the long years, pliant to his drifting thoughts and ready to open a window on any one of the multitude of moments in his life. And that, in itself, was a source of pleasure. In what were supposed to be his declining years, there was a developing sense of clarity, as though those pieces of his life were steadily incorporating into one complex whole, offering a promise of something arcane, eternal and wonderful.

At a whim he could summon excerpts from great literature, recall the beauty of inspired works in theoretical science, the thoughts of Aristotle, the observation and in-sight of Byron and Shaw, or he could remember the magpies that used to choral outside his bedroom window each morningat age seven. Ten thousand instances of beauty and wonder captured from the earliest days of youth, right through to the present; or darker memories—memories of a world caught in the grip of a desperate struggle, sweeping misery and suffering across the face of the globe. And yet, even from that awful chaos, the retrospective eye, detached as it is by time's passage, was able to discern profound mystery and meaning like diamonds scattered and sparkling amid the scorched ruins.

That life was a mystery, he was glad of the fact, and if there had to be a mean-ing for life then for him it was to work towards unravelling that mystery, and thereby to enjoy his existence.

He remembered a lecture he had attended while on weekend leave, in Glasgow, 1940, delivered with such energy and passion that from that day forward his view of this world had forever been altered. W.Macneile Dixon had been the speaker's name, a name he wasn't likely to forget. For it was he who had suggested to all who filled the auditori-um on that cold November afternoon, that life, all life, being a creation of the universe was as one with and inseparable from it, and that life was in fact the manifestation of the cosmos' need to perceive itself. It seemed so elegant a piece of thought at the time, its subtlety had sown a minute seed which had grown into an unquenchable desire to probe the mysteries of existence. Probing, he realised, was not the same as understanding; but that was fine with him, and better left to more capable minds than his own. It was enough to be aware of the great mystery and be enchanted by the wonderment of it. But he could see so clearly now, the perfect symmetry of the notion. He knew he had in common with every other single living thing, one essential, binding commonality: Each could see in every other their self, and the whole, since all were an integral part of 'the one.'

"The one what?" Daniel asked.

"Never mind," said the Colonel, reeling in his thoughts. "I was only thinking aloud."

"Oh." Daniel twisted around in his seat so he could more comfortably talk to the Colonel. "I met Jack last night. I got up around three this morning for a glass of water and there he was, standing in the front room. Surprised me a bit."

"That sounds like Jack, all right," the Colonel observed with a chuckle. "He's a one-off. Did you talk?"

"Yeah." Daniel's brow furrowed. "The damnedest thing." He paused, considering how best to describe the event.

"Did he spook you, Daniel? He does have a flair for the theatrical." "A flair! I'll say. I suppose you know what gadhaitcha is?"

"I can't purport to having a thorough understanding, but it's akin to the ancient Greek legend of Nemesis, perhaps. Though it has a far wider application. Like the gad-haitcha man. He's pretty much equal to our bogey man. Or an object can be gadhaitcha, too. He talked about that?"

"He reckoned the gadhaitcha man was prowling around. Told me not to worry though, that he was after somebody else. Yeah, I don't mind admitting I was a little spooked," he laughed. "But finding Horrie dead in his room this morning. . . it is something of a coincidence, isn't it?

"Is it?" asked the Colonel, holding Daniel's gaze.

"I don't know," he replied, searching the old man's face. "I don't know so much that I could discount it out of hand."

"Then you exhibit a sound attitude. Jack is tuned to a different wavelength than most of us. I believe he sensed death in the house, perhaps even at the very time of Horrie's departure, and translated it into his own thought matrix as gadhaitcha. Is that difficult to accept?"

"No. I suppose I believed it from the start, but I was looking for a way to disprove it because. . . well, because if he was accurate on that count. . . he said something else which had me wondering."

"Oh?" The Colonel's interest increased. "What was that?" "When I said good night to him, he answered, "Good luck". "You misheard him."

"No, I didn't. I'm sure. And the more I think about it, the more deliberate I know it was. I was out of the room for not even fifteen seconds, and when I went back in, the room was in darkness, and he was gone."

"A flair for the theatrical, as I said," the Colonel chuckled. "I believe you. I wouldn't lose any sleep over it, though. If he said good luck, then that's what he meant. Good night, good luck, what's the difference?"

Daniel's brow smoothed, "Yeah, that's right. Cripes, what the hell am I going on about? Just with Horrie and all, I guess. . ." he shrugged. "My imagination."

Twenty minutes out of town, Gerda turned right at a signpost indicating "Ochre Beach 1km." which took them, bouncing and shaking, along a dirt track between two enormous wheat fields, stretching wide and all the way back to the coast.

The track terminated in a dusty parking area atop scalloped cliffs, sculptured in varicoloured clays ranging through red, orange, yellow and white. Half a dozen vehicles were parked there, mostly four-wheel drives and station-wagons, and to the left, club members worked busily at assembling their gliders.

Before the Colonel disembarked from the van he instructed Daniel in the opera-tion of a video camera, then observed his attempts via the on-board monitors as he prac-ticed zooming and focussing on the local seagulls as they planed along the escarpment in the up-draught.

"You'll do," he said. "Just remember, no sweeping around. Switch off when your subject has gone, and re-focus before you shoot the next. And don't go thinking you're some sort of artistic genius with that thing. This is bread-and-butter work," he concluded sternly.

Daniel eased the Colonel down the ramp and wheeled him over to where the fliers waited, apparently ready to fly. In a short time everybody was ready to commence. Gerda, the Colonel and Daniel had positioned themselves adjacent to the designated take-off point, and, when the signal was given, recorded the gliders launching into the wind.

For around twenty minutes the hang-gliders soared, wheeled and swooped around the vicinity, and Daniel felt sure he was doing an admirable job of capturing the grace and excitement of this hang-gliding lark. Just the right angle, perfect focus and framing, and he was sure his technique in tracking those sweeping passes was unusually proficient for a first-timer. The Colonel would be impressed, he knew, especially with the pod of dolphins he located close in to shore. It would give a certain environmental per-spective to the story.

When everybody was back on terra firmathe Colonel decided to experiment with a mini-cam, which was fixed to the A-frame of one of the gliders using gaffer tape, and set running to take DHULDO footage while the flier executed a few low passes over the shoreline and escarpment. With this accomplished, Daniel was given the task of setting up a tripod-mounted camera, while Gerda retrieved a microphone and recorder from the van, to be employed in the promotional interview.

Gerda came over to see that he had set up properly, and checked the focus while he stood to the side with his hands in his pockets, hoping for approval. She took her eye away from the viewfinder and caught the Colonel's attention.

"We are ready," she announced, and slapped Daniel firmly on the shoulder.

"Very fine." she said with a wink.

The club spokesman stood, looking wooden and awkward as he spoke to the camera with Gerda watching through the lens, telling everybody what a thrilling sport hang-gliding was, and how the club's professional instructors would expertly coach all newcomers, while the Colonel fiddled with sound-levels on his recorder.

Six times the spokesman managed to botch the carefully-constructed spiel, but on the seventh take he succeeded, and after handshakes all round it was time to pack up and go home.

The drive back to Port Moreton was filled with discussion, primarily with Danielasking the Colonel about previous assignments he had undertaken. He was quite taken with the novelty of video documentation, and the variety it offered.

"I wouldn't mind doing something like this, myself," he said, looking over the interior of the van in appraisal. "Must have set you back a few bob?"

"Not as much as all that," replied the Colonel, evasively. "A lot of this stuff I got second-hand." He checked his wrist-watch. "Would you mind switching on the radio? I'd like to catch the news.

Daniel reached over to the dash board radio and switched it on to hear: "indicative of the usual infighting among members of the Opposition, the Prime Minister said yesterday. Now to local news.

"A man was attacked in his home during the early hours of this morning after answering a knock at his door. Barry Ivan Curino, twenty-eight, a carpenter and a resident of Port Moreton, was assailed with a long-bladed implement which he described to police as resembling a machete. The brief but ferocious attack by the unknown assailant caused serious and life-threatening injury, say doctors at the Marion Regional Hospital. Mr Curino's condition is listed as serious.

"Anybody having any information, or who may have seen anything suspicious at around three o'clock this morning, in the vicinity of Compass and Lanyard Street, Port Moreton, are asked to contact police immediately. A reward has been posted.

"And at Bingham, a burst water-main has caused extensive damage to houses...

Five

Amber's day had been a shambles. It had begun when she awoke, lying on top of her bed, fully clothed. Fatigue and depression had held her motionless while she struggled to recall how she had spent the previous evening. She remembered meeting Daniel down on the beachand the terrible emotions which had coursed through her until she thought she was losing her mind. The last thing she remembered was changing out of that silly dress and into a pair of jeans. . . but what after that?

Time was slipping away from her. With an effort she forced herself up off the bed and moved lethargically in preparing herself for the day. She was already fifteen minutes late when Gwen rang to say she had suffered with toothache over the weekend. She had to drive to Marion to visit the dentist and was therefore unable to come into work. This meant that Bevan, her pick-up and delivery man, had to mind the second-hand store while she filled in for Gwen at the curio shop, thus backing up deliveries by one day and throwing her sense of order even further out of kilter.

She had been unaccountably irritable throughout the morning, and when people came into the shop to look around she wanted to scream at them to either buy some damn thing or get out. There had been a teenage boy who had searched the shelves for half an hour before choosing a pewter beer mug, a birthday present for his father, he said. The thirty-five dollar price-tag was a little difficult to read, and when he counted out all his money, much of it in coins, he had offered thirty dollars to Amber in payment.

"It's thirty five," she had pointed out, impatiently, and the boy had looked at her in dismay. He inspected the price-tag again, to see his mistake. "It's all I have," he explained. "Could I give you five tomorrow? It's dad's birthday today."

"Come back when you have the money," she had told him, and watched dispas-sionately as he gathered up his money and departed.

"Bitch," she had chided herself a minute after the boy had walked out the door. "Rotten, lousy bitch."

There had also been the tourist coach which pulled up at the restaurant just after midday. After their meal many of the passengers had taken a stroll up the street, and upon discovering the curio shop they had flocked inside to browse, taking the "careful" signs as licence to prod, spin, lift and otherwise handle every article taking their interest, which accounted for almost everything.

One customer had bought a clockwork music box for her granddaughter, which was a good sale at thirty-seven dollars, but when a young boy had tried to wield the mace that accompanied the sixteenth century suit of armour, and destroyed a china urn worth two hundred and eighty five dollars, she had seen red and stridently demanded that the child's mother pay for it.

An argument had ensued, the mother claiming that the mace was positioned too close to the urn, and, anyway, the thing was grossly over priced!

The other tourists had gathered around the sphere of action by this time, ab-sorbed by this real-life drama which, no doubt, would make a fine anecdote to amuse their friends. Amber was not concerned with the onlookers, and she would not write off any damage and turn the day into a complete disaster.

She threatened to call the police, which noticeably disconcerted her opponent, and seeing her waver she pressed the advantage, constructing the scenario of the mother being led away by police while her boy watched guiltily on.

She couldn't believe she had said it, but it was the decisive blow. In a huff of resentment and outrage the woman produced a cheque book, hastily scribbled on it the required amount, and signed it. "You'll be hearing from my lawyer, young woman," she had said in handing it over.

Amber refrained from commenting, accepted the cheque, which she knew would almost certainly be cancelled, and watched as the woman strutted out of the shop, the small boy struggling to keep up.

When the others had filed out the door, failing to make another purchase but mumbling appreciatively about the contest, Amber collapsed into the chair behind the counter, exhausted. For some time she thought about nothing, allowing the silence to soothe her. She looked out at the street, bright and hot, where the only movement was the heat haze rising from the bitumen. When a seagull swept up past the verandah, her thoughts followed its upward path until the town stretched out beneath her mind's eye, deserted in the afternoon heat. A country town with one pub, one supermarket, one business street; and she owned two businesses on that street. Junk shops. It all seemed suddenly so pathetic. Would this be her life, working here until old-age claimed her, then to retire and live off her investments until the end of her days? Life looked to extend out into the distance like some vast, desolate landscape.

She had been content to prove her independence by running the business and supporting herself, and that, in itself, was the whole point.

She was doing that, had been doing it for years, and now it was becoming obvious that she needed something more. There had to be more. There had to be a way to quench those visceral stirrings which somehow seemed full of strange, sweet promises. Why had they come to unsettle her so?

Unexpectedly, she thought of Daniel, and there was a sensation of a thousand tiny electric currents delicately firing deep inside of her, simultaneously producing a con-fusing mixture of pleasure and discomfort.

She didn't care about him, she tried to reason to herself. He had helped her with the window, that was all, and later on the beach he had rejected her, turning her night into a misery. But her effort to evoke anger only intensified the strange feelings. She would have to see him again, something deep inside told her it was the only way to appease this terrible yearning. At dinner-time, she thought, I'll make him notice me. She remembered the dress she had worn the last time, and how silly she had felt once she had arrived there. Stop it you fool, are you out of your mind? I can't do that. I can't!

~

Daniel came into the front room after washing for dinner. The Colonel was sit-ting beneath the reading-lamp, hunched over the same tome he had been reading the last time. With half an hour to wait until mealtime he considered switching on the tele-vision but decided against it, not wanting to disturb the old man. Instead, he walked to the book shelves to look over the titles. There were a lot of Reader's Digests, a swag of paperbacks, mostly whodunits, and a number of old, hardback volumes with interesting titles. He selected one of thesewith the unassuming title of Guy Manneringand took it over to an armchair to inspect further.

"Dolphins, said the Colonel without looking up. Daniel looked across to the old man. "What?" "Keen on dolphins, are you?"

"Oh, that," he replied, remembering the pod he had videoed. "I thought it might be good to illustrate the ecological aspect."

"Did I tell you to shoot the aquatic life?" "No, but-"

"Then why do I have three metres of tape showing dolphins where there should be oversized kites flying oversized boys?"

Daniel had no reply.

The Colonel looked up as he turned a page, smiled thinly. "It's actually a very nice shot, but whichever way I think about it, there's no way of tying it in with what we have. It's a commercial, not a documentary. I'll be saving it though. It may be useful sometime in the future."

"Really? Good. I thought you were dark on me for a while there." The Colonel chuckled. "That's what you were meant to think.

Disobeying orders? There was a time I could have had you shot." Daniel didn't quite know how to take that. It was an odd sort of joke, if that was what it was. He returned to his book.

A car was heard to pull up out the front, and a moment later Gary staggered in through the door, covered in grime and splatters of concrete, and obviously drunk. "Hel-lo chaps," he said merrily. "Am I in the wrong houseor is this the municipal library?"

Another car pulled up at the front of the house. Gary craned his neck to see who it was. "Ah-ha," he said, hicupping. "My capitalist sister, hic."

"Knock off early today?" the Colonel asked.

"Yeah. Knocked off at two and went for a few beer, hic . . .beers." Amber sat in her car, wandering if she hadn't been a bit hasty in her choice of clothes. She knew there would be doubts once she got here, but in front of her bedroom mirror she had known that this was how she wanted Daniel to see her. Besides, she had tried on everything else.

The skirt was okay. It hugged her waist and draped nicely over her hips and bum, and the little star patterns were nice too. It was the top she was worried about. It was white, so it matched well with the dark skirt. It was lacy around the waist and the neckline, which dipped quite low, and was supported only by two little straps. But it was very thin and it fitted very snugly over her contours. That was the worry. What if her mother said something to embarrass her?

She knew she must not hesitate any longer. She got out of the car, slammed the door closed with determination and set off towards the house. As she neared the front door it opened in front of her. Gary held it open and bowed with a sweeping hand gesture.

"Entree vous, mademoiselle Ambeur. Ow arr yew today?" She stepped into the room and saw that she was the centre of attention. Daniel was there, and he was looking at her, but she nervously avoided meeting his eyes. "Gary. Are you drunk again?" "Oui oui. Jest zee leettle beet pissed." he replied, tweaking her cheek.

"Stop it. Oww! That hurts."

"I see madam is going with zee rivets look this season," he continued in his simulated French accent. "Very nice, I think. Perraps if we jest adjest zee left tit up a fractzio for zee balance, hmm?"

He made as if to do this and received a kick in the shin. "You bloody dare! she growled, to which Gary snickered.

"Okay," he said, dropping the act. "I'm totally stuffed. It's been a long day. I think I'll go and crash out for a month or two," he said, walking off in the direction of his room.

Daniel was knocked out by Amber's appearance. "Your brother is a real character," he commented, filling the vacuum Gary had left in his departure.

"He gets a bit weird when he's had a few. . . dozen," she replied with a little laugh. There were a horde of butterflies in her stomach, all trying to escape at once. She didn't have to imagine his face now. It was right there, and he was looking right at her. She knew her own face was flushing. "I'll just go and say hello to mum."

Daniel nodded, watched her walk towards the kitchen and disappear through the door. He looked back down at the book in his hands and tried to give it his full attention. She was being friendly again, he thought. Perhaps everything was all right between them and she wasn't offended at all by the way he had behaved last night? Well, that was a break, there was no need for him to apologise now. Maybe it was all in his imagination and none of his thinking on the subject had any truth in it? It was confusing. He had been here only two days and already he was in a spin with this girl. It didn't seem normal. He had better keep his distance, he decided. If things could get this mixed up after only one afternoon. . . but the way she looked in that outfit. God she looked good!

Right on six o'clock Beth emerged from the kitchen, carrying plates of fish and chips. "Come on boys," she called gaily. "You must be hungry by now. Where's your fa-ther?" she said to Amber, who followed with the other plates.

"I'll look out back," she answered.

Beth went back to the kitchen while Daniel and the Colonel seated themselves at the table. In a moment Amber returned with Ted, just as Beth came back out with the salad bowls. Amber and her mother both converged on the same chair.

"I'm sitting here tonight, dear," Beth said, quickly occupying the chair. Why don't you sit around next to Daniel to even things up?"

Amber gave her mother a sharp look before she skirted around behind Ted to sit in Gary's usual position.

"Where'd you get to last night?" Ted asked her. "I decided to go out for a pizza."

"Oh. Was it a good pizza?"

"I didn't get a pizza."

"What did you get?"

"I didn't get anything." "Why not?"

"I wasn't hungry." "Then why did you-" "Dad!"

"Sorry, love. I just thought that if you went out for a pizza you must have been hungry, that's all. And if you were hungry, why didn't you stay for dinner?"

"Because I decided to go for a pizza, just for a change, but I realised I wasn't hungry when I got there."

"Oh, well, there you are then. That explains it, doesn't it."

"I wasn't aware there was a pizza shop around here," Daniel said. "There isn't," Beth replied, and everyone but Daniel laughed. "We used to have a guest here," said Beth, explaining. "Irwin Pommel. Funny little chap, he was. He was mad on pizza, and he would drive twenty miles to the nearest pizza shop and bring it back to eat in his room. He would do this at any time during the day or night, and whenever he was missing we would know he was driving to the Pizza Bar at Picton.

"It was Gary who started it, but whenever anybody went missing, we all got to saying, oh, they're out for a pizza. Just one of those silly family things, Daniel."

"Thanks for explaining. For the moment I thought I'd lost the plot."

"Speaking of plots, "Ted put in, "Horrie's funeral is on Wednesday. Dan, you're excused, of course. But I want you, Amber, and Colonel, you can come, can't you? to be at the Methodist church cemetery at eleven a.m. Okay?

It won't take but a little while, and we can see the poor bugger off in the proper fashion."

"Eleven?" said Amber. "Who'll look after the shop?"

"Close your blessed shop for half an hour. It won't cripple you, girl. "Perhaps Daniel would mind the shop for you," Beth suggested. "No, it's all right, I suppose. Just for half an hour, though." Daniel remained silent. He wasn't going anywhere near Amber's shop.

"Now tell everyone what happened at the council today, dear," Beth prompted.

"I was coming to that, love. Give a man a chance. You've spoiled the effect now, you see? I was going to sneak up on it, casual like, but now all the element of surprise has gone out of it."

Ted cut off another portion of butterfish and put it in his mouth, chewed it nonchalantly. He looked around at everyone to see that he had their attention. When he decided enough time had elapsed, he said,

"About that thing with the council. I drove out to see them today and told them I wasn't happy, that they should get another inspector down here and take a proper look. It was a supervisor, see? One of them white shirt types. So he takes a gander at the report and tells me that there's nothing wrong about it, that I'll just have to face facts.

And that's when I did what you said, Dan boy. I said I was getting a private bod in for a second opinion."

He lifted a chip from his plate and popped it in his mouth. Chewed it thoroughly while everyone waited.

"And?" demanded the Colonel.

"Well, he came over a bit strange, you know. Said if I insisted on wasting my money, perhaps he could send another one of his chaps after all. Said as how I was a ratepayer and everything, he supposed I was entitled."

"That's good, dad," Amber commented. "But I don't see what that will accomplish?"

"No? Well you're just an innocent girl, my love. No one would expect you to."

Amber fixed Ted with a scornful look. "That's not even funny, father dear."

"All right," he acquiesced. "Dan here suggested that they might change their mind once I told them I was going to a private inspector. It points to something fishy, see? It's a glimmer. Now we get in our private chap, any-way, and if his report conflicts with the council's we've got something to fight them with. We can stall them for months while we wait to go to court, at the least."

"You thought of that?" Amber asked, turning to Daniel and briefly holding his gaze.

"I have a natural distrust of bureaucracy." "So what happens now?" Beth asked Ted.

"We wait until the council guy comes out, then we get our man. We just have to hope we're right about this."

"Whatever happens, Ted," said the Colonel. "At least you can say you tried your best."

"That's right, dear," Beth said in support. "We'll be all right, whatever happens."

When dinner was over the men departed while Amber helped her mother clear the table and pile the dishes beside the sink. Amber ran the water and mixed in the detergent while Beth stood behind her with hands on hips, regarding her daughter with a cunning look in her eye.

Amber's attire had not escaped her attention. The skirt was pretty. The skimpy, lace top, however, wasn't quite her idea of how a young lady should dress, but she wasn't about to upset Amber again by commenting. If she wanted to catch Daniel's eye, that would certainly do it, and, she decided, that was all right with her. It had long been her concern that Amber showed so little interest in men. Besides, Daniel seemed a nice young man. . . and he owned property.

"Leave it," Beth commanded.

"It's all right, mum. I can give you a hand."

"Leave it, I said. You'll mess your skirt. Out of my kitchen, now. I don't want any-one under my feet."

Amber retreated from the washing-up and wiped her hands on a tea-towel.

Where was he? she wondered.

Daniel had returned to the front room, declining Ted's invitation for a beer on the balcony. He knew that if he wanted a chance to talk to Amber, here was the best place. But what was he going to talk to her about? There was nothing to say now, was there? And he certainly wasn't going to apologise for something she had started.

The Colonel flicked over a page and ha -hemmed, clearing his throat. I'm doing the exact opposite to what I decided, he thought, just as Amber pushed open the kitchen door and walked through.

She stepped into the room then stood, looking around. "It's quite cool in here," she said, her voice a little strained.

"Yes, very pleasant," he replied, aware of how super-ficial that had sounded.

"What are you reading?" She came forward and bent over, as if to read the book title.

Daniel averted his eyes, though not before taking notice of Amber's beautifully formed breasts beneath the lace. "Just something I picked off the shelf. It seems pretty dry stuff. I might try something else."

"Oh." She straightened and turned, sweeping her skirt around with her hand as she went towards the shelves, leaving behind the scent of lilacs.

The Colonel ha-hemmed again, and put down his book. "I think I'll go out onto the balcony for a while," he said to Daniel, and wheeled himself towards the door.

Daniel couldn't take his eyes off of her. She stretched her lithe body in reaching high up for a book, holding that position for longer than was necessary, though he wasn't to know that. When she brought it down she remained standing next to the shelves, holding the book in one hand while deliberately turning through the first few pages.

She's going to drive me nuts, he thought, and said: "It was very pleasant down at the beach last night, didn't you think so?"

Amber looked up as though distracted from her book. "Pardon?" "The beach, last night? I thought it was, ah. . . pleasantly ah-" "Balmy?"

"Moderate," he said. "Yes, balmy."

Amber closed the book with a slap. Again on tip-toesshe reached up to replace it.

"I'm sorry if I seemed a bit brusque last night. I was. . . I had some things on my mind." You idiot! he thought. What did you say that for?

"Not at all," Amber replied airily. "I didn't notice."

Of course you noticed, he thought. How could you not notice ignorant behaviour like that? And he remembered now, his original reason for wanting to talk to her. It had nothing to do with apologising for his behaviour, or even with giving her the opportunity to do the same. It was about getting behind that haunted look he had rec-ognised in her eyes. But tonight she seemed fine, and now it all seemed a bit absurd. Where had he gotten such a far-fetched notion?

Amber continued to scan the book shelves until she began to feel foolish, but she didn't know what else to do. She couldn't for the life of her think of anything to say, and her nerve was about to give out altogether!

"I was thinking," Daniel said. "I usually enjoy a stroll around this time of day. I was wondering if you might like to come along?"

He watched as she thought it over. She wasn't looking at him, but seemed more concerned with the dust on the shelves, which she brushed at with her fingers. "All right then," she said at last. "Down by the water would be nice."

Daniel led the way up the path and held open the gate while she passed through, her heart pounding so hard she hoped he wasn't able to hear it. It was still very warm out of doors, but the sun was only about an hour off the horizon and he hoped there might be a sea-breeze after sunset.

"How was work today?" he asked as they set off together. "Terrible," she laughed. "Everything went wrong." "Oh? One of those, was it? What happened?"

Amber gave him a full account as they negotiated the streets along the hill-side, how she had woken up late, how Gwen was unable to come in to work, and about the argument with the customer over the broken urn. "I hope your day was better than mine," she concluded.' "An outing with the Colonel and his protege, Gerda," he said with amusement in his voice. "It was fun. But I didn't realise you ran the curio shop, too. I thought maybe you just used the lock-up there to house your truck."

"Own," she corrected him." I bought it a couple of years ago, and it's doing rather well."

"That's great," he said, for lack of a suitable-response.

They walked in silence for a moment, Daniel considering how he might begin to explore a young woman's personality, how to test his disturbing theory without over-stepping the mark and arousing suspicion, while Amber struggled with conflicting emotions; the debilitating ambivalence of wanting to turn back, alone, in order to relieve the stress of this situation, and the desire to continue on in the company of this man who was the source of that anxiety. But at least that terrible yearning which had wrenched at her insides throughout the afternoon had been satisfied. For that reason it felt right. She would manage her discomfort and somehow conquer it.

When they emerged at the street corner adjacent to the top of the bluff, Daniel asked, "Do you want to cross over and take a look at the view?"

"Mmm," she said, nodding. "I like to come here."

They crossed the road and came up near the edge to lean against the railing and look out over the ocean. Daniel chanced a sideways peek at Amber while her attention was drawn to a ship out on the water. He wondered if he had ever seen a more beautiful sight. A solitary gust of wind came across the cliff-top, damp and smelling of sea salt. When it struck Amber's hair lashed about her face and head, instantly reminding him of the disturbing dream which had woken him during the night, and the memory of it still carried something of that portent.

They remained silent as they looked out over the coastline and the sparkling, blue expanse of water, constant in its movement. It was a comfortable silence, Daniel thought. Amber seemed completely at ease, but there was no need to rush it. This stroll had been a good idea.

Without turning from the view, Amber said, clearly, "I'm sorry I spoke to you the way I did."

"Forget it. We all have our bad days."

That had sounded condescending. Now she turned to examine his expression, but it revealed nothing to her. "I don't know why. . ." she began, but she left it unfinished, realising she couldn't explain something she didn't understand herself.

"Don't worry about it," he said, smiling. "There's no-"

"I'm not!" she responded impulsively. "I wanted to apologise, that's all."

"All right," he said mildly. "Shall we go on down to the beach?" "Yes," she answered, studying the ground by her feet.

She was finding this difficult. As she walked beside him down the steep slope she felt sure that her nervous state was being betrayed in her awkward gait. She felt awkward and constricted. Thankfully her legs operated of their own volition, remembering the mechanics of walking, but she was sure they moved in a stiff, irregular manner.

It was very disconcerting, and there was such a thrill in her stomach, though not an altogether unpleasant sensation.

"Do you want to walk out on the jetty?" he asked as they arrived at the foreshore.

"I think I'd rather sit down," she said in a small voice.

"All right. What about under the jetty, where it's cooler?" Amber

nodded and slipped off her shoes, ready to negotiate the sand.

He led the way down onto the beach and across the sand, to a position just above the water-line in the shade of the boardwalk. Daniel sat with his back against a pylon, his legs stretched out in front of him. Amber folded her skirt under her as she knelt on the sand, then sat back to prop on one arm with her knees tucked up sideways.

After listening to the sound of the waves for a while, Daniel said, "I've figured out that you have a room at the guest-house, but do you have somewhere else too?"

"I spend the weekends at the house," she said, brushing her hair away from her face. "I also rent a flat. Down there," she pointed along the beach.

"Where I saw you last night?" She nodded.

"And you live there alone?" "Yes."

Yes, he thought, and if my guess is right, Amber, alone is the only sanctuary there is for you. I'm surprised you consented to coming along with me this evening. Why did you? Am I wrong about you? I sure hope so, my lovely, because then we can go our separate ways, without me playing the role of the kind stranger and having to shoulder the guilt if I discover I can't exorcise your particular demon.

When he turned his head to look over at the squealing children playing in the surf, she grasped the opportunity to study him. He seemed quite an ordinary man. Not big, but his musculature looked strong and supple, well proportioned like the men in the magazines. He had a kind face, perhaps even handsome, and she was forced to concede that his pony-tail suited him well. It served to distinguish him from the red-neck, ocker bastards around here, anyway. She liked the way he looked, she decided. There was a certain elusive and fascinating quality about him.

When he turned back, he noticed her quickly look away. Had she been sizing him up? The possibility amused him. The way she looked she could have any man she wanted. She was probably wondering what the hell she was doing down here with an unemployed nobody like him, he imagined.

"It's hot, isn't it!" Amber observed, feeling at a loss with the silence between them.

"Yeah. We should have brought some swimming togs." Amber climbed to her feet. "I'm just going for a paddle." Daniel's eyes followed her as she walked down to the water's edge. She hitched up her skirt and stepped into the advancing wash, getting up on her toes as it splashed cold on her legs. She was a vision of beauty. It was a pleasure just to watch as she cooled her feet, splashing the water out in front of her and scratching her toes in the wet sand as the water receded.

He was aware of what he was doing to himself. He knew that if he allowed him-self to continue in this way, he would eventually sucker himself into thinking he was fall-ing for this girl. It could not happen. It was the last thing he needed. To allow himself any sort of involvement, particularly with a doomed and totally fanciful combination like this, could only be a further source of turmoil in his life. Christ knew there was already a bundle of that! He was the last of his family, he thought ruefully. He had to start cutting out a proper life for himself, start settling his troubles. And the house, sitting up there on the hill, depreciating with every passing day while he continued to languish with indecision. It was time to wise up, to finish with the empty day-dreams and effect some determination in his life.

He could feel his resolve strengthening as these thoughts filled his mind. He would see what was ailing this girl and get back to the guesthouse. There was some serious thinking to be done before he left town.

"The water is really nice," Amber declared, affecting girlish pleasure. She knew what she must do. She would face down her anxiety and try hard to be friends with Dan-iel. It was an important decision she had made, and exciting. She really felt she could do it.

She had surprised him; run up to him and knelt down beside him, now arch-ing her back with elbows held high and outstretched as she combed her fingers back through her hair. He tried to ignore the ripe bud impressions pressed against her thin top.

"Not cold?"

"No, it's lovely," she affirmed. "Let's go for an ice-cream, shall we?"

"Okay," he agreed, wondering what had gotten into her.

"Do you mind paying, she asked with an apologetic simper. "I didn't bring any money."

"My treat? Of course. I get to play the gentleman and buy the lady what she wants. An old-fashioned custom, but I kind of like it." "Me too," she bubbled, feeling suddenly much happier.

They walked up to the esplanade where a kiosk served refreshments on the raised terrace. Daniel purchased the ice-cream cones and they took them to sit at a plas-tic table beneath a brightly coloured umbrella.

"What made you get into the second-hand and curio game?" he asked as soon as they had seated themselves. Daniel had made up his mind to get to the heart of the matter quickly, with no pussyfooting.

Amber glanced at him thoughtfully over top of the ice-cream cone. . . continued only to lick.

"I think it's a very interesting business. How'd you get started?" "A friend. When she died she left me the second-hand shop. I used to work for her. She was such a dear, sweat lady."

"Oh. I'm sorry about your friend, but she left you a great asset. A means of survival. I guess you learned the business from her? And you've since bought the curio shop. That was smart. . . buying out the opposition."

Amber sat back in her chair, inspected her ice-cream and licked at a dribble as it ran down towards her fingers.

"I expect there's more to a job like that than meets the eye," he persisted.

"I did a couple of. . . almost two years at business college."

"You didn't finish?"

Amber only shook her head. "Why not?"

She shrugged. "I didn't like it much, and there was the job at the second-hand store. I wanted to start earning money for a change."

"Yeah, well it turned out to be a good decision for you. You've done pretty well for yourself. Keeps you busy, I bet."

"Not all that busy. Gwen and Bevan are good employees. Just keeping on top of the situation is the main thing, making sure to stock only what people want to buy."

"Well it certainly makes sense. I bet you're a good businesswoman. Long hours and careful management. You do devote a lot of time to your work, don't you. Five days plus, what. . . Saturday afternoon, Sunday morning? That doesn't allow much time for yourself."

She was looking at him warily, now. Why was he so interested in her work? There was a vague sense of something strange going on, but perhaps it was just her. He was taking an interest, that was all.

"It's no more than is necessary," she said, a touch defensively. "To run a business like that you need to keep the doors open as much as possible. I have to survive, don't I?"

"Absolutely. I agree," he said, seeing a trace of something now. "But it doesn't worry you that it takes up so much of your time?"

She sensed a trap. Was it real or a product of her own fears? she wondered. He was getting close to something tender. What was it?

"No, why should it? People have to work."

He knew he was on the verge. This was where the demons dwelt in people's lives, if those lives were broken. Their private lives, their ability to connect with others. . . intimate connections. If there was damage, then there would be the accompanying shame, and it could never be permitted for another human being to get close enough to discover the source of that shame. He sensed the barriers going up, and already he was cursing his dubious talent for doing this thing.

The signs were emerging.

"Yes," he said, noticing the worried eyes that watched him. "And all that work makes it all the more enjoyable when you let down your hair at the end of the week, doesn't it. It does for me. Where do you go with your friends to enjoy yourself?"

Why are you doing this to me? she thought through rising panic. Oh God, no. He can't know! But why else would he. . . A great, black void seemed to be swallowing her from the inside as she realised what a terrible fool she had been making of herself. How could she have even thought she could be just a normal girl? I have no friends, you bastard! But you already know that, don't you. I'm the local slut, the subject of every perverted joke or story in the district. I am the joke!

What was happening in her eyes? "You probably go to the pub and meet your friends there, eh? Have a good old knees-up. I bet you have lots of close friends, don't you?"

Amber stood up so fast, her chair flew backwards and tumbled with a clatter against the bricks. Her eyes shone with fury and consuming horror.

"You bastard," she bawled down at him, and threw her ice-cream at him. "You fucking bastard. Who told you!" Her voice was shrill and distraught.

"Amber, I'm sorry. Nobody told me anything, I promise you." "I trusted you!" Her hands could find no place to rest, darting from hair to face, to her shoulders in a self-hug, then to arms folded and holding her midriff as though in unbearable pain.

"I don't know what it is," Daniel said urgently. "I'm sorry it hurts you so much, but whatever it is, you have to let someone in. It's the way of it, Amber. I can help if you let me."

Amber was listening, but only partially understanding. Her insides writhed with terrible surges of emotion and her mind could not accept the words of her betrayer. She fled from the table and ran off down the street.

Daniel thought about letting her go on her own, but realised that it might be a mistake. He chased after her as fast as he could, and at the street corner opposite the hotel he managed to catch her by the elbow.

When he turned her towards him, she refused to look him in the eye. There was no resistance in her, she was strangely pliant, as if she were pretending she didn't exist.

"Amber. We need to talk," he said almost tenderly.

"Yeah, I bet, talk." And she twisted out of his grip, stared defiantly at him.

"I said talk and I mean talk," he continued calmly. "Look, Amber, I don't know what's going on, exactly, but I know when someone is torturing themselves. And if there isn't anybody else, then let me help you. Please."

"You're telling me you don't know?" Daniel shook his head while she continued to glare at him. "Liar!" she screamed. "You miserable bastard. Don't know, hey? Don't know? Well come on, I'll show you the social life of this quaint old town. . . show you how many friends I've got. Come on, buy me a beer." She tried to drag him across the street towards the hotel.

"Amber, I don't think-"

"Come on you bastard. You can buy a lady a beer, can't you?" Short of dragging Amber bodily home, Daniel didn't know what else to do.

"You're not going to make a scene in there, are you?"

"No," she said, straining, dragging him by the arm. "You want to talk so much? We'll damn well talk in here."

Amber shoved him through the door of the front bar so that it banged up against the wall, announcing their entry to everyone in the room. They were all working stiffs, as Daniel had expected to discover: labourers, fishermen, farmers, tradesmen, council workers and a number of women among the throng as well. Several turned to see who had banged the doorwhile the rest continued to fill the room with loud conversation, laughter and cigarette smoke.

When Amber came out from where she was hidden behind Daniel, there were several double takes as the men took note of Amber's revealing attire.

"Go on, buy me a drink," Amber insisted, pushing him towards the bar.

"All right, all right," he protested, and with Amber following he found a path through the crowd. As he advanced he noticed two women at a table against the wall suddenly stop talking, to begin making furtive gestures towards Amber, surprise and something else registering on their faces, which he couldn't decipher.

"Excuse me, pal," he said to a big man in overalls who was blockinghis route, and he finally made it through to the bar.

He propped with his elbows resting on the counter and looked along each side of him to observe some of the faces as he waited for service. Through the general din, odd phrases began reaching his ears: "Goes off like a rocket, mate"... "a right little raver" ... "certified nympho, they reckon" ... "who's the guy?"

He had ordered the beers and was just paying for them when a man came up close to his ear and said, "You lucky devil."

He turned around in time to see the man walking away. Shrugging, he decided to forget it and paid for the drinks.

"Here," he said turning to Amber and giving her her beer. "There's a table over there in the far corner."

As he followed her towards the vacant table a young woman in tank-top and jeans at the second table they passed looked up, scowling at Amber. "Toe-rag," she spat.

"Hey," he called to Amber. "Let's get out of here."

"No," she answered over her shoulder, and continued on to the table.

Amber opted for the corner seat, looking out on the room while he sat facing her.

"How about it, Amber?" came an anonymous voice above the hubbub.

Daniel twisted around in his chair to see what was going on, and found most of the room was staring at them.

He turned back to Amber. "What the hell is going on?"

"These are my friends," she said, putting on an unpleasant smile. "This is where I come to relax and enjoy myself."

"Hey, Amber! Come over here and sit on my face," came another call.

"Right, that's enough," he said, standing. "Come on, you've had your joke." He extended his hand to entice her out of her chair.

"And you don't know anything, right?" Her eyes shone with renewed fury.

"Hey, don't take her away," someone called out. "I'm getting a hard-on perving on them tits." A chorus of laughter filled the room.

"Why don't you shut your filthy mouths, you morons!" he yelled, turning to face the crowd.

There was a moment's lull and some nervous laughter. "I said we're going." He took her hand and pulled her up out of her chair.

She smiled mockingly at him as he pushed her in front of him and began guiding her towards the exit. A guy in a sleeveless football jumper leaned out as they passed. "Hey, Amber. Car-park in ten minutes. I've got a nice piece of sirloin for you."

There was a bone-splitting crack as Daniel's fist connected with the man's jaw, and a thud as he hit the carpet.

Someone called out "Hey, what'd you do that for? No need to get sore just because your piece of crumpet likes to share it around." When the man emerged from the throng, Daniel's heart sank. He had to weigh at least twenty stone. His bald head was tattooed with an octopus, and some teeth were missing from his leering grin. Behind his huge shoulder, he was even more dismayed to see Amber watching him, her lips fixed in a cruel sneer.

"Get out of my way, we're leaving," Daniel said, but the man knew he held the floor.

"This guy wants to leave," he said to everybody, swinging his great frame around. "That was my buddy you just king hit, pal."

Daniel knew the score now. This guy was going to wipe the floor with him, given half a chance. He leapt forwards and landed a good blow across the bridge of his nose, and before he had reacted, another one on his jaw. After that, things got a bit too busy to really know what was happening.

Amber watched as the much bigger man recovered to hit Daniel so hard in the face it almost sent him to the floor, and felt the thrill of satisfaction. She wanted him hurt. He had hurt her and he deserved a share of the pain.

It wasn't long before Daniel was overpowered. He was being hit repeatedly in the chest and stomach and was ready to fall, but his assailant held him standing. That's enough, she thought. No more.

He was slammed headlong into a concrete post, then kicked in the face, once, twice, three times...

No, stop. Stop. Please stop! A wave of nausea swept over her. Daniel was let go and he slumped to the floor. The man swung his boot, hard at his head, and there was a sickening dull sound as it connected, jarring his head savagely back.

"Nooo" Amber wailed, finding her voice, but the kicking did not cease. "Stop it! Please, God. You're killing him."

She raced forward when it was evident the kicking was going to continue, and collided with the now frenzied brute to send herself sprawling over top of Daniel in a desperate attempt to protect him. "Can't you see he's unconscious, you animal!" she bawled.

The man stood, looming over her with a smile on his face. "You better scrape up your boy-friend and go home, then." He gloated for awhile longer before lumbering away toward the bar.

Amber carefully lifted herself off Daniel, to bring herself to a kneeling position beside him. "Oh, Dan, I'm so sorry."

She looked up to those who were still gathered around. "Would somebody please help me?" But mostly they only remained watching on. A couple walked away.

She tried to get her hands under his shoulders to lift him. She managed this but found she was unable to move him. "Please," she implored.

A barman pushed through the crowd of onlookers and squatted beside Amber to look at Daniel's condition. "Bloody hell," he said, seeing that Daniel's face had been opened up in several places and was covered in blood. A tiny squeak emerged from Amber's throat.

"Have you got a car?" he asked. She shook her head.

"There's a taxi just pulled up out front," someone obliged.

"Go and tell him to wait," he ordered. "Now, come on you mongrels, two of you lend a hand here. Anyone with guts enough to take on Big Jake deserves a ride home, I reckon."

There was general agreement with this, and volunteers came forward. Daniel was loaded into the back seat of the taxi while the driver protested having bleeding, unconscious passengers in his cab.

The barman silenced his grumbling by handing him a twenty-dollar note. "Just take him where the lady says and shut up," he growled.

Amber got into the back seat with Daniel, rested his head on her lap as tears began to spill from her eyes.

"Where to, lady?"

Where to? She hadn't even thought. . . How could she take him home to the guest-house looking like this? How could she possibly explain?

"I said, where to?"

"Oceanview flats," she barely managed to say before breaking into convulsive sobbing.

"What number?" the driver persisted.

"Na una anine."

Amber didn't know why she was crying. . . for Daniel, for herself? there was no way of knowing. She didn't care if the taxi-driver glanced in his mirror at every opportunity. She had never cried like this before. It came from the depths of her being and racked her entire body as great waves of long pent up emotions gushed out of her, finding release at last.

She gave in to it, unable and even unwilling to hold it back. It felt so good to be able to cry again. And she cradled Daniel's head in the crook of her arm as tears streamed and fell to mix with the blood on his battered face. He had fought for her. He had stood up for her, alone against all those bastards, and had been beaten senseless for it. He really did care, and he hadn't known anything of her shameful past after all. Something strange and compelling stirred within her. Nothing of the sort which in the past had threatened to tear her apart or drive her to desperation. This was something new and, even so, not at all frightening. It was warm and sweet and. . .yes, tender: a heartfelt tenderness as she looked down on him and softly stroked his face.

Six

Only when it became evident that his passengers could not depart his taxi unaided did the driver grudgingly lend assistance. He hooked his arms under Daniel's shoulders and followed as Amber struggled, walking backwards with his legs held either side, through the front door and down the passage to lift him onto her bed.

"This isn't in the job description, you know," complained the driver in a surly manner.

Amber reached beneath the bed and pulled out her handbag, found a twenty-dollar note and thrust it towards him, saying, "Would you close the door on the way out?"

He took the money, looked at it peevishly as he turned it in his hand, grunted and left the room.

Amber gathered up all the pillows from around the room and strained with Daniel's weight while she arranged them behind his head and shoulders. She thought that this was the correct procedure, and it seemed like the right thing to do. Satisfied that she had made him as comfortable as she was able, she rushed to the telephone in the kitchen and hurriedly dialled for the doctor.

When she returned, she stood, looking at him from the doorway, wondering what else she could do for him.

She went to the ornamental chair against the wall and dragged it over beside the bed, where she lowered herself into it and sat stiffly beside him, her hands clenched tightly together on top of her knees. Standing again, she leaned across to inspect his injuries, chewing pensively on her bottom lip as she noted the depth of the wounds. A small, quavering sound escaped her throat and she quickly left the room, returning a few minutes later with a bowl of warm water smelling of an-tiseptic, and a wad of cotton wool. Sitting and pulling the chair up close, she moistened the cotton wool and leaned over to begin gingerly cleaning around the broken skin, her mind cruelly conjuring up thoughts of permanent injury and brain damage which elicited plaintive lamentations from her as she worked, while every time she dabbed, fresh blood filled the cut she had just cleaned.

He had seen her horrible face, she recalled, just before he had thrown the first punch at that brute. *What have I done? What sort of a callous bitch am I? His face. . . his lovely, kind face. Every time he sees the scars in the mirror he'll remember the black-hearted witch I am.*

"I didn't mean to. . ." It came involuntarily, and finished with a squeak as she fought to hold back resurgent emotions which threatened to consume her last ounce of strength.

He had wanted to talk to her. He said he knew when people were torturing themselves, and that he would help her if she would let him. Why hadn't she heard him then? Why, only now, did she hear those words?

He had acknowledged her pain and she hadn't listened. He understood what no one else ever could, and only now did his words touch something deep and painful inside her.

She was forced to cease tending his wounds and steadied the bowl on her knees as her shoulders began to shake, and again, tears began to flow.

As she sobbed she thought what a miserable thing she had become, how her life which had once begun to show promise had turned so dark and perverted until all hope had been extinguished. And then it came, a dread memory which emerged from the depths of her mind with such violence that she reeled at its horror and began to moan uncontrollably. Her hands released the bowl, letting it spill to the floor as she clutched beneath her ribs at the awful thing ravaging her insides.

"Oh, Dan." she called desperately. "Help me, Dan, please. Oh, God, Dan. Help mee-e-e" she moaned lamentably. "I think I've k-killed someone!"

She pitched forwards out of the chair to fall across the bed, reaching out to him and wailing unrestrainably at the horror her own mind assaulted her with, the bed rocking with her convulsions and the walls resounding with her strident cries.

When Daniel's hand moved under her grip, she snapped her head up from the bed to see through tear-blurred eyes that he was regaining consciousness. In a sudden, fearful flurry she tried to lift herself from the bed and flee in the one action, in her frenzy colliding with the chair and tangling her legs so that she was sent sprawling across the carpet. He mustn't see me like this! was her one, panicky thought as she got her feet under her and scrambled for escape. She ran across the passage and into the bathroom, locking the door behind her, then slumped down beside it, bighting hard into her hand in effort to subdue the anguish which strove to pour out, wrenching her whole body and escaping from her as low, mournful ululation.

Daniel opened one eye, then the other. He thought he had heard a banging noise. Where was he? A bedroom, obviously, but whose?

Frilly curtains over the window, a framed picture of horses on the wall facing him. A dressing-table with hairbrushes and cosmetics on top. A sharp pain behind his right eye made him wince.

This was Amber's room, he guessed, and he carefully turned his head to the right to see the overturned chair and the mess on the floor. Something was not right.

"Amber!" he called, and immediately wished he hadn't. It brought a lightening pain to his chest.

He was propped up on a pile of pillows, he realised. She was showing surprising concern for someone she had just fed to the sharks, he thought ruefully.

"Amber?" he called less strenuously, not quite avoiding pain from his ribs.

He heard the sound of water being splashed. . . . a wash-basin perhaps. All right then, someone was here.

He experimented by moving his arms, found his shoulders were sore and strained. His legs seemed okay, it was just the rest of him that felt like it had been through a mill. He heard a door open in the passage.

"Amber? Is that you?"

She moved slowly through the doorway, taking small steps and holding her hands clenched at her breast. Her eyes were puffy and red.

"How are you feeling?"

It was obvious to him she had been crying. "Oh, I'll be just fine. I've been beaten up by bigger galoots than him in my time." He tried a smile and discovered it hurt his lips.

"You're not all right. I've called a doctor," she said, looking sullen.

"Oh? Well, that was thoughtful you."

"I know I deserve that. Go ahead and shout at me if you want. I won't fight back."

He studied her. She stood halfway in the room, about six feet from the bed. Her eyes were downcast and her feet were together in an altogether forlorn pose. But he didn't want to feel sorry for her. Why the hell should he?

"My head will hurt if I shout at you."

"I'll get you some aspirin," she said quietly, and left the room. He gave a sigh and put a hand to his face, testingly. It came away daubed with blood. "Terrific," he breathed angrily. "I don't believe this."

In a short while Amber returned with a tumbler of water in which

three aspirin fizzed. She found Daniel examining suspiciously loose teeth.

"I put three in," she almost whispered, and stretched from a distance to hand him the glass.

He accepted it, being sure not to make contact with her as he took possession, and making a point of not thanking her. He drank it down and strained to reach the bed-side cabinet with the empty tumbler.

Amber moved to assist him, but hesitated at the last moment. "You have an accident?" he asked, directing his gaze at the mess on the floor.

She quickly knelt to pick up the bowl and the cotton wool, and righted the chair as she stood.

"You've been crying."

Amber wiped her eyes, looked down at her feet and sniffled. "You make it hard, don't you? I'm doing my best to be angry with you, but how can I when you stand there looking so goddamned miserable?"

"I'm sorry, Dan. Really." She looked up at him. "I'm so sorry."

"Yeah, well. . . I can see that. If it makes any difference, so am I." A questioning look came over Amber's face. "You? Why?" "Because I'm a jerk, that's why." After pausing awhile, he said,

"The way I treated you. All those stupid questions without knowing. . . no, with-out caring if I was hurting you. I'd call this right whack ," he said, indicating to his face. "I've got no right to be angry with you. But if you want to shout at me, go ahead. I won't fight back."

He looked over to her, saw the corners of her mouth begin to curl a little. He offered a grin. "Ouch! Oh, shit. My mouth feels like minced meat."

Amber came quickly over to him as he doubled over, put her head down to see what was wrong. "I'll get some ice," she said worriedly.

"No, no. No ice," he said, straining. "Stay here." He straightened up again and began to chuckle. "Oo, ah, shit."

"What's wrong?"

Her look of puzzlement and the question itself sent him into a barely restrained bout of laughter, which he managed to keep to an agonising chuckle.

Amber watched bemusedly on as he cursed and writhed in mirth. The pain seemed to make him laugh, and the laughter brought more discomfort which made him curse and laugh still more.

"But what are you laughing at?" she asked, beginning to giggle herself, and having no idea why.

"Oooh, ooo, aaah-haa-ha-ha," he expressed leaning back into the pillows and taking a steadying breath. "Ooh. . . phew. . ." He appeared to be regaining control.

"Nothing. Nothing in particular." He chuckled again and took another breath. "Just the whole situation, that's all. Did we or did we not set out for a peaceful stroll along the beach this evening? And take a look at us now. What's wrong with this picture? Oooh," he sighed, don't let me laugh any more. It hurts."

He groaned and sighed for a while longer, until he had fully recovered. When he returned his attention to Amber, he found her watching him closely, a serious look in her face.

"It could be the bump on the head," he replied to the look. "I do feel a bit light-headed."

Amber moved the chair up to the bedside and lowered herself into it. "I suppose so."

After a moment's quiet, Daniel remarked, "You like horses then."

Amber turned to look at the picture. "I didn't buy it especially for the horses. I'm not sure why, exactly. It just appeals to me. Daniel studied it for a while. There was an old, European-style town in the background, at the base of a hill. He could make out what looked like a church steeple. There were seven horses in all, including a foal chasing to catch up. . . with its mother, perhaps. The forest behind them looked old and foreboding, the story-book kind where witches and goblins lurked, but out in the yellow grass, all was wildflowers, bright sunlight and safety. He had to look away when dark blotches started to obscure his vision.

"What's wrong?" Amber asked, watching him rub at his eyes. "I think that great clod loosened my brain."

"Where's that damned doctor?" she hissed. "I'm going to clean up your face some more. I'll be back in a sec."

Amber picked up the bowl and went to the bathroom cabinet for more antisep-tic, when she returned she found Daniel lying back with his eyes closed.

"You okay?"

"Just resting. I'm a bit tired."

Amber sat the bowl on her lap and began cleaning where his wounds had been bleeding again. He opened his eyes to look at the studied expression on her face. She really was beautiful, he found himself thinking.

"You ought to see your face," he said with a chuckle.

"You ought to see your own," she smiled.

"Please, don't start me laughing again." He closed his eyes and enjoyed the attention he was receiving.

"I should have taken you to the hospital."

"Don't worry, you're doing great. And I bet the nurses aren't half so pretty as you."

"Don't be silly," she said, dabbing his nose. "There, that's all I know to do until the doctor gets here."

"Hey," he said as she stood to take the bowl away. "Believe me, I'm not angry about this, okay?"

She nodded and gave a little shrug at the same time. "Okay," she repeated, affecting a narrow smile, and continued towards the bathroom.

Had he really said that to her? Had he really said she was pretty? The last of the shadowy remnants receded from her mind with the unexpected thrill those words had evoked. No man had ever said she was pretty. . . never pretty!

She looked critically at herself in the mirror above the wash-basin, and combed her hair back with her fingers where it had fallen around her face, sceptically noting her pale features and those few, annoying freckles sprinkled over her nose. "If he says you are, then you are," she said, poking her tongue out at her reflection.

Before leaving the bathroom she searched for and found a pink lipstick, which she hurriedly applied to colour her pale lips, thinking how nice it felt to have him here, even under the circumstances.

"Amber? I think the doctor is here," Daniel called from the bedroom, noticing the movement of headlights on the curtains.

When the doorbell chimed he watched her hurry past the bedroom doorway to get the front door, and in a little while she led in a tall, elderly man carrying a large, leather case.

"My my," the doctor intoned in mild surprise and peering judiciously at Daniel's face. "How did this happen?"

"A difference of opinion with a gorilla," he replied without humour.

He sat in the chair beside the bed and set down his case. "Any other injuries?" he asked, reaching over to pull back Daniel's bloodied T-shirt.

"The ribs are a bit tender."

"Hmm." He lightly felt around Daniel's ribs, causing a grunt of discomfort.

Daniel glanced up to see Amber standing at the foot of the bed, wringing her hands and wearing a worried scowl.

"Hmm." The doctor released the T-shirt and turned his attention to Daniel's face. "Any loss of consciousness?"

"A bit."

"About fifteen minutes," Amber corrected.

"Any trouble with your vision?" "Yes," said Amber as Daniel said no. "A bit," he amended.

The doctor shone a light in his eyes, then asked him to follow his finger as he moved it from side to side.

"Will he be all right?" Amber asked, breaking the silence.

"I expect so," replied the doctor, as he studied Daniel's eyes more closely with an instrument composed of a lens and a small, bright light. "You've taken some heavy knocks, er. . . ?"

"Dan," Amber answered.

". . . Dan. You're concussed and you ought to be in hospital for observation."

"I'd rather not, doc. How about if I just take it easy for-

"Rest." said the doctor, cutting him short. "Complete rest, and quiet. None of this take-it-easy business, you understand?"

"I'll take care of him, doctor," Amber volunteered.

The doctor turned to her. "Keep him off his feet for two days. Severe headache, dizziness, nausea, excessive sleepiness, bloody urine, anything untoward and you phone me, understood?"

Amber nodded gravely.

"You may have a cracked rib there," he said, turning to Daniel. "Are you breath-ing comfortably?"

"Yes."

"Okay. Best you stay on your back the way you are. If it gives you any grief, have your girl-friend drive you to

the clinic for an x-ray." The doctor's presumption brought a smile to Daniel's face. He glanced over at Amber to discover she was smiling, too, but she looked down to conceal the expression when she saw him watching her. The doctor bent to open his case, and after searching around he came out with a bottle of antiseptic, a needle wrapped in cellophane and a coil of thread likewise wrapped. "We'll stitch up those wounds for you now. Or does your girl like the rugged look?" Daniel found himself laughing. "Ooo-hoo, doc. Give me a break.

What do you think, sweetheart?" he said, playing along.

"Maybe you could stitch his mouth closed," she replied with a flush of colour in her cheeks.

The stitching took several minutes, and while the doctor concentrated on his work, Amber sat on the end of the bed, watching on uneasily and squeezing Daniel's foot as an act of support.

When it was done, the doctor stowed away his equipment and snapped shut his case. "Remember now, rest. That's not the same as taking it easy, you understand."

Daniel nodded and found it hurt his head.

"Paracetamol for the sore head," he said turning to Amber. "You take good care of him," he said, feigning sternness.

"I will."

"Good," he smiled. "Now I've got two flues and a pre-natal to attend to. Good night to you both."

"I'll show you out," Amber said, following. "Thanks, doc," Daniel called.

When she returned from seeing the doctor out, Amber stood back from the bed, seeming uneasy. "Can I get you anything?"

"No, thanks. I guess I'm okay. I suppose I'd better let you have your room back and get-"

"No," she said, taking an impulsive step forwards. "Did you think I was lying when I said I'd take care of you? This was my fault. You have to let me make amends."

"Amber, you're not to blame for this. Christ, this sort of stuff has been happen-ing to me all my life. I have a knack for it."

"Let me look after you, Dan. I don't care what you say, I feel responsible and I want to do something to make it right."

"Are you sure?" he asked in a serious voice. "Yes."

He sighed deeply. "Am I glad you said that. I'm not sure I could have gotten up off this bed. Just until I feel better, okay? I can't put you to too much trouble."

Amber came slowly up beside the bed, hesitated awhile before sitting on the edge of the mattress. "Is it too bad?" She leaned over close to inspect the doctor's hand-iwork. "Did it hurt? It looked dreadful."

"Not as much as having my foot crushed. That's some grip you've got, girl." He chuckled, and made a grab for his paining head.

"I was trying to comfort you," she said indignantly, then baulked, realising what she had said. "I mean, you know, lend support."

"Yeah, I know. Thanks. It was a nice thing to do. It did divert my attention," he said, chuckling again.

Amber met his mirthful eyes and found it impos-sible not to smile back at him. "Stop it. I didn't squeeze that hard."

When she smiled at him, he thought his heart was going to melt. He knew she was terribly troubled, but he couldn't stop what he knew was happening inside him. It was pointless to try, and he felt as vulnerable then as he had ever felt in his life. He just did not have the strength to resist, as his better judgement tried vainly to warn him.

"What is it?" Amber asked, concerned at his sudden quietness. "I'm a . . ." He wrestled with his conscience. He ought to tell her what was happening, for his own sake as well as for hers. It would be best for both of them if he left, tonight, if his feelings weren't reciprocated.

"What, Dan? Tell me. Are you feeling ill?"

"Yeah, you might say that," he replied, smiling awkwardly. Amber moved to put her hand on his arm, hesitated midway, then lowered her hand to his forearm. "Can I do something?"

"You don't understand" he said, looking at her concerned expression, her silken hair and her clear, steady gaze. "I think perhaps I should leave."

Amber peered hard at him, her countenance gradually altering to a mask of poorly-disguised disappointment. "Oh," she said quietly.

Assuming he didn't want her touching him, she withdrew her hand from his arm. Already she could feel the loneliness seeping back into the atmosphere of her flat. "All right, if you think you would be more comfortable."

"It's not that, Amber. Look, this is a bit of an odd situation, wouldn't you say?"

"I suppose so," she agreed reluctantly.

"And I know everything isn't exactly smooth sailing for you, is it?"

To this Amber lowered her eyes, conceded the point with a barley perceivable shake of her head.

"I can't add to your problems, it just wouldn't be fair."

"I don't know what you're talking about," she said sullenly, tracing over the star patterns of her skirt with a fingernail.

"I'm sorry, that's my fault entirely. I'm saying this all wrong. I'm going to have to just come out with it."

Amber engaged-his eyes expectantly. "I wish you would."

"I don't believe I'm about to say what I'm going to say. But I'm in so damned deep now, it's too late to turn back."

"Dan. Tell me what it is and maybe I can fix it."

"Okay," he said, screwing up his courage. He made a painful face. "Amber. I know I have no right to say this to you, but if you don't lean over and kiss me, immediately, there's a very good chance I could go stark raving crazy."

Amber felt stunned. For a while she was unable to speak. Daniel tried to judge her reaction. "I'm sorry. It was a completely stupid thing to say."

"No one has ever asked me that before," she said levelly. "I shouldn't have said it."

"Was that why you wanted to leave?"

"Yes," he answered, and tilted his head back in the pillows to stare up at the ceiling. He knew she was staring at him like he was some kind of three-headed creature from another planet, so he kept his gaze up there. It was her turn to talk, and he would just let the silence continue.

He felt her weight shift on the bed. Was she going to leave the room? That was the end of it then. . .

Her face entered his field of vision as she leaned over to him, placing one arm on his opposite side for balance.

"But I think I want to kiss you."

"Think? This mug must be quite a sight," he reasoned. "It will heal, Dan. You have a very nice face."

She was fearful, excited, too. . . quite beyond the limits of her experience. But she knew she wanted this.

After a nervous, faltering moment, she bent herself slowly to him and met his bruised lips with her own. She felt his hands come up to hold her waist, and the exquisite thrill of delight it produced, drawing her closer until she pressed needfully against him. After a while she raised her head to look at him. She felt a little dazed, but wholly alive and strangely separated from reality, every nerve in her body singing with a newly-dis-covered sensation.

"Something wrong?" Daniel asked, looking deep into her violet eyes.

"That's just it, Dan. Nothing is wrong." "Then kiss me some more." "Dan..?" She stopped him, and her voice came as if from far away. "What?"

"I've never felt like this before."

When she bent to kiss him the second time, he seriously suspected he might lose consciousness again. His lips hurt from the punches they had stopped, but the hun-ger and tenderness of her mouth seemed to transform pain into transcendent pleasure.

After a long time, they parted, and this time there were no words between them, only a long silence as they searched one another's faces.

Cripes, he thought. I've screwed up big this time.

His hand moved to brush back the yellow-orange hair which had fallen around her face. She responded by holding his hand against her cheek, having discovered the pleasure of his touch, and nestled her face into his palm. She remained this way, search-ing the unfath-omable depths of his hazel eyes, wondering how he had done this incred-ible thing to her. It was as if a hidden door had been opened up inside of her, one which she never dreamt existed.

"Thank-you," she said silkily, letting her eyes close. "What did I do?"

She opened her eyes again, affected a small frown as she looked down on his face. "I don't think I can explain. Ask me again sometime, and I'll try."

"Mmm," he agreed with a sigh, now letting his own eyelids fall closed.

Amber suddenly recognised the weariness in his face. "I should let you get some rest, you poor thing."

"Mmm. Poor me," he chuckled listlessly. "Do you really think it's a good idea, me staying here?"

"I do," she said firmly. "P-l-e-a-s-e?" she crooned playfully. "Let me look after the poor, sick man?"

Still with his eyes closed, his lips parted slowly into a smile. "You won't be cruel and yell at me like you did at the shop?"

"N-o-o-o." she soothed, and broke into a giggle. "I won't yell at you again," and she bent to gently kiss his forehead. "And I won't try to hurt you again, ever," she said, kissing his nose. "And I'll make you got well, really fast, I promise."

She pressed her mouth to his with all the tender-ness she felt welling up inside of her. They kissed pas-sionately for a long time, until she felt him weaken and relax his hold on her. She remained pressed against him and rested her head on the pillow beside him, her hand on his chest and his arm draped around her.

He was falling into a heavy sleep while she looked on with something resembling fascination shining in her eyes. She felt luxurious, contented and peaceful as she lay there in the silence, watching. His breathing came in long, low susurrations as his injured chest rose and fell beneath her palm. And she could feel his heart beating, steadily pumping his life's fluid through his warm body. . .pressed so close to her own. "Dan?" she whispered. "Dan?"

He was asleep in her arms, just like in one of those romantic stories which made her feel so lonely and sad late at night, here alone in this very bed. I'm in love, she thought. I'm really, finally, wonderfully in love. What else could it be to make her feel like this?

An idea came to her, sending a tingle of excitement deep to her vitals. She lay clicking her thumbnail against her teeth as she stared at his face. It seemed rather silly, yet the urge was irresistible. How long she had secretly desired to say it to someone, and how long she had feared the moment would never arrive in her miserable life.

"Dan," she whispered once more, and when she was positive he was asleep, she uttered the words at last. "I love you Daniel." Inspiration came to her. "I love you and nothing will ever come between us." And she lay blissfully beside him, wondering what new joy tomorrow might bring.

At around midnight, Amber gently pulled the front door closed behind her, walked down her driveway and set off along the esplanade. Her car was still parked outside the guest-house and had to be brought home. There was something else, too. When she had noticed Daniel's room key protruding from his pocket, she decided to bring home some clean clothes for him, and his blood-stained ones she would wash, personally. Her heart swelled in her chest as she thought how pleased he would be with her thoughtfulness. She would show him how well she could care for him.

Her inner harmony was enhanced by the warm, still night. There was the scent of flowers in the air, from rose-bushes and azaleas and a variety of other blooms profuse in the window-boxes of the residences she passed. Nearby, on her left, the surf pounded the shore in a continuous boom and swoosh as it ran up onto the beach. The word rapture entered her mind as her feet trod the warm bitumen, and it seemed just the right word to her. The night had taken on a magical quality, like no other night she had ever known. For her the stars, bright and scintillating in the vast heaven shone down with divine grace and benevolence, announcing to all the world that she, once cursed with a cruel affliction, had passed beyond her torment to walk the face of the earth alone no more. If there really was a God, for all the suffering she had endured over the years, tonight she could forgive him, so great was her happiness.

The streets were dark, deserted, though peacefully so, without any suggestion of emptiness. She walked down past the jetty and saw that there were several anglers out there, enjoying the night as she was. She followed the road up the side of the bluff, and stood at the top by the rail where, only a few short hours ago, they had stood to-gether, and she remembered with a twinge of discomfort how desperately nervous she had been, how terribly close she had come to inventing some lame excuse to run back to the house, and there, no doubt, lament her cowardice. Thank God she had seen it through; how different would have been the night, how full of loneliness and bitter re-gret. But only quietude filled her now that all had come to pass so well.

The surface of the water below gleamed with the reflected light of the moon, full-round and radiant above. She loved to watch the silvery sparkles. As a child she had learned that if she stared into them for long enough, they would appear to lift up from the surface of the water to glitter and dance in the air like something magical. Fairy sparkles she had thought them, but no one else could ever seem to get the knack of seeing them.

While she enjoyed the glistening ocean, someone moved out of the shadows and moved stealthily up towards her. Their movement was fluid, casual and totally silent.

Amber had an odd feeling and looked to her left. Her eyes sprang wide and she let out a frightful squeal.

Jack stood calmly at the rail beside her, smiling with much amusement.

"Jack!" she exploded, stamping her foot. She clutched her chest, feeling quite faint. "God. You nearly frightened the life out of me." She began to laugh as her heart stopped racing, and Jack laughed along.

"You sure are a jumpy lot." he grinned.

"Jumpy? I sometimes wonder if your feet actually touch the ground. How do you do that?"

"I just walk," he said, shrugging. "What you doin' up here alone?" "I was on my way back to pick up my car. It's such a beautiful night, though, isn't it?"

"Yeah." Jack looked all around, then up to the sky. "Him full moon. All the crazy people come out tonight, eh?"

"What are you looking at me like that for? You're out here, too!" "Yeah, but I'm an okay kind of crazy."

"What a thing to say. Does that imply I'm not. . . ?" She thought about it awhile. "Anyway, you're not any kind of crazy."

Jack's laugh sounded like a chugging motor. "No? Then why am I out here on the streets in the middle of the night?" His eyes seemed to be alight with some kind of mischief.

Amber shrugged

"To walk you back to the house," he answered. "There's some white fellahs back in there. Drinkin' in the vacant block where you walk. Don't go that way, girl. They're pissed and actin' stupid. You be takin' a risk, for sure."

"Are you serious, Jack?"

Jack didn't see the need to answer that.

"But you couldn't have known I was coming? It's after midnight, for Pete's sake."

"Why not?" he countered impassively. "Well. . . I don't know. How could you?" "You never thought the phone was going to ring just before it did? Everyone's got it."

"Well I still don't see how, but it's very kind of you, Jack. Thanks." Jack shrugged. "Come on. We'll go 'round the top."

Amber walked with him over the hill, then along a laneway between the houses which led to a street parallel with the one she would normally walk down. Some howling and hooting noises carried above the roof-tops as they walked along.

"That them?" she asked.

"Yeah. Young fellahs. Somebody'll call the cops soon, for sure." A few yards further on, Jack asked, "How's that Daniel fellah goin', anyway?"

"What do you mean?" she replied guardedly.

"I mean, how's that Daniel fellah goin'? That's what I mean. I heard he went a round with Big Jake. He didn't come home."

"So?"

Jack grinned into the darkness. "He's all right, that fellah. He knows some things, I reckon."

"Yes, he does." Amber said thoughtfully. "How much do you know?"

"You were there. That's how come he got fightin'. He didn't come home, so I reckon you got him camped at your place."

She grabbed Jack's arm and stopped him. "Does anyone else know? At home, I mean."

"Dunno. How would they? Come on," he said, starting them walking again. "Got to be some place soon."

Jack walked her to the front gate of the guesthouse. There she wished him good night and watched as he walked off down the street to disappear back into the night.

The house was in darkness when she eased open the front door and tiptoed across the room, every floorboard squeaking and creaking so loudly she felt sure her parents would hear from their room. The corridor was lit, as usual, and she made her way quietly along to number five and inserted Daniel's key into the lock.

When she opened the door and flicked an the lights she was struck by the severity of the bare walls and sparse furnishings. In her own room she had hung colourful curtains, pictures and filled it with knick-knacks from the store. But this was so stark. To let him come back here to recover was simply unthinkable.

His only apparent possession was a small clock beside the bed. In a drawer she discovered his shaving kit. Yes, she hadn't thought of that. All the other drawers were empty, so she tried the wardrobe and found his canvas bag. She knelt down and drew back the zipper, enough to see a clean T-shirt and jeans at the top. Might as well take the bag, she decided, and pushed the shaving kit inside and zipped it closed.

As she heaved his bag onto the car seat beside her, she felt very happy, and suddenly very eager to return home. She had been gone for quite some time, it occurred to her as she pulled away from the curb. What if he woke up in pain and found she wasn't there. . . She pressed her foot a little harder to the accelerator pedal. What if he needed help? He could have a bad turn with his internal injuries; there could be haemorrhage and she had promised to look after him!

By the time she sped into her driveway and switched off the motor, she had worked herself into an anxious state. She grabbed his bag and hastily attempted to va-cate the car, to be jerked suddenly backwards onto the seat as the straps tangled in the gear-shift.

"Shit!" she whispered vehemently, as she fumbled hurriedly to disentangle it. Finally it came free.

She pushed the door carefully closed, so as not to disturb Daniel should he still be asleep, and tried to run to the door with the bag held awkwardly in front of her. . . something lumpy inside it bumping sharply against her shins.

She left the bag just inside the door and hurried on down to the bedroom, knowing that she was being foolish but nevertheless succumbing to the irrational fear that something might have happened while she was away.

She halted with a thump against the door-frame, and there, still in the same position as she had left him, lay Daniel. Was he breathing? She hurried over to the bed, bent over and listened carefully. Yes. . .the soft, steady sound of his breath came to her ear. Realising she had been holding her own breath, she let it go with a sigh, and almost giggled in relief.

Where would she sleep? she wondered. The couch? No. She didn't want to sleep there. She knew what she wanted to do. It was a warm night, but she would have to sleep with her clothes on.

She switched on the bedside lamp near the window, and turned off the main lights, pleased with the tranquil atmosphere that produced. She went around by the window and sat on the edge of the bed to slip off her shoes, thinking: I've never slept in the same bad as a man before. Well this would be the first time, she conceded readily, and stretched herself out on top of the bed. It was uncomfortable, especially without a pillow.

She sidled over toward Daniel, tugged at one of the bottom pillows, without success. Only when she got up on her knees and pulled with all her might did it come free, and then with such suddenness it had her tumbling backwards and nearly off the edge, barely saving herself by making a desperate grab for the counterpane at the last moment.

She began sniggering, and had to cover her mouth until it was over. She must get some sleep, she thought, sobering, and placing the pillow up close to Daniel, she edged herself over to settle next to him. Again his nearness brought a wave of pleasure. She rested her head and, for a while lay quietly, watching him sleep. Her own sleepwould come soon, she knew: she felt totally exhausted. Lifting her head from the pillow to see, she reached over to rest her hand over his heart, so that she could feel it beating. She nestled up closer and released a long, weary breath, feeling more wonderfully re-laxed than she could ever remember.

"Good night, Dan," she said softly, and waited for sleep to gather up the last weary remnants of this long, eventful day.

Seven

Daniel awoke to find Amber asleep next to him with her arm lying across his chest. The lamp in the corner was switched on, and the digital clock beneath it caught his attention as it winked to 7:45. He remembered from Sunday morning that she opened the store at 8:30, and he assumed she must have forgotten to set the alarm in the confusion of last night.

He moved his neck gingerly in turning to get a clearer look at her. To disturb her seemed a terrible shame; she looked so peaceful, even childlike, lying there with her hair fallen over her cheek and her thumb pressed against her lips, blissfully detached from the troubles and urgencies which relentlessly accompanied human existence.

He had woken up in some peculiar situations before, he reflected. There had been brokendown doss-houses, couches and bare floors in the dwellings of people he had met during a frantic night of carousal. Prison cells on occasion, and more times than he cared to remember, park benches or even under a bush in a town square some place where he had arrived in the dead of night and been stranded, or simply too bone-weary and dispirited to continue the journey.

Events flooded back from the years to arrange themselves in his mind as a mocking account of his life;

a montage of locations, faces and circumstances strewn across the length and breadth of the land in numbers too many to grasp as anything other than a silent host on fleeting parade, most, if not all, evoking only unwanted mem-ories laced with the nettling disquiet of self-imposed exile, the piquant emptiness which accompanied his rambling and the constant struggle to preserve a tenuous lead over the nameless ghosts which continually dogged his heels, until there seemed no place else to go for that new fresh start without retracing old footsteps.

And here I am, he thought moodily, back at the point of my departure with this beautiful, troubled girl asleep beside me. I have no right. And why now—why did it have to be now, when, finally, I accept my accursed fate? What last torment lies in wait this close to my escape?

He turned his attention to Amber, thinking, I wish I didn't have to rouse you from your slumber my love, back into this infernal arena. I wonder what dreams you make behind those lovely eyes? He gently squeezed her hand. "Amber. Amber, it's going on eight o'clock."

She gave a small sigh and wriggled closer to him. "Amber. Shouldn't you be getting up?"

Her eyes opened and she stared blankly for a moment, blinked twice before awareness began to show.

"Were you dreaming? I'm sorry I had to wake you." "Mmmm," she groaned, stretching her limbs out straight. Then replying sleepily, "A sailing-boat. You and me and the sky and the ocean."

"You dreamt about me?" he said, making his voice rise to express his delight. "I'm flattered."

"How do you feel this morning?" She brought her knees up and pushed herself sideways to kneel beside him. "Your eye is all swollen and there's a big bruise on your cheek."

"Thanks a bunch. You're a real charmer first thing in the morning, aren't you?"

Bighting her lip and making a face, she stared apologetically at him until he smiled.

"Well, at least one of us looks beautiful this morning." "Don't," she said, turning away coyly, then rallied with a smile and tentatively met his gaze. "You don't really mean that."

He pushed himself up from the pillows and assumed a stern pose. "You tellin' me I don't know my own mind, woman? No more of your sass, you hear? Else I'll be forced to beat you."

Amber giggled gleefully. "Oooh, no, sir. Please don't beat on poor little me. The exertion might be too much for you."

"Oh yeah, you think so, do you?" he said, laughing, and he grabbed her by the arm.

"Don't, Dan, you'll hurt yourself. I'll come quietly."

He supported her weight and lowered her gradually to him until they were em-braced and kissing tenderly. When they parted, Amber suddenly widened her eyes in a gesture of shock and spun to face the clock.

"Oh, no," she groaned disappointedly. "It's eight o'clock" "That's why I woke you, sleepy-head."

"Yeah, but you could have told me," she responded, looking cross. "Excuse me. But then I wasn't the one who forgot to set the alarm last night, was I?"

"No time," she said, climbing off the bed to dash to the wardrobe. "I've just got time to shower and dress. And I haven't even made you any breakfast!"

"That's okay, I can cook."

"You can't cook fresh air, 'cause that's what's in the cupboards. And, anyway, you have to stay laid up. Don't you dare move," she said, making for the bathroom with clean clothes draped over her arm. "I'll work something out, you'll see."

"Hmm," he expressed thoughtfully, looking around at the confining walls of the room. The prospect of spending even one day in here was out of the question; although substantially larger, it didn't demand much of the imagination to recognise the similarity to a prison cell. No. He wasn't spending the day in here, alone. The beach was just a few steps away; a swim in the ocean would do a world of good for a sore body, he reasoned, and for the numerous cuts and abrasions.

After ten minutes Amber emerged from the bathroom wearing a lightblue dress, and hurried to the wardrobe to search for a pair of shoes to match with it.

"Fifteen minutes," Daniel informed her.

"I know. . . I know already," she replied querulously, at last finding a pair of white flats to slip on. She stood and smoothed the dress down around her, looking critically at her reflection in the mirror.

"You look gorgeous."

Amber spun to face him, indecision showing in her face. "You don't think-?"

"It's the perfect dress for working in this heat," he reassured. She smiled and quickly came around to the side of the bed, leaned over and kissed him. "I'll come back with some food later. I won't starve you," she sim-pered, stroking his arm. "Oh, I almost forgot!" She rushed out of the bedroom and went to the front door, where she had left his belongings. She returned wearing a satis-fied smile and dropped the bag on the bed. Daniel's face dropped when he saw it.

"I brought you your things," she said, pulling back the zipper. "No, don't!" he gasped, but it was already too late.

Amber's attention was drawn to the anxious expres-sion on Daniel's face, while he stared aghast at the exposed calico bags, a thick wad of money protruding from the top of one of them. She followed his line of sight until, with a sharp intake of breath, she discovered the source of his anxiety.

Silence ensued while Amber lifted out the partially opened bag and dropped it on the bed. With a mixture of horror and amazement she put her hand back into the bag and withdrew a shiny, silver hand-gun, holding it with obvious distaste in the tips of her fingers. Now she turned her wide, questioning eyes on him.

Daniel heaved a long, rueful sigh and fell back into the pillows, submitting to his inextricable predicament. "Oh, Amber," he sighed. "It's a long story."

Amber let the gun fall onto the bed beside the bag of money, continued to stare at him as his gaze remained up at the ceiling.

"I'm late for work." she said softly, and knelt beside the bed to retrieve her handbag. When she stood she remained, watching the unreadable expression in his face for a few seconds longer. "I have to go," she said finally, turned and left the room.

He listened as the front door shut behind her, and when her car started and reversed out of the driveway, he understood that she had returned in the night for her car and obviously thought to bring his things over. An unforeseeable event, he mused, feeling utterly defeated.

As the first wave of self-pity swept over him he growled deep in his throat. He pulled off his blood-stained T-shirt and swung his legs over the edge of the bed, carefully pushed himself to standing and began emptying the contents of his pockets onto the bed.

The beach was all but deserted as he tried to stroll unaffected by the numerous sites of injury to his body, and the water looked clear, blue and inviting. He waded out to chest-deep, then leaned back into the liquid coolness, groaning relievedly as the water buoyed his weight. "God," he said, looking up into the azure sky. "How can anybody who created things like this be such a bastard? Not that I don't believe I'm talking to myself."

The sea was perfectly calmand he let himself float motionless in it, listening to the sound of his breathing and the hundreds of clicks, pops and creaks emanating from unseen marine life.

What would happen now? He didn't get the impression that she had been in any way frightened. If she had been, it would be reasonable to assume she would go to the police. That would be the perfect end to it—a perfect end to him, he thought bitterly. He was too tired, too soul-weary to make a dash for it. If the coppers rolled up, he pictured himself surrendering meekly to his fate, being hand-cuffed, pushed into the back of the car and driven away like some poor, hapless bastard whose energies had been spent to the last. If that was how it was going to be, then fuck it, there was nothing to be done.

She hadn't asked for an explanation! Why not? She hadn't panicked, hadn't de-manded that he leave or any of those things. She had only gone off to work with hardly a word. Christ, what must she be thinking? She could be thinking anything, and that was the problem. Her imagination would be constructing any number of odious scenarios to fit with the evidence: mobster, assassin, drug courier, anything! Not that bank-robber was something to be especially proud of.

He tried a few testing strokes towards the shore and found that the stiffness had eased somewhat. What should I do? I can't let her work through the day thinking there's some kind of monster lurking in her home. She'll be afraid to come home. . . she'll be afraid of me. Perhaps I'd better leave, he thought, but then, that didn't present itself as a very satisfying solutioneither. To merely walk off, leaving everything still hanging in the air unanswered, that was no way to resolve this thing.

"You're in love, you idiot," he said, stepping out of the water. "You can say good-bye to rational thought."

As he walked back up to the flat he picked up the newspaper lying on the drive-way and took it inside, observing a small headline on the front page which announced: Attack Victim Dies. Poor sod, he thought, remembering the news item he had heard in the Colonel's van. He unfolded the paper to check that it was the same person. Curino, yes. Barry Ivan Curino. Lanyard Street Port Moreton. Complications. . . renal failure.

He dropped the paper on the coffee table, headed for the bathroom and a cold shower.

While under the shower he realised the situation was beginning to eat at his insides, he couldn't simply wait to see whether it was Amber or the police who came in through the door; and, in any case, he had to have the opportunity to explain it to her.

Pulling on the clean jeans and T-shirt Amber had brought him, he went to the kitchen where the telephone was mounted on the wall over the breakfast bar. In the tele-phone book he searched for and found the number of the second-hand store. He dialled and waited. In a moment a man's voice answered.

"Good morning. Port Moreton second-hand." "Is Am. . . ah, Miss Powell there,please?"

"She's over at the curio shop at the moment, sir. Can I help you with anything?"

"No, it's okay. Thank-you."

He hung up the phone and immediately realised he should have asked for the number of the curio shop. He flicked back through the pages of the book. In the C listings his eye was caught by a name which had been deeply underlined in pencil, enough to have gone through the paper. Curino B. I., 14 Lanyard Street, Pt. Moreton. She knew the guy? He wondered at the unhappy coincidence and continued his search. woman's voice, not Amber's, answered at the curio shop. "Hi, is Miss Amber Powell there please?" "I'm sorry. You've just missed her."

"Oh. . . well, can I leave a message then?"

"You can if you like, but she won't be in for the next couple of days. I think she's a bit poorly. She doesn't usually take time off. Not Amber. You are a personal friend, aren't you?"

"Yes. I believe I'm talking to Gwen, is that right? I'm Daniel Gilmour."

"That's right, I'm Gwen. If you have any sway with that girl, maybe you could convince her to make more time for herself. She's going to worry herself sick, other-wise."

"I don't suppose many people can tell Amber what to do." Gwen laughed phleg-matically, and ended in a short bout of coughing. "Oh, my goodness, no. That girl has a stubborn streak a mile wide. I could tell you a few things."

Daniel was warming to the old girl, but this was bordering on gossip. "I bet you could," he replied. "Say, you wouldn't happen to know where she went, would you?"

"She told me to ring her at home if there were any problems, so I suppose that's where she has gone. Not that I'd disturb her time off. There's nothing I can't man-age here."

"That's just what she tells me. Well I guess I'll try her at home then," he said to wind up the call.

"Or the guest-house. Do you have the number?"

"Yes, thank-you, Gwen. Bye-bye."

He hung up the phone, smiling, picturing Gwen as a blue-rinse granny in a floral frock and puffing ciga-rettes behind the counter.

He considered what he had learned. Amber taking time off work was apparently a rare event. He might have expected her to stay at work all day while she decided what to do about having an armed criminal in her house, but taking a holiday was definitely an unexpected response. Perhaps there was still time to gather up his things and get out.

He went to the living room and sat down on the couch, thinking of all the possi-ble moves he could make, all the while knowing that he wouldn't make any one of them. While he pondered the situation, he looked over the room, at the polished wood floor and woollen rugs, the television and video-recorder, ste-reo, the high-quality landscapes on the walls, potted plants in brass containers and a set of Japanese swords mounted in a wooden rack under the window. She had some nice things, he mused. Twisting right around, he realised he had overlooked a large tapestry hanging on the wall behind him. He smiled in recognition of the subject matter. It was the legend of Wunjunu, and a fine piece of work, depicting in four sections the petulant child leaving the campsite, the an-gry youth tearing up the countryside, the disconsolate man being counselled by the spir-its of nature, and the grief-stricken old man, wading to his final resting-place beneath the beckoning waves.

Someone should make a statue, he thought. Where in this country had anyone thought to build a statue depicting Aboriginal legend? It was always some white explorer or a jumped-up British aristocrat looking stern and visionary.

His thoughts were interrupted by the sound of a car palling into the driveway, which set his heart racing and painfully tightened his muscles in animal readiness for flight. But there was no chance of escape, nor even the will to bother. If she had called the police he would simply accept whatever happened. His life was such a mess already, what the hell difference would a load more trouble make? . . .Sod all!

He listened intently as the car door opened and closed, then another. Footsteps over the paving bricks, moving haltingly towards the door. When the door swung sud-denly inward, it caught him by surprise and Amber stood in the doorway, hugging a large grocery bag in one arm while trying to reposition the strap of her handbag on her shoulder.

Her initial surprise at seeing him sitting on the couch quickly turned to disregard as she pushed the door to and walked stiffly towards the kitchen, passing without so-much as a glance in his direction as she went by the back of the couch.

He watched as she set down the shopping and her bag on the bench and com-menced stocking the cupboards, still refusing to acknowledge his presence. Her face was set in a resolute expression of preoccupation, and the silence between them continued as she commenced pulling old cereal boxes from the cupboard and shredded them before consigning then to the waste bin.

"All right, okay. If you want me to go, I'll go. "The only reason I waited was be-cause I figured I owed you an explanation. Well, to hell with that idea." He stood and walked around the couch to follow the passage down to the bedroom.

Lifting the pistol from the bed, he threw it furiously into his bag, then stood, looking at the calico bags which he knew contained $215,000. . . enough to live comfortably wherever he chose to go. Sydney or Melbourne were plenty big enough cities for a man to lose himself in. He could get a bus out of Marion this evening and be across the border by midnight. But what about the house? "God, I can't even think straight," he hissed angrily, and raising hid hands to cover his face, he let out a ragged breath.

He stood quietly until he had composed himself, then quickly began bundling everything into the bag. Once filled, in frustration and finality he zipped it forcefully closed, snatched it up and turned to depart.

He had taken a step before catching sight of Amber, standing, watching from the doorway. Distress was evident in her face, and uncertainty in the way her timid pose made her seem diminutive and vulnerable. The sight of her rocked him.

"Jesus, Amber, are you all right?"

"I don't know what to do," she cried miserably. "I don't know what's wrong with me and now you're going to leave. You said you'd help me."

Her legs began to buckle under her, and she grabbed for the doorframe as Dan-iel rushed forwards, dropping his bag and grabbing her in a supporting embrace. "Shhh, Amber, honey. Don't cry."

He almost had to carry her to the bed, and upon getting her there she let herself fall backwards and began to cry out mournfully, covering her face with her hands and tuck-ing her knees up to her chest.

Daniel watched helplessly on for a moment, at a loss to know what to do, then went quickly to the bathroom. He returned with a damp flannel and, at first began wip-ing her arms, then coaxing her hands away, he began wiping her forehead, cheeks and eyes. She soon stopped crying and lay, looking up at him as he continued to apply the cool flannel to her face.

"Amber," he said softly, but frowning gravely down at her. "I'm very worried about you. I think you should find professional help." She turned her head away and con-templated the dark forest and the horses in the picture on her wall. Then she grabbed his wrist and removed the flannel from his grip, guided his hand down to press his palm flat against her midriff. "It hurts," she said choking back a sob, and still staring at the picture.

"A pain, you mean?"

She shook her head. "Like I'm being torn apart. I don't think I can stand it any more, Dan. I really don't."

He gently began massaging the spot in a small, circular motion. Amber moaned softly as fresh tears spilt from her eyes. "I've arranged to take some time off work."

"That's good. You need the rest," he soothed.

"But I. . ." She turned from the picture to look at him. "I feel like such a fool. Look at me. Look at you. What are we doing?" she asked, holding his gaze.

"Don't you know, really? Or do you just have to hear me say it?" She held his hand still against her. "I'm afraid, Dan. You're the only man I would ever let touch me like this. I love the way you touch me and I'm not even afraid of saying it to you. I know you think I'm a whore, and you're a complete stranger with a bag full of money and a gun, and I'm too afraid to ask because I'm scared that knowing will be more than I can take.

"Dan, what those animals tried to make me out to be. . . it's not true. It's not. Please believe me. You have to believe me."

"Of course it's not true, honey," he said, gripping her hand in reassurance. "I never thought it was. I know small town vindictiveness when I see it. It must be a night-mare for you."

"Hold me, Dan, please, before I start crying again. I don't want to cry any more." She reached up to embrace him as he sat on the bed, then leaned over to her. "I've never been able to talk about it with anybody before. I've been so alone, so sick inside. They raped me, Dan. The bastards raped me and made me ashamed."

When he felt the tremors begin to course through her body, he squeezed her as tightly as she did him.

"Oh, God," she whispered, her voice quailing. "I never thought I would be able to say it to you. What they did to me. . . I wanted to die, and I think some of me did. I'm not a very nice person any more. I want to be a nice person again, for you. I want it so much but I'm rotten inside. I killed someone."

The words barely had time to register with him when she struggled violently to free herself from his embrace and sat, bolt upright with a bewildered look on her face. She turned to look over her shoulder at him, then turned quickly away again to look at her feet dangling over the edge of the bed.

"It's true," she said firmly. "Sometimes I remember but most of the time I can't. The bank manager, he got me drunk and raped me in his office at night. I think I was insane. I went to his house and made him think we were going to have sex again. The sick bastard wanted me to tie him up, it was perfect." She looked back over her shoulder again, her eyes didn't seem to be focussed on anything in the room. "And the other one hurt me and made me do things. Horrible things, Dan, and then he made disgusting stories to tell the whole town. Made me into something dirty, not even a person. Curino. But the bastard didn't die. And now I'm only a dirty toe-rag. I'm a murderer, too, and now you're repulsed by me and I won't even try to stop you from leaving." She moved to stand up.

"Amber, don't."

She remained sitting on the edge of the bed but wouldn't look back.

"Why did you tell this to me?"

"Maybe because we're both criminals," she answered reflexively. "No, I don't really mean that. Something inside told me I could, and if I had to hold it in any longer I think I would have to kill myself. I'm not a human being any more. I'm something that's alive but doesn't really want to be. Why the police haven't caught me and put me in pris-on for ever, I don't know. I thought they would have by now."

"You want to be caught," he said tonelessly.

She lowered her head a fraction, stilled her feet from swinging above the carpet. "I'm not fit to be among decent people. I think I must be truly evil. Look at what I did to you."

"That simply isn't true, not true at all." When Amber didn't respond, he said in as matter-of-fact a voice as he could manage, "I suppose I should tell you. I guess you don't know Curino died overnight."

Now she turned to look at him. "Good," she spat. "I hope he burns in hell."

"Amber, don't pretend to be a hard-case. I feel numb after hearing what you've told me. As you rightly point out, I am a criminal, even though I don't like the sound of it, but I don't think that you are. You've been terribly hurt and you've responded in an equally terrible way. I can only see that the score-card has been balanced. But then I'm in love with you, and I could be biased. In any case, I have no right to judge anybody, least of all you."

Her gaze parted from his to look down at the bed cover.

"Don't be in love with me, for your own sake. I'll hurt you. But thank-you for saying it. It was the one thing I wanted to hear, but I know you can't love me."

"Because you're not worthy of being loved, is that it?"

Amber nodded her head sadly. "I'm all eaten up and black inside." "Amber, look at me. I have something to tell you."

She did as he told her, and she watched him with glistening eyes. "I robbed a bank ten days ago, not caring whether I was caught or even killed in the process. It was what I had planned as a last exploit in my own lousy life, to restore my family's home as an act of contrition for the way I deserted them many years ago.

They died in a road accident and it was almost a year before I found out. I wasn't sure what I was going to do after fixing the place, but I know I couldn't live there alone with unwanted memories. The whole scheme was totally irrational but I was impelled, by guilt, I think, to go through with it. I never allowed myself to look beyond the completion of that one task because, in the back of my mind, I already knew what lay there. Can you guess?"

Amber was staring deeply into his eyes now, seeing something akin to her own pain residing in him. Her lower lip was pinched between her teeth as she nodded her head ever so slightly. "Nothing," she said quietly.

"Nothing," he repeated dully. "A bottomless, empty nothing. It was my inten-tion to put an end to my solitary, pointless existence." "No.

You mustn't do that, Dan. You'll find some happiness if you just keep on."

"And that's just what I kept telling myself through the years. I can't. . . I can't just keep on existing like this. I haven't the strength any more, perhaps not even the will, Amber. I have a very strange feeling about us." His look intensified as he searched her eyes for understanding.

Amber nodded slowly, not taking her eyes from his. "Have you always been alone?" she asked soothingly.

"I think I was born under that curse. I know you understand how alone one per-son can be. Amber, I'm in love with you, and being here with you makes me forget the empty void of my life."

She reached out her hand and gently caressed his cheek. "You're crying, my love. You know how this will end. How can

I let you be hurt. I don't want you to be hurt any more, least of all by me."

"You can only hurt me by lying to me. Tell me my leaving will make anything any better for either of us."

"Oh, Dan, I can' t. But–"

"Then we should stay together, whatever happens. We'll extract our share of happiness from life, now, while we have this chance."

"I'm happy now, Dan, and I love you more than I know how to say. Do you really think we have a chance?"

"Perhaps not much of one. I honestly don't know. But for my own part, at least, better a small chance with you than none and without you."

"Yes," Amber expressed solemnly. She took a breath and turned to him, as if about to say something further, then let her breath escape without a word.

"What is it?" he asked.

A silence followed, during which Daniel watched on while she composed her thoughts. After a while, she began to speak softly, her eyes seemingly focussed on the intangible.

"I've got this thought that won't go away. It's like we've sat here this way a thou-sand times before, playing our roles over and over as some form of horrid entertain-ment for—for—I don't know. But it's like something is happening and it's out of my power to change anything. It scares me, Dan, but I feel calm inside too, a calm so deep it goes into forever. Does that sound very stupid?"

"No. I know what you mean because I've felt it too. It occurred to me this morn-ing while I watched you sleeping, how unlikely the odds of our being together like this.

It's very strange. For me there are no more choices either, as if a current has caught. . . us?"

"Yes, the two of us. Do you believe in fate, Dan? Destiny?"

"A week ago I would have said no. But now. . ." He shook his head in uncertainty. "I don't know how to explain what has happened. It does seem right though."

"It seems exactly right," Amber hastened to acknowledge. "And that's the frightening thing about it. It's as if I already have the memory of us. I feel I knew you and loved you already, but not in the past. I can't see the future though, I can't even imagine where we are being taken, swept along in the current like you say. My mind won't let me look ahead, Dan. It's like tomorrow doesn't exist any more."

Daniel studied her worried countenance and saw where her thoughts were taking her. "Then if todays are all we have, let's take them and be glad of them. You know the fates haven't been terribly kind to either of us. The way I see it, we're both overdue for a share of cosmic goodwill. Maybe this is where it starts." He reached out to offer her his hand. "Come over here with me awhile."

She brought one leg up onto the bed as she twisted right around at the edge of the mattress to face him. She looked at him closely and offered a timid smile, then took to tracing small circles in the bed cover with her fingernail.

Daniel lowered his arm and tilted his head sideways, trying to gain her attention. "What's the matter?"

In a small voice, she said, "Are you thinking about having sex with me?"

The question caught him off guard, and he blew loudly through pursed lips, to-tally nonplussed. Amber shot him a nervous, sideways glance and quickly looked away again.

"I don't know how to answer you. I suppose it might have crossed my mind. Yes. . . but I think I was kind of hoping there might be a spark of spontaneity between us, without one of us saying something brilliant like are you thinking about having sex with me. You make me feel like some sort of fiend."

"I'm sorry," she simpered, her Welsh lilt suddenly emerging, and she let herself fall backwards to land with a thump beside him. "That was tactless of me. I don't know anything," she said, annoyed with herself and rolling her eyes back in her head.

Daniel began to laugh, "Ooo, that looks grotesque. Can you see your brains when you do that?"

She giggled brightly and let her eyes return to look up at Daniel's smiling face. "It's like a haunted castle in there, all dark corridors and cobwebs and everything."

"Yeah? Give me a look."

He put his face right up close to hers, so that her eyes encompassed his whole field of vision, and he looked into the blue-violet depths. It was meant to be a joke, he was going to say something funny so they could laugh again, but he was suddenly spell-bound, captured by the depth and beauty he saw.

"It's like looking into your soul," Amber said in a hushed tone. "It's so timeless and peaceful. Let me come in there with you."

She pressed her lips to his and groaned softly with mounting desire. Neither wanted the embrace to end as they gripped each other tightly in a desperate and dizzying exchange of giving and receiving. The gentle touch of his hand against her thigh was not unexpected nor unwelcome, and it filled her with exultation.

Yes, Dan, she willed in her heart, make love to me, and her own hands sought to find a way of returning the pleasure.

In a wave of passion and desire to fulfil her needful expectation, his hand obeyed her beckoning flesh to initiate penetration beneath her garments. He felt her shudder and tremble against him, but her nails bit painfully into him as she arched convulsively, and the tiny wail in the back of her throat sent a cold chill to his core.

"Honey?" He pulled back to see her face strained with anguish. Her eyes were pleading and her mouth worked ineffectually at trying to form words.

"Honey, what's happening?" he asked desperately.

She had been holding her breath. It came now in short, urgent gasps. "H-h-h hold me, D-Dan."

He hesitated briefly, alarmed at the way her eyes were glazed and inward focussed. He held her tightly, fearfully, vaguely aware that the trembling he felt came from his own body.

"Amber, hold on. I think you're in shock." He could feel her arms, limp, around him, the lack of response in her body. "I'm here, I've got you. Don't go anywhere I can't follow, you hear me?"

Her arms suddenly tightened around him, and her breathing came in deep gulps. ". . .hear . . .you," she managed haltingly.

He lifted his head from her shoulder and stared into her eyes. "Are you back?"

She nodded her head in an exaggerated fashion. "I'm sorry I scared you." She raised a hand to her forehead stared at him wide-eyed. "I'm a basket-case, Dan. I should be in a mental asylum."

"You can joke about something like that?" "I'm not joking."

"Then shut up!" he roared angrily. "Oh, Christ. I didn't mean to shout."

Amber saw him fighting to contain his emotions. His face began to contort under the strain and she reached out to stroke his injured face.

"Those bastards did that to you, didn't they. If they weren't already dead, I'd kill them myself." he said in a fierce whisper.

"Sssh," she soothed. "It's all right now. I love you. We can try again."

"I can't risk that again," he said, looking horrified.

"I want to make love with you, Dan. And you'll help me won't you? I know you're the one that can. You know I've never made love with anybody but you. Because that's what we were doing, wasn't it?" Daniel nodded. "Yes, we made love. How was it for you?" he asked with a hollow laugh.

"Up until the lights went out, I think I was about to catch fire," she said with a sudden flush in her cheeks.

He looked at her in wonder, and broke into a smile. "You're something, Amber. You really are. I feel like the luckiest man alive, right now."

"I'm glad I can make you feel like that. I know there's no other man in the world for me. If only things could be different for us, my love."

Eight

Above Regent Street, on the third floor of the Marion regional police station, Detective Sgt. Ron Gasgoyne and his partner, Detective, second-class, Stanley March, worked perfunctorily at filing reports and updating records, a job neither man cared for in the least, but, as Gasgoyne felt grudgingly obliged to point out every Tuesday, the one day set aside for this dreary task: If it ain't writ, it ain't worth shit; a maxim he had drilled into him at the academy during his cadetship, some twenty inuring years past.

March punched a wrong key on his typewriter and cursed vehemently, reached for the correction fluid while his senior chuckled amusedly from the desk adjacent. "Freudian slip," March drawled. "Put Joey Mason down for bunglery instead of burglary."

"An understandable mistake. Let it stand," replied Gasgoyne, stretching back in his chair and reaching into his shirt pocket for his cigarettes. "Somebody should recom-mend a good career guidance counsellor for that boy. You nearly finished with that lot?"

"About twenty minutes. There's still my notes from the marijuana crop. Why?"

Gasgoyne nodded towards the clock on the wall and lit up. "I fancy a break."

"Bit early for a counter lunch, isn't it?" March replied, grinning. "Not if we drive to Port Moreton. I want to take another look at Lanyard Street. Those idiots should have something to report by now. It's been over twenty-four hours and they haven't even come up with so much as a footprint. A little motivation might be in order," he sneered, giving a glimpse of smoke-yellowed teeth.

"What about the door-knock?"

"Bugger all. Seems everybody was tucked up peacefully in bed at the time. No-body saw or heard a thing. Still, there's a few residents to catch up with yet. So, are you coming or just breathing heavy?"

"Just let me finish this, okay?"

Gasgoyne blew a stream of smoke into the air, expressed reluctant approval by flicking ash towards his waste-paper basket, and watched it fall short of the target. "Pull your finger out, eh?"

Beth slid the apple and apricot pies onto the oven rack and closed the door, checked again to see that the thermostat was set at four-fifty degrees, then went to the sink to begin cleaning up the mess. She stood thoughtfully for a moment, looking out across the township and the river flood plain beyond. Her daughter and Daniel had gone off together after dinner last night. This, on it's own, was an innocent enough occur-rence, in fact it pleased her immensely that the two of them had hit it off, especially after Amber's obvious angling, and it brought back fond memories of her's and Ted's romance all those years ago. But it had been after mid-night when she heard Amber's voice out in the street, shortly afterwards to hear her tiptoeing across the creaky floor-boards. And when Daniel hadn't been at the table for breakfast, Beth had looked into his room on the pretext of hanging a clean towel behind his door, to discover his belongings, all but the tiny travel alarm clock, had been removed.

She hadn't told Ted because she was ashamed with herself for having looked into Daniel's room the way she had. She had never done that to a guest before. But now the facts spoke for themselves.

Daniel had stayed overnight with Amber, and one or both of them had come sneaking in the middle of the night for his things. It was so unlike her daughter to act in such a mysterious a way. Was she so afraid of what her old mum would think? she wondered. If they had become lovers, and if it made Amber happy, well, that was okay. She was old enough to be managing her own life now. But it was a disappointment that Amber seemed hesitant to tell her mum; she could have telephoned at least.

And when Beth had walked down to Main Street to casually visit Amber at the shop, she found she had left earlier in the morning, after announcing that she was to take two days off work. This had been the great surprise. Amber had not taken one day off work since she had started with old Mrs Grieves. Beth's curiosity was Siqued, and it was with considerable effort that she refrained from telephoning Amber's flat to coax an explanation from her, and to tell her it was all right with her if she had Daniel staying with her. Amber knew there was no need for secrets within the family. What on earth had gotten into the girl?

The sound of the front door closing released her from this reverie, and she waited to see if it might be Amber, come to tell her the news.

When no one entered the kitchen, she gave a mental shrug, plugged the sink and turned on the taps. Oh well, she consoled herself, perhaps she would see them for dinner, tonight.

"Hi, ma."

Beth turned to find Gary standing, grinning inside the door. "What are you doing home, dear? Nothing's wrong, I hope." "The concrete trucks are on strike. We're stuffeduntil they start back."

"Oh. How long might that be?"

"Who knows? They're pushing for a wage increase. The boss says he'll ring when things get moving again. It suits me, anyhow. This weather is knocking us around a bit."

"Get yourself a drink from out of the fridge. I've made a couple of jugs of lemonade for tonight, but there's plenty."

"Great," he replied, moving to the fridge. "Has Dan turned up yet?

I thought he might want to come down the road for a beer."

"Why don't you give it a rest, Gary? If you want to ruin your health, just drink poison and have done with it. And, no, I haven't seen Dan today."

"Hmm, that's suspicious. You don't suppose my sister would know his where-abouts?" he quizzed, filling a glass to the brim. "Could be she has finally found herself a fellah. The way she was tarted up for dinner last night."

"Don't talk like that, Gary. You should see yourself when you go out on the prowl on the weekends. Now there's a sight. A right Charlie you look."

Gary laughed. "You're annoyed with her, aren't you, mum." "No, I'm not,"

"With Dan then?"

"Dan's a nice lad. I like him fine. I guess I'm just being a mother." It had to happen sooner or later, ma. At least now we know she isn't, you know, into other girls."

"Stop your nonsense, boy. Go and get your shower and get out of those clothes. I want you to drive me over to her flat."

"But she'll be at work, won't she?"

"I've been to the shop already. They tell me Amber is taking a couple of days off. And, don't tell your father or I'll brain you, but Dan's things are gone from his room. I heard Amber here late last night."

"Aye, aye." Gary grinned, making his eyebrows bob up and down. "Do you really think we ought to disturb them. They might be–"

"Go and clean up," Beth cut him short. "And don't let on to your father."

Amber brought Daniel's plate of bacon and scrambled eggs to the breakfast bar while he sat, smiling at her. "Yum, am I ready for this." "I can make more if it's not enough," she said, fetching her own plate and coming to sit opposite him. "I bet you're a big eater."

"Yeah, but this is plenty. I usually am a big eater. I think my stomach has shrunk. It happens when I'm travelling."

He scooped a large forkful into his mouth and made blissful expressions as he chewed.

Amber grinned uncontrollably, "Cut it out. It can't be that good." "Absolutely splendiferous!" he announced enthusiastically.

She giggled delightedly. "You old flatterer, you." "Please. Not so much of the old." "Hey, how old are you anyway?"

"I can't talk with my mouth full. How old are you?" "Shut up and eat your break-fast," she responded playfully.

They ate in silence for a while, taking quick glances at one another when they thought the other wasn't aware, until their eyes caught and locked, and they openly watched one another's every move.

"This is nice," Amber said finally. "I like having you here. We can snuggle up on the couch, after, and watch a movie together. Do you want to do that?"

"Sounds good. What movies do you have?"

"I've got Mad Max, Macbeth, Falling Down, um. . . Vanishing-Point, Blues Brothers and um. . . I forget the rest. I'll look in a minute."

"You've seen them all, though, haven't you?"

"But that doesn't matter. We can still snuggle and talk." "What? And spoil a perfectly good movie?" he said, poker-faced. There was a flicker of resentment in her face before she replied.

"Don't, Dan. Don't joke like that. I know I'm meant to laugh, but I can't laugh at the thought of you not wanting me."

Daniel's expression was contrite. "No. Under the circumstances I suppose cracks like that aren't too clever, are they. The truth is, nothing would give me greater pleasure than to spend the afternoon on the couch with you, movie or no movie."

Amber smiled warmly and was about to reply when there came a knock at the door. It brought a look of dread to her face.

"It's only me," came Beth's voice from behind the door.

"It's mum!" Amber exclaimed in a whisper. "Shit." She clamped a hand over her mouth in censure.

"Better let her in then," Daniel suggested.

"Coming, mum," she called, making a nervous face at Daniel and sliding off of her stool. "How am I going to explain?" she whispered.

"Tell her we went for a drink and I got into a fight. At least it's the truth."

"That's not quite what I meant, Dan." She gave him one last worried look and went to the door.

"I brought you over a pie," Beth said as soon as the door swung open. "Apple and apricot."

Amber stood holding the door, staring at the proffered pie. "Gee, it looks nice. How did you know I'd be home?"

"I was down the street and popped into the shop to say hello. Are you going to invite me in, or do I die from exposure on your front step?"

"Oh yeah, sorry. I wasn't thinking," she said, nervously stepping aside and clos-ing the door behind her mother.

"Oh, hello, Dan. What a surprise," Beth intoned liltingly. "My goodness, what happened to you?"

"He got accidentally caught up in a fight at the pub when we stopped in there for a cool drink last night," Amber answered while her mother looked at her askance. "Really. This big fight broke out and in the confusion. . ."

Beth noted her daughter's glowing face. "Of course, dear. It happens a lot."

"But I had to bring him home because he was hurt, and I got the doctor who said he must rest so he's resting. Here." she finished lamely.

"That's fine, dear. Do you like apple and apricot pie, Dan?" "You bet. My mother used to make them."

"Good. Then don't wait for Amber to offer you some. Just help yourself when-ever you're hungry," she said good-naturedly on her way to the kitchen. "How much of what my daughter just told me is true?"

"Well, as a matter of fact, Beth, apart from the accidentally bit, all of it."

Is she taking good care of you?"

He looked over to Amber who leaned against the wall, watching this exchange in silence.

"Probably better than I deserve," he answered, and succeeded in eliciting a subtle smile from her.

"I hope you gave as good as you got," said Beth, inspecting his face. "You might not think it to see him these days, but my Ted was a fair scrapper in his time."

"That's the first I've heard," Amber rejoined. "My father?" "Oh, yes, believe it. He would never admit to it, mind. But when he was courting me, he would take on anybody, no matter how big they were, if they took more than just a passing interest in me.

"I used to act disgusted with him, of course, but I secretly thought it was very exciting to have a man fighting over me." She aimed a knowing look at her daughter. "It's one way a man can show you he loves you without actually having to come out and say it."

Daniel chuckled quietly. "You're a very perceptive woman, Mrs Powell, but I don't have any qualms about expressing my love for Amber. I'm in love with your daugh-ter, Beth. I hope you don't find that objectionable."

Beth turned to Amber where she leaned with her back against the wall, watching Daniel with undisguised adoration. "And unless I'm mistaken, my daughter is in love with you."

Amber came up beside him and placed an arm around his shoulders in affirmation. "Yes, I love him"

"Then that's as it should be. How can I object? I think it's wonderful." Beth rounded the breakfast bar and kissed Amber on the cheek. "Really wonderful, darling. Now I must be going. Your brother is waiting outside in the hot car."

"Stay a bit longer, mum, and I'll bring Gary in. There's a bottle of cool drink in the fridge."

"No. I've got to get back and start preparing dinner. I won't be expecting you two tonight. You'll want to be just the two of you, I expect. I've taught her how to cook, Dan, so don't let her get away with frozen pizza and such. There's no excuse for not cooking a proper meal for a man."

"Is it really necessary to try and embarrass me like this?" Amber objected.

"No, dear. You're right." Then turning to Daniel she asked, "Have You been up to take a look at your property yet?" having suddenly remembered his eligibility as a husband.

"Not yet. It slipped my mind, actually," he said, slipping his arm around Amber's waist.

"You ought to drive him out and take a look, Amber. A family home, you said?"

"Mum!" Amber stamped her foot. "Cut it out. You can be so obvious sometimes."

"Life is short, dear. You'll realise that, one day. No point in beating around the bush. Anyway, I must be off now. Your father doesn't even know I've gone out."

When Amber returned from seeing her mother to the car, she made a comical face, expressing great relief. "I can't believe it. It's too good to be true," she rejoiced, rounding the bar and resuming her seat opposite Daniel. "I thought she was going to be angry with me. Do you know what she said to me out there?"

Daniel shrugged. "Get rid of that bum?"

"No," Amber laughed. "She really likes you. She said she was glad I had found someone who could make me happy. I can't believe she actually said that!" she gushed.

Daniel feigned disappointment. "Yeah, right. As if I could possibly make you happy."

"Ooooh you. . . I didn't mean that. That's not what I meant," she played along in a sympathetic voice, and hurried around to embrace him. "I've never been so happy, truly. I'm so happy I could burst."

They kissed for a long time, then parted to look at one another. "If you're feeling well enough, I'd like to take you to see your house. Wouldn't that be nice? We can watch a movie tonight. Besides, it'll be more romantic with the lights down low," she purred.

"Yum," Daniel replied, smiling affectedly. "You've won me. That's a terrific idea. And we can make this afternoon a picnic."

"Oh, yes!" she bubbled. "I've got a basket. I'll make some sandwiches and we can get a bottle of wine on the way. What fun!" Daniel grinned broadly as he dared with his sore mouth to see her enthusiasm.

"What?" Amber asked, puzzled.

"You're beautiful," he said soberly. "And I don't just mean the way you look. You're beautiful, right through."

Amber stroked his face adoringly. "Don't, Dan. Now I want to cry again, and my eyes will get all red and puffy and I'll look horrible." And her eyes glistened as she bent to kiss him again.

In short time, they had prepared the sandwiches and put them into Amber's basket, together with cheese, dill pickles and a pair of wineglasses. At the last minute Amber decided she must change her clothes for something more suitable, precipitating a period of pained indecision for her before she emerged from her room wearing a pair of cherry-pink shorts and a sleeveless black blouse tied at her waist.

"You must spend a fortune on clothes," Daniel commented, admiring the outfit. "I look like a dag alongside you, wearing this old stuff. One change of clothes, I have, and the other's are identical to these."

Amber regarded him for a few seconds. "You would look nice in a proper shirt," she said thoughtfully. "Would you take the basket out to the car? I'll be out in a tick."

While Daniel made to comply, Amber went back into her bedroom and retrieved her bag from beneath the bed, smiling fondly to herself as she opened her purse and began counting her money.

When she arrived at the car, Daniel was in the passenger seat, positioning the seat adjustments. "Not a bad car," he determined as Amber slid in behind the wheel. "Remem-ber the morning I saw you at the deli, the morning your window got busted?"

"I remember," she said, an enigmatic smile curling her lips as she started the motor.

"I remember thinking, that chick is up tight and hoity-toity, but the red Renault really suits her."

Amber was backing onto the esplanade, she braked suddenly and shot him a stern and questioning look. "So you're saying I'm haughty or something?"

"Well, you might not recall, but you sure gave me some dirty looks the first couple of times we met."

Her look thawed, and she got them under way. "Yeah, you're right. I'm sorry about that. I guess I can be a bit, I don't know, petulant sometimes?"

"The petulant child," he said pensively, turning to look out to sea. "What do you mean by that!" she replied petulantly.

"I didn't mean you, I mean the wall hanging you have. Do you know the story behind it?"

"No. I found it in the curio shop when I took it over. Do you like it?"

"Very much. I must tell you the legend of Wunjunu sometime. That's what the tapestry is about."

Amber drove in behind the hotel to park near the bottle shop. "You choose the wine, okay? I'm just going up the street for a minute."

"Hey, you're on holiday, remember?"

"I know, I know. It's got nothing to do with work. I won't be long." She climbed out of the car and set off across the car-park while Daniel sat, following her progress, enjoying what he saw. After a few yards she glanced over her shoulder, smiled sweetly when she saw him watching her, and continued, thrilling in her new-found happiness.

At the bottle shop Daniel searched for a suitable wine, but not knowing much about wines he made an educated guess and selected a medium-priced white. The check-out was unmanned so he pressed the service button and waited.

After a minute a young man in a white shirt and tie appeared from a doorway leading back into the hotel. "Sorry. I just ducked in to pour a few beers. One of the staff is off today."

"No problem," replied Daniel, noticing that he was being scrutinised rather closely.

"You're back on your feet quick. I figured you for a hospital case, last night. Twenty bucks," he said, pointing to the bottle. Daniel pulled the twenty from his pocket and passed it over. "But you wouldn't remember. I was forgetting, you were out cold when we put you in the taxi."

"You did?"

"Yeah. Hey, I wouldn't go in there now." He hooked his thumb over his shoulder. "Big Jake is in there."

"The one who. . ." he pointed to his face.

"Yeah." The barman nodded meaningfully. "He's a complete mongrel, but no one's game enough to tell him that to his face."

Daniel's mind ticked over for a few seconds before he asked, "Where's he parked?"

The barman's eyes narrowed. "Hey, mister. I'd like to help, but I don't know if I ought to get involved. My job, you know? It's kind'a like being a doctor or a lawyer or something."

Daniel reached for his wallet, saying, "Well thanks for helping out last night, anyway." He pulled a fifty dollar note from the fold and pushed it across the counter.

The barman cooked an eyebrow. "No worries, buddy. Did you know you broke his nose? It looks like a twisted turd," he laughed. "It must hurt when he bumps along in that green and white Toyota four-wheel-drive with roof-racks 'round the back."

"I sure hope so." said Daniel, nodding. "Well, gotta go now." Amber returned to find Daniel rummaging in the boot between boxes of brick-a-brack, a garden gnome and dozens of wire coat-hangers.

"What are you doing?" she asked, clutching a gift-wrapped parcel to her chest.

Daniel pulled his head out and smiled sheepishly. "Ah. . . Do you have any tools, hon?"

She refrained from asking the obvious question and flipped back the rubber mat on the floor of the boot to reveal a compartment lid with a finger-hole in it.

"Oh, right." Daniel flipped up the lid and was delighted to see a hammer sitting atop the jack and wheel brace. "Just the ticket," he said, seizing it.

Amber's bemusement was apparent in her expression. "What do you want with a hammer?"

"Guess who owns that four-wheel-drive parked under the tree over there? Does the name Big Jake ring any bells?"

"Oooh, Dan," she moaned with an upward inflection and noted the determination in his eyes. "I suppose you have to," she sighed. "All right, wait until I bring the get-away car over first."

Amber got into the car and tossed the parcel onto the back seat, started the engine and backed out while Daniel moseyed over to the Toyota.

He started at the front, the headlights and panels first, then onto the wind-screen, the mirrors and side windows. As he came around to the back, Amber got out of her car and rushed over to him. "Wait a minute," she said urgently. "Save some for me!" And relieving him of the hammer, she started in on the rear window, tail-lights and back panel.

Peals of laughter escaped her as they dashed back to the car. Daniel caught a glimpse of the barman as he gave the thumbs-up from the corner of the bottle shop, and as soon as he was in, Amber accelerated them away while she continued to laugh effusively.

Daniel watched her with a wide grin on his face as she drove them rapidly out of town, trying to concentrate on her driving but laughing so much the tears impeded her vision.

"I like to see you get out and enjoying yourself," he quipped. "You should do it more often."

"Bloody hell, Dan. I don't believe I did that," she said breathlessly. "I'm too old to be a delinquent, aren't I?"

"Too old to be a juvenile, anyway. But you show real promise. Nice technique on the backhand."

"Thanks, but I shouldn't have done it. It was a bit scary. I started getting angry and I didn't want to stop. Do you do things like that often?"

"Nope. I've never done that before, either. It was too good an opportunity to pass up, though, wasn't it?"

"I suppose so. Yeah," she said more confidently. "The bastard deserved it. Hey, am I going the right way?"

About a kilometre out of townDaniel directed Amber along a narrow track which led down to the river, and turning onto it they drove along beside the Wunjunjurra, passing beneath long rows of overhanging gums growing on the embankment to their left. There was no perceivable movement in the water and it reflected perfectly the blue sky and the few, white puffs of cloud drifting high above the plain.

Amber wound down her window to feel the wind on her face, turned to smile at Daniel who was looking across at the opposite bank, where a flock of ibis stalked fish in the shallows. He returned her smile, reached across and began caressing the back of her neck with his fingertips, to which she responded with a sigh and a sensual wriggle, while she tried to keep her attention focussed firmly on the road.

Five miles further on they came to an intersection where the main road south cut across and went over the river on a single span bridge, by-passing the small town of Horseshoe Bend which nestled in a deep hollow at the base of the foothills. Negotiating the intersection, they descended into the town, following a long curve which led over an ancient-looking bridge across the Wunjunjurra and on to the main street, past a football oval, a post office and a number of brick houses and stone cottages.

Daniel pointed out a signpost on the right, beside a stone-built schoolhouse, reading Gum Gully 6km, Rushbrook 8km, and Amber turned onto the narrow strip of bitumen which led up the side of a steep ridge.

As they started the climb, Amber looked quickly across to Daniel who appeared to be in a contemplative mood. "You must be feeling strange after all this time away," she said, just loud enough to be heard over the engine.

"Strange. . . yes. I feel sick, if you want to know the truth. I've thought about this moment so many times. That was my old school back there. Jesus, the memories are so strong."

The road climbed for over a mile before the gradient eased to a gentle slope, and here Amber pulled off to the side of the road and switched off the engine. It was a moment before Daniel realised what she had done.

"Why are we stopped?"

"There's plenty of time. Are you okay?"

Daniel shrugged, looked out over the countryside. "Nearly seventeen years, Am. They're all dead now. I'm the only one left and I've squandered my life. It doesn't seem right, does it."

Amber placed her hand over his.

"My sister, Ally, she was the promising one. She always knew what she wanted to be. A doctor. She would have made it, too. No doubt about it. She would have been a terrific doctor. A nurturer, you know? My folks reckoned I might make a good sailor. Hugh, I never did understand that. I suppose they couldn't think of anything else to say to their little aberration."

Daniel continued to search the hilltops while Amber watched him closely. "Why did you leave, Dan? What did you do?"

"I was eighteen years old, hon, and the country stretched out beyond my vision with the promise of adventure. And like most young men of that age, I suppose I needed to prove my independence. But the more I roamed, the more detached I became, and then it wasn't so much travelling to some new destination as needing to leave the one I was in. I was running, you see? From here, from one town or city to another, from one collection of crazy circumstances to another. I never understood why. My life has never made sense to me, never served any purpose, and it didn't take very long before I just got swallowed up by the great, impersonal vacuum that exists out there. Then, inevitably, I suppose, the day arrived when I realised I couldn't come home. The point of no return, as they call it. I was too afraid to show my family what I had become. I had ostracised myself." He turned to Amber. "It really is a crummy little story. It's about how a dreamer like me can get the stuffing kicked out of him when he has to live in the real world."

"No one should have to live like that, Dan. Don't try and put yourself down like that, because I won't listen to it. You've survived, and despite what you've put yourself through, you're still a warm-hearted, wonderful person, and I couldn't love you the way I do if that wasn't true."

"You put forward a good argument," he said, grinning suddenly. "I'm convinced. Let's go."

Amber looked at him dubiously. "You sure?" She knew he was holding back.

"The poignant interlude is over," he announced derisively. "Come on, I've embarrassed myself enough for one day."

She shook her head disbelievingly. "All right but first, why don't you reach over and grab that parcel off the back seat."

"Eh?" He turned around to see the gift-wrapped parcel she was talking about, reached across and lifted it over. "What is it?" he asked, offering it to her.

"Open it," she beamed. "For me?"

Amber nodded, and he stared at it with an exaggerated look of wonder in his face. "But it's not my birthday!"

Amber giggled. "Will you cut the act and just open it?"

He fiddled with the bow for a few seconds, then tugged the end which released the knot. Parting the paper he found a western shirt, embroidered with scroll-work on the cuffs, pockets and collar. He lifted it up to view it better, genuinely delighted.

"It's a great shirt. Thanks, hon."

"Do you really like it? I can change it if you don't."

"No, don't do that. It's a beauty. Grey is the right colour too," he said, turning it one way, then the other. "Can I put it on?"

"Of course you can, silly," she said, grinning. She was enjoying this immensely.

He struggled out of his T-shirt and began pulling on his new shirt, noticing Amber inspecting his bare torso. "Oh, I get it," he said suspiciously. "This whole thing is merely a ruse to pull over and have me undress so you can have your evil way with me. Very cunning, but I'm not that sort of boy."

"But you'd like to keep the shirt, wouldn't you? All you have to do is be nice to me," she intoned silkily, and reached over to feel his tight stomach.

"Don't start anything you can't finish."

Amber withdrew her hand, looking hurt. "Bastard," she spat. "I was only joking. A joke," he insisted plaintively.

"No, not a joke. You might have expected me to think so, but we both know it wasn't."

She started the engine and quickly prepared to leave, ignoring his attempts to gain her attention.

"Hold it, Amber."

She paid him no heed and pulled back onto the road, accelerating rapidly.

"Amber, it was a fair enough statement. You know what I meant." "Yeah," she snapped bitterly. "What you meant was I can't touch you because there's no point, you can't fuck me. You might get a hard-on and have nowhere to put it!"

"What the hell kind of talk is that? Jesus, you sound like a goddamn whore. Stop the fucking car, now!"

Amber stamped hard on the brake pedal and skidded the car to a haltjust where the bitumen finished and the dirt road began.

"Where do you get off saying shit like that to me?" Daniel bawled. "Do I have to calculate every word I say to you for fear of being indelicate? Christ! I can't believe I heard what I heard from you. For someone who claims to be inexperienced, you've sure got a mouth on you. You sound like one of them fuckin' hard-line, man-hating feminists who think that the easiest way to injure a man is to ridicule his sexuality. I'm totally amazed."

"So what do you think you did to me." Amber countered. "Do you think I'm stupid? You say something hurtful and then you claim it was a joke. Well I don't have to take that from you, or anybody. Do you think you're the only one with feelings?"

"Screw feelings. Who the fuck needs them?" Daniel growled in frustration. He opened up his door. "I need some air," he said, climbing out of the car.

"That's right, run away. Just like you did your whole life. Poor little boy who lost his way!" she screamed after him.

Daniel turned and glared threateningly at her. Amber realised she had gone too far and clamped her mouth shut. Her heart quailed in her chest as she saw the smoulder-ing light in his eyes.

He turned away and walked off down the road.

Amber sat silently behind the wheel, watching him go. "I didn't mean that, Dan," she whispered, feeling suddenly very alone and miserable. Long moments passed as Daniel's presence faded, diminished with each step away from her that he took. She knew he wasn't coming back. He was stubborn, she had wounded him and he would not be coming back.

Already the tiny pangs were beginning to stab inside her. Soon they would be-gin to surge and tear at her. She had to act quickly to repair the situation before it was too late, before both of them had set their minds irrevocably to a desolate end. That was the danger, she knew. She recognised in him the same fatalism which ruled her own life. Once the mind had accepted a thing, it homed in on that course inexorably, no matter what the cost to one's self or to those who were unfortunate enough to be near.

She started the engine and set off with uncertainty, trying hard to think what to say to him when she caught up. He was angry, that made it difficult, he probably wouldn't even want to listen to a word she had to say, and for that she couldn't blame him, after the cruel thing she had said. She ached inside with torment, but she couldn't be sure if it was her own or his. She would do anything to make it right again. Anything to stop the pain she had unleashed.

When he heard the car coming, he moved over to the edge of the road, but continued walking without looking back. As she drew level, she leaned across to him and called, "Dan, please don't hate me. I don't realise what I'm saying sometimes. You mustn't think I meant it, it just came out. I was trying to get back at you, that's all. It was a horrible thing to say, and it's not even true, not any of it.

"Isn't it?" Daniel replied, halting.

Amber stopped the car. "No, of course it's not."

He leaned against the fender looking weary and unhappy, and stared contemplatively into the scrub beside the road. "I'm not so sure about that. Maybe it is."

Amber got out of the car and walked around to him, stopped short of touching him in an ambivalent move and let her hands fall to her sides.

"I'm empty inside, Amber. I don't want to fight with you any more.

I haven't the strength, so keep your nasty remarks to yourself, okay?" "Yes, Dan."

"You've got a vicious tongue. Learn to think before you use it, for Christ's sake. You ought to hear yourself."

"I'm sorry, I know you're right. I'm impetuous."

Daniel glanced at her to see a smile emerge on her otherwise contrite face.

"No. Cut it out, I'm serious," he said, showing signs of exasperation. "You made me angry enough to explode back there, I hate being angry. Really. It's like a nuclear melt-down or something," he said, tapping the side of his head. "It's the stupidest and most destructive human emotion, and I can do without it, thank-you very much."

"I thought you were going to hurt me," she said evenly. "You wanted to, didn't you."

He shrugged. "Perhaps."

"But you didn't. If you did, I couldn't have blamed you. I've been rotten to you. But you didn't because you're gentle inside. I know that about you." She reached out and tugged at his open shirt, looked up earnestly as he turned to face her. "Will you forgive me? I wish I could make you forget what I said. I wish I could. It really makes me sick inside, Dan. I'm so sorry. I'm terribly selfish, I know. I'm awful to you and I want you to stop my hurt. But I can't help it. Please forgive me."

"Of course I do. I already had after the first twenty steps. I know how you are. . . remember? All that stuff you have to carry around in you, and your chemistry is right out of whack, too. You'd know that if you had been to a doctor and explained your condition."

"My condition?" she asked, searching his face.

He sighed heavily, realising it would have been better if he had kept his mouth shut. "You get nervous and wound up, right? Sleepless, restless nights? I know you get anxious and emotional, depressed and lethargic too, I bet. And stop looking at me as if I'm a bug or something. I've seen some of your emotional states, myself, and you've told me about the intenseness you get in your solar plexus. Your body chemistry is the most likely cause of all that, and I'm certain it has been terribly unpleasant for you over the years. Tomor-row you're coming with me to see a doctor, and we'll let him decide."

"So I'm nuts, is that what you're saying?"

"No." he laughed. I'm nuts for bringing it up. Come on, let's get going."

"No, wait!" she demanded, stamping her foot and raising a small cloud of dust from the roadside. "Tell me what you mean. How come you know so much?"

Daniel looked at the way she was standing, and for a moment saw a wilful little girl—a very beautiful little girl. "I've learned a lot about people over the years, Amber. How they think and why they think what they do. We're not as cerebral as most of us choose to believe. Much of how we behave is governed not by the will or logical thought, but by the chemical soup that we are.

All I'm saying is Nature might have spilled the hot sauce when she made you. But I'm very fond of hot sauce," he appended, being sure to cover himself. Without warning, Amber suddenly sprang at him, throwing her arms around his neck and pushing him backwards over the bonnet, giggling and kissing his face repeatedly.

Daniel felt her urgent need as she pushed against him, and his own blood was rapidly rising to the boil. She moved rhythmically against him, and he suddenly realised that she had unfastened her shorts and was now working adroitly at unfastening his jeans. "Wha-" he attempted, but she covered his mouth with her own, and instantly the current flowed between them.

He held her tightly in one arm as his free hand slid her shorts and panties clear. She gasped at his shoulder, duplicated the manoeuvre on him and twisted with supple strength until she was bent against the bonnet of the car, with him over her.

"Please," she whispered hoarsely, her eyes wide and beseeching as she pleaded to the heavens for a merciful reprieve.

His lips pressed to hers, tenderly now. She moaned tremulously as she received him, wrapped her arms tightly around him and held on with all of her strength. "Oh, my love, yes. I knew we ... we could. I knew ..."

In that moment, each felt a strange sensation, a wave of warm emotion so powerful that it made them shudder as one as it passed through them, and although neither gave voice to their thought, both felt they had touched the other's soul.

Amber began to cry, as did Daniell, but they were tears of great happiness, a greater happiness than either could have expressed by words. They laughed as they cried, embraced and wiped away the tears from each other's eyes, and kissed with an all-consuming passion.

They rocked and stroked one another, touched, caressed and explored the depths of each other's eyes until the passion mounted beyond containment to crash in a momentary obliteration of the senses, of self, and perhaps the entire universe.

For a timelessness they remained in a luxurious silence. Amber gazed up into the azure sky, amazed and enchanted by the total stillness residing in her. A rosella darted through the air above her, a flash of yellow, green and red. Her mind held the image with immaculate clarity, as if her senses had suddenly been heightened beyond their normal ability. She smiled dreamily as she felt Daniel's embrace close around her, his warm kiss against her neck. He began to laugh and she felt it rumbling pleasantly through her.

"I think we both must be nuts," he said against her ear, and she began to laugh, too.

"You're supposed to whisper endearments now, not psychiatric reports," she giggled.

There was the sound of an approaching car, but it took them both a moment to register it. Daniel was the first to turn his head towards the crest of the hill.

"Shit!" He pushed himself up.

"Try pulling your pants up," Amber managed through a very large smile.

He grabbed her by the arm just as the approaching car crested the hill, yanked her from of the bonnet, and they fell in a tangle, down behind Amber's car. Amber was laughing gaily and, ignoring the situation wrestled him down to pin him beneath her, and began kissing him in rapid succession.

The car whizzed by, spreading a plume of dust in its wake. "Amber, come on. That's enough. Jesus, we're lying in the dirt by the roadside, half naked, and these peb-bles hurt like buggery. You're supposed to be looking after me, you wanton woman. Wait until I tell your mother about you."

"But, Dan, we did it! Don't you realise?" she said standing and beginning to search around.

"Hey, yeah, that's right." Daniel got to his feet and began dressing himself. "This is great. We'll celebrate with the wine as soon as we get to the house." He walked over and gave Amber a big kiss on the cheek. "I suppose congratulations doesn't quite say it."

"It was wonderful Dan. I didn't know it could be like that. Let's do it again."

Daniel puffed out his cheeks in expelling air. "Not here, honey. Think how much more comfortable it would be on your bed. . . how much more private. Hey, are you on the pill?"

Amber's eyes widened as she drew a sharp breath. "Oh, no. I didn't think. We'll have to stop at the chemist on the way home," she said, extending her search to include under the car. "Dan? I can't find my knickers."

Daniel burst into laughter, and she looked up from where she was to see what was so funny.

"There," he said, pointing to her white lace panties caught atop the radio ariel.

"But how did they get up there?" she asked incredulously.

Detectives Gasgoyne and March ducked under the police tape at the Lanyard Street crime scene and entered through the front door to stand, casting their gaze over the small living room. On the grey carpeta trail of dry blood led from the threshold out to the kitchen, and at the centre of the kitchen floor a dark patch indicated where the victim had lain, apparently left for dead by his attacker. Against the wall, directly underneath a blood-stained telephone, more blood was smeared where he had finally slumped after dialling for assistance.

"Nasty business," Gasgoyne remarked, hitching his belt over an ample paunch. "Branson?" he called, and in a moment a tall, bespectacled man appeared from the hallway off the kitchen.

"Sir?"

"Tell me you have something."

"Perhaps," he mumbled, shoving his hands into his dust-jacket pockets. "Entry was obviously through the front door. Next to impossible to find distinguishable prints therefore, as you would know. Not a skerrick inside, but this," he withdrew a small plastic bag from his pocket. "Caught on the screen door."

"What is it?" Gasgoyne asked, taking possession and holding it to the light.

"Hair. One strand," Branson answered. "Two hundred and forty five millimetres in length. Probably female, if you notice the colour. It's quite a distinctive colour, wouldn't you say?"

Gasgoyne passed the little bag to his partner. "So? It's a front door. How many people do you suppose come through there in a week? He was something of a ladies man, from what I can gather."

March handed back the bag. "Anything else?"

Branson shook his head. "I've done what I can. The lads have searched every yard, vacant block, every tussock, bush and tree for a mile. We found a knife, but it's nothing like what we're looking for."

"What about the door-knock?" Gasgoyne tried sullenly.

Again Branson shook his head. "Tried nearly everyone. There's still a couple, though. Both out of town visiting relatives. The local sergeant has agreed to chase them up for us. He'll look in again, tonight, and call you if anything turns up."

"Bloody terrific," Gasgoyne cursed. "You'd have to be Sherlock flamin' Holmes. One victim, a nondescript assailant in a ski mask, a vague account of something like a machete, and one orange hair which could have blown in on a southerly. What's the bet it belongs to a neighbour's cocker spaniel?"

"It pays not to overlook a thing, however insignificant it might seem," Branson expressed earnestly. "But it quite definitely is a human hair. It could just be, it belongs to our quarry."

Gasgoyne hurrumphed. "And pigs might fly. Well, it appears there's nothing more we can do here. If we hurry, we might make it in time for that counter lunch," he said to his partner.

Nine

For the last quarter of a mile the countryside had exhibited the scars of a recent bushfire. Probably from the previous summer, Daniel guessed, judging by the regrowth
of grass and shrubs; but the trees still stood dormant,
black and skeletal in their ranks as Amber drove them
slowly through the eerie silence which hung over the
vicinity.

"It's just over the next ridge," Daniel said quietly,
and only then did Amber become fully aware of the
change which had been slowly mounting to charge the
atmosphere around them.

She searched for something to say, but could find
nothing. She was afraid to give voice to her apprehen-
sion, lest it prove true, and to say anything else would
merely sound glib or foolish. She glanced quickly over to
see Daniel sitting back, apparently relaxed and looking
ahead at the blackened crest before them. The back of his
fingers drummed nervously against the door.

"There's a gate on the left," he said. "About twenty
metres after that big pine. You see it?"

"Yes."

"Ha, the fire didn't even touch it. Must be two hundred years old. A grand-daddy of a tree. I never did man-

age to climb to the top of it." The land levelled at the crest, and Amber slowed, searching for the gate.

"There," he pointed, and she noticed two tall gate-posts between which a long, wooden gate lay broken on the ground.

"Some bugger has driven through it," he observed calmly. "The C.F.S. trying to head off the fire, maybe. The chain is still padlocked."

"I can't see a house," Amber queried.

"No, you can't from here. There's a sort of a trough down the slope that the house sits in. Look between those trees, you can just see the top of one of the chimneys."

"Oh, yeah." She drove carefully over the broken gate and followed the wheel tracks down and across the slope to the left.

At the edge of the trough, the track cut right again, but at this point the house came into view: Only the stone walls and chimneys remained standing, and between them all was a black, twisted pile of wreckage. The scene was made incongruous by the tall, green trees surrounding the homestead, and an untended garden had grown wild with colourful blooms.

At the sight, Amber stopped the car to stare down at the ruin.

"Oh, Dan," she said sadly, and again could find noth-ing more to say.

"We might as well go on down," he said, turning to her without expression on his face or in his voice.

They descended slowly and came up to the front of the house where Amber parked by an overgrown garden path and a timber railing fence. They sat quietly for a while as they looked over the ruins amid the surrounding growth.

"There's a lot of ground water," Daniel said. "It seeps from the side of the hill and we hardly ever had to worry about watering the garden. We sunk a well at the base of the hill and pumped up all the water we needed. As good as that spring water you have to pay for in the supermarkets. Better, I reckon." He pushed open his door. "Come on, I'll show you around."

He climbed out and waited for Amber to circle the car and join him by the garden path. She came up alongside him, put her arm around his waist and allowed him to guide her between the tangled profusion of plant-life.

"It must have swept in from the side," he said. "Along the slope. Jesus, there's nothing left. It'll all have to come down."

They skirted the wreckage and stood at the back cornerbeside a water storage tank. From here they had a panoramic view of the gorge and the undulating ranges sweeping away to the horizon.

"Look." Daniel pointed to a bench seat and table sitting beside an enormous rose-bush. "If I drag them over to the middle of the yard we can have our picnic."

Amber hugged him. "Okay." And walked back towards the car to get the basket.

By the time she returnedhe had repositioned the table and bench, well back from the house, between two tall poplars, and there was a bunch of roses arranged in a dirty china vase at the centre of the table. She walked towards the setting, swinging the basket beside her while he leaned casually against the table, smiling.

"Nice," she smiled affectionately.

"A hidden talent," he shrugged. "Let's have those sandwiches, this country air has given me an appetite."

Amber searched his face as she came up to him. It bothered her that he seemed so unmoved. He had to be feeling terrible disappointment.

"I forgot to pack the corkscrew."

Daniel lifted the wine bottle from the basket and looked at it.

"Hmm. I'll see what I can find."

She laid out the sandwiches, pickles and cheese while he went to search in the ruins. When she had done that she sat, waiting quietly, letting her gaze wander over the landscape. A smile came to her face as she imagined a small boy with so much space to explore, roaming over the countryside dreaming boyish dreams beneath the wide, blue sky, climbing down to the river to catch frogs and tadpoles to bring home in a jar. But it was very isolated up here, lonely little boy. Yes, he had that quality in him, still.

"I had to push it through," he said, startling her, and he came around to sit beside her. "I'm no expert, but it looked like a reasonable sandwich wine."

He poured the first glass and handed it to her. "What do you think of the view?"

"It's glorious. I bet you know every nook around here."

He looked around for a moment. "Yeah, maybe. It's a lot of space. Once you get used to space like this, you never really feel comfortable without it." He picked up a sandwich and took a bite. "Every child should have the benefit of being raised in an envi-ronment like this. It has a way of balming the soul and freeing the spirit."

"That's nice. . . 'Balming the soul and freeing the spirit.'" She put her hand on his leg. "You love it up here, don't you."

Looking out to the steep slopes of the gorge, he nodded. "I understand what Aboriginal people mean when they say they are a part of the land and the land is a part of them. I carried the image of this place with me, all through my travels. More than just the scenery though; the spirit. . . the soul of this place. I expect that sounds pretty silly." "Itdoesn't sound silly. Tell me more."

He looked at her as though he wasn't sure whether he was being teased or not, then turned again to the landscape. "I learned to believe in magic, living here. The magical quality in nature, I mean. I believed in it because I could feel it like you feel the sun on your face. This land is really alive, Amber, and it has a soul, a kind, nurturing soul which is life-giving. Only a child or someone who has lived all their life in such a place can accept thatwithout being persuaded to think otherwise through ordinary skepticism and arrogance, both inherent to our modern culture. Most of us have lost the ability to connect, really connect with the magic which exists in nature. I discovered it as a child. It was an intoxicating revelation which mellowed and deepened with time. It has become like an old friend, and it has sustained me through my darkest days." He glanced to see if Amber was still listening and found her attentive, her blue-violet eyes watching him closely.

"You know, all I ever had to do, whether I was in a prison cell, sleeping on the ground or in a ramshackle shelter in the middle of nowhere, or anywhere! All I had to do was to remember this country, and the spirit would warm me, soothe me, even nourish me; whatever was needed. . . Enough to keep me going. I can't describe it well enough. It's as if this land shared it's spirit with me, and I carry it with me wherever I am. All I ever had to do was close my eyes and I could be in any part of this country I wanted to be. And being here again, now. . ." He shook his head, searching for the words. "After all this time, Amber. Being here again. . ." he repeated, hauntingly.

Amber wiped a tear from her eye but remained silent, willing him to continue, sensing that there was something emerging, something he had to say.

". . .it's like the fulfilment of a promise; the end of a long and arduous journey into hell and back; a quixotic quest completed and the answer to a paradoxical question finally revealed. Christ, I wish I could explain it to you . . .to myself!"

"Keep trying, my love. Please? It's important."

"Yes. Yes, it is. I must find the words to explain this feeling." There was a long pause as he plunged himself into the search for an explanation. He wasn't aware that Amber was instinctively stroking his hand to assist his concentration.

"It was the journey," he said in a whisper. "I never knew why I left. Not really, and I always regretted doing itEut I was impelled. It was the journey that was important, not how big a success I made of myself. God, it's so simple. To leave with a question and travel for years, only to find the answer, here, at the point of my departure. An answer I never could have recognised without having made the journey. Everything I said to you before, about the magic of this land and the spirit of nature, I've never expressed it quite like that before—never had reason to. It was always just an unconscious, instinctive feeling. But what I said is true, I know it is. There is a greater power separate of ourselves at work over the world. Knowing that releases a great burden somehow. When your own kind is plundering the planet like a sapping cancer, it's hard not to feel a great burden of guilt. It sounds crazy to you, I know. It would have to, because it wasn't your demon, so to speak. But I found a balance, of sorts. Without really knowing it I was plumbing the depths of society, its murky depths, its underbelly, and found humankind hurting so badly, but still willing to struggle for life. This will sound mad, for sure, but Na-ture holds no grudge. It recognises the need to survive and retreats as is necessary until the balance swings back, probably after we've drowned in our own waste. Quite simply, we'll destroy ourselves or learn to live harmoniously with the rest of creation. . . and that includes ourselves."

"Are you saying as a child you felt guilty for what mankind was doing to the planet?"

"That's part of it, yes. I was a very strange child," he said, smiling self-consciously.

"But that's awful. Why?"

"Because it's the greatest shame there is. Hitler's Germany, Stalin's Russia, the atomic bombs dropped on Hiroshima and Nagasaki. Tito, Samosa, Phol Pot and all the other despots. All monstrous, but it doesn't compare to the rape of a global ecosystem. Guilt by association, Amber. The workings of a child's mind who regards Nature as a personal acquaintance, a spiritual guide, a teacher, a friend, a provider, a source of beau-ty and wonder and more besides. I lived here in splendid iso-lation and communicated hardly at all with the outside world, until the irresistible urge to travel seized me. The world wasn't the shiny jewel I imagined it to be, but I persisted with all the curiosity that I had, until the innocence was knocked out of me and I started to resemble the poor creatures I thought I despised. I learned. Those people became my family and I grew to love them. Downtrodden and desperate as many of them were, there wasn't one among them who wasn't willing to share what little they had, even if all they could give was a piece of advice. Even the hardest bitten I've met, their humanity still lay buried deep inside, sheltering, I could say, from the hostile world they had to endure, or else perish. And it's not even the people who are at fault, not consciously, I think. We've created these systems. . . systems of government, of trade, of finance, of law, of industry, reli-gion and data exchange, and they've gotten out of control. No one man can stop them. No thousand men. Even a new messiah would be hard pressed. It's like Frankenstein's monster run amok. Perhaps alike to the seven-headed hydra Nostradamus described in foretelling the downfall of mankind. The systems grind on like a massive, inexorable machine, mindlessly subjugating and crushing its creators between the wheels without the slightest regard. And now people obey their systems like drones, or pay dearly, in the form of marginalisation, poverty and dispossession. . . certainly with their loss of *humanity*."

Daniel remained silent, intent on some inner vision. Then his eyes appeared to catch sight of his immediate surroundings and refocussed.

"I'm sorry," he smiled sheepishly. "I don't know where all that came from."

Amber sipped her wine, studying him over the rim of her glass. Returning the glass to the table-top, she said, "I could listen to you for hours. It's exciting, the way you see the world. Or perhaps I mean frightening. I don't know."

"It's both of those," he said, unscrewing the jar of pickles and taking one. "And mind-bogglingly complex when you look at it closely. A shocking mess, unfortunately."

"Do you believe in God, Dan?" "Only if he believes in me." "No, don't joke."

"Sorry, but it wasn't exactly a joke. It's a tough question. How about if you tell me, first? Do you believe in God?"

"I think so. Yes, I do. When I'm frightened and alone I pray as hard as I can," she said with a shy smile. "But then I think how selfish I am, because I only seem to pray when I'm in trouble. But it always helps. It's having someone to talk to, someone wise and understanding on your side. God is hard to imagine though. How can He or She watch over everything? It seems impossible to think of one mind watching over everything. Everything means the whole universe."

"Yes, that's exactly the point, "Daniel expressed seriously, then leaned over and kissed her.

"What was that for?" she asked, surprised and pleased. She reached over to touch him.

"Because I love you."

She slid over and repaid him with a hug, resting her head on his shoulder. "I think you're evading the question, sweetheart."

"No I wasn't." He put his arm around her. "You said, how can one mind watch over the universe, right?"

Amber nodded, her head on his shoulder, then quickly kissed him on the neck. "Right."

"Well, what if the universe is God? The vast complexity of the cosmos, right down through the quantum level, allows plenty of possibility for the existence of an integrated network which might relay information. The universe, or the space between it, could contain self-awareness. . . a Godlike intellect."

"Say that again, Einstein," she chuckled.

"The bible says God is everywhere, in everything. I think Jesus was reported to have said it. It could well be the literal truth, depending on your understanding of what God is.

You, me, that tree, that hill, the sky, the universe itself. All contain God because everything is God. Perhaps way back in the beginning of time, in some unfathomable way, the universe attained self-awareness."

"I've never heard that one before, but it sounds wonderful. Does that mean God is part of me and I am part of God?"

"Yep. And therefore I am you and you are me, in a sense." "What, because we're all connected through God which exists in everything?"

"Do you like it?" he asked.

"I love it. It sounds just right. I like the bit about you and me being one the most. I can believe that. When we were making love, that's what it felt like to me. It was as if only our bodies prevented us from becoming one. But for a while there, it was as if we really were, don't you think so?"

"Yeah, it was extraordinary, hon. That's just exactly what it felt like. I've never experienced anything like it." "Really?"

"Absolutely."

"Mmmm, I love you," she said, hugging him tightly. "Aaah, ouch. Am. . . easy," he groaned.

"Oh, your poor ribs. I forgot. How are you feeling? You really should be resting like the doctor said. If anything happened to you I'd never forgive myself."

"I'm okay. Slight headache is all."

Amber snatched his drink from the table, poured it on the ground. "No more alcohol. I've been a terrible nurse, but not any more. I think

I should take you home to rest."

Daniel sat, grinning at her, enjoying her show of concern.

"I mean it," she persisted. "He said you had concussion. If you've got a headache, I'm taking you home."

"It's only a tiny little headache. Let's just sit here awhile longer, okay? Sitting can't hurt."

She viewed him with suspicion for a moment. "We-1-1, if you're sure. It is very nice up here. But don't go pretending to be a tough guy, just to impress me. That sort of thing doesn't impress me at all." Daniel chuckled mirthfully, but soon sobered, staring at her in thoughtful silence, and in return her eyes explored his face.

"Why are you looking at me like that?" she wanted to know, feeling suddenly and unusually vulnerable under his gaze. "I've come over all funny."

Daniel appeared to be debating with himself. No answer was forthcoming.

"Tell me." she insisted.

"I'm sorry, hon. I don't think I can. Not just now."

"You can't do that!" she replied in a rising voice. "You look at me like that and not tell me why? That's not fair. You were thinking something bad about me, weren't you." She sat up, looking alarmed. "Weren't you. That's why you won't say."

"That's not it at all, Amber," he answered placatingly.

"Then why won't you tell me?" she demanded, looking hurt and angry at the same time.

"All right. If you're going to get worked up, I'll tell you." Amber's gaze faltered, disengaged his eyes to inspect the shirt she had bought him, the scrollwork on the pockets and cuffs. When he reached out for her, she leaned over against him, raised her hand to place it over his heart.

"I was only daydreaming," he soothed. Her head rested against his chest and he felt her respond with a nod. "I've got enough money to rebuild on this land, and still have a bit left over. I was thinking, if nothing happened with, you know. . . about that guy dying. I was imagining what it would be like if we came up here to live and raise a family."

Amber put her arms right around him and squeezed gently. "Oh, Dan," she murmured, and nestled her head against his chest.

Time passed without reply, and Daniel held her to him while he looked out at the scenery, feeling increasingly uncomfortable for having expressed this most private thought to her.

She would reply when she was ready, he supposed, and allowed his thoughts to drift back down the years, recalling the happy events which had taken place here, when his family were alive. If he had come here alone, he knew there would have been only remorse, but Amber was with him and it had made all the difference. Again he had the unsettling feeling of fate having played a role in his life. All past experiences somehow led right to this moment, another base touched in a life already mapped out to the end by an unseen hand.

Everything before his eyes glowed with a soft, preternatural radiance, there was a life-sustaining effusion emanating from everything around, an essential presence as old as existence itself, humming a vasty arcane symphony of life and symmetry, as if the atoms themselves, the building-blocks of nature which gave substance and form to the world, had, at this moment, determined to resonate in harmonic accord. He had come homeand the country welcomed his return, reaching out to him with its great soul in fond embrace and reassurance that his pilgrimage was finally at an end, and that it had been a necessary ordeal in the fulfilment of his life's journey. *Nothing is in vain, it said. We never parted, even in your deepest despair, when you thought you were alone.You have returned with new wisdom, closer to your destiny, and there is abidance with us still. We cannot be separated. Across the oceans or across the stars We endure beyond all time and distance, beyond life or death. We are constant, eternal and in love We continue together. We are the One.*

A light breeze caressed his face. The enchantment was broken, leaving in its wake a haunting wonderment. He looked down at Amber. She was asleep in his arms with her face turned upwards to him, smiling peacefully as though she were caught in a rapturous dream. Tears began to spill from his eyes, coursing down his cheeks in meandering rills, and the mixture of sadness and joy which gripped his breast set him to sobbing as he fought to hold back a torrent of long-suppressed fears and turbulent emotions.

In his mind's eye the faces of his family came to him, his mother, his father, his baby sister. Each as he remembered them in those last days before his fateful departure. They smiled consolingly, their faces conveying love and sympathy for his sense of abandonment, telling him that it was all right that he had gone away, that there was no need to carry the guilt any longer. You went to find your own life, as everyone must, and it's all right. It's all right. . .

"It's all right," Amber reassured, holding him tightly and speaking softly beside his ear. "Let it out, my love. I thought you were going to hold it in for ever."

"They're not gone." he wept. "Not really gone. They're alive in me, at least."

"Yes they are, my love. My poor, lonely wanderer. And now I'm with you, too.

"Build the house, Dan I'll live here with you. We'll what I dreamt. You and me sitting on the verandah while our beautiful children frolicked in the sunshine. It was such a nice dream, Dan. Such a wonderful dream, and when I woke up and saw you crying, I knew it was going to be all right." She was sniffing back tears of her own now, and she suddenly hugged him much tighter, with renewed urgency. "Dear God," she prayed. "Give us this chance, I beg you!"

Ten

It was late in the afternoon by the time Amber and Daniel arrived home to her flat. Daniel had cajoled her into letting him take her down to the river, and despite her initial protesting that he ought not to be exerting himself, she relented with an affectionate smile and gave him her hand.

He had led her down the slope behind the house to the edge of the gorge, then along a narrow trail which angled steeply across the rock-face to take them down to the valley floor where eucalypts towered, statuesque beside the river, backdropped by rock walls washed with the colour of leached minerals and mottled with lichen. The under-growth buzzed with unseen life whilefrom the tree-tops came the occasional chuckle and choral from a kookaburra or magpie, and the shrill of parakeets as they wheeled in from out of the azure sky.

In the warm sunshine they had lain on the grassy bank beside the Wunjunjurra, to marvel at the extraordinary beauty of the land and to bask in its permeating aura, at once balming, enchanting and infused with something altogether peaceful and exhilarating.

The river sparkled and gleamed in the bright sunlight, the diaphanous water tinkling merrily as it moved swiftly over bedrock and rippled around boulders damp and green with moss. And while they lay there together, staring up to the clouds as they sailed silently over the landscape, Daniel related to Amber the story his grandmother had told him, thirty years ago, on the very same spot, the legend of Wunjunu.

Amber listened, spellbound by the sound of his voice, the lulling murmur of the river and the magic of the surroundings. He talked softly and with deliberate clarity, yet there seemed a great distance in his voice, and Amber had the incongruous impression of his words coming to her as if over a vast distance of thousands of years, carrying with them the ghosts of forgotten lives, and the far echo of a culture as rich and complex as the country itself, sadly in peril of being lost among the corridors of time.

When the story was told, she kissed him, and there, on the grassy bank beside the river, they had again made love. Without fear of interruption they availed themselves of one another with a need so great they shared an intoxication which saw the afternoon pass unnoticed around them, in a warm, golden haze of contentment.

~

At six in the evening the telephone on Detective Gasgoyne's desk chirped beneath a scatter of papers. He let it ring seven times while he leisurely lit up a cigarette and made a hopeful expression to March as he returned from the coffee machine carry-ing two cups.

It was the sergeant from Port Moreton on the line Sergeant Collins. He had just returned from interviewing the previously absent residents of Lanyard Street, and he had uncovered an interesting piece of information. One lady he interviewed was a mem-ber of Community Watch, she was also an insomniac and in the habit of walking her Pomeranian dogs late at night. On Sunday morning, at around three R'clock, she had passed by number fourteen and had seen a red car parked at the front. She couldn't say what make of car, only that it was red. She did, however, notice the licence plate because it reminded her of the logo of a motion picture company from the 1950's. The prefix letters read RKO, and although the exact numbers which followed escaped her, she was quite certain they included an eight and a five.

Gasgoyne thanked Sergeant Collins for his contribution andhung up the telephone with a grin.

Gasgoyne's repertoire of facial expressions numbered two, a grin and a sneer, unless blankness counted. "Good news or bad?" March was forced to ask, handing his partner his coffee.

"We might be in business," came the stolid reply. "Some old sticky-beak got a partial make on a red car parked outside the poor bugger's house at 3a.m. on Sunday morning. RKO, with maybe an eight and a five among the digits." Gasgoyne sat look-ing expectantly at his partner for a moment. "Well, what are you waiting for? You're the computer expert, aren't you?"

"Oh, yeah, right. Um. . . RKO, eight and five. Red. Could be registered locally, right? If I find it I'll get a copy of the owner's licence photo."

"Yeah. That'll be good," replied Gasgoyne, about to turn away. Then, as an afterthought he said with a sneer, "I always wanted to arrest Bozo the clown."

"How's that?" asked March, baffled.

Gasgoyne chuckled derisively. "Branson's precious strand of orange hair. I don't suppose you'd care to make a bet? I'll give you five to one."

"No thanks," said March in departure.

Gasgoyne sat thoughtfully for a moment, leaned over to open his bottom draw-er and reached in to pull out a well-worn folder which he lifted and let fall heavily onto his desk. He wasn't sure why he had done this, but he opened the cover anyway and thumbed desultorily through the pages, knowing that this was unnecessary because already he knew every word of it.

This was a case file he had compiled two years earlier. The investigation into Lester Bishop's murder had been a low point in his career. He had worked for months on the case and had come up with nothing— nothing, that is, except a detailed scenario of what had taken place on the night, and a tarnished reputation as an aging cop without skill enough to handle anything more sophisticated than bouncing dull-witted villains into the cells.

As he turned the pages he seized on the single, relevant detail the murder weapon had been a long-bladed implement, as in this case. Undiscovered. He wondered if he wasn't grasping at straws, if it was only wounded pride that forced him to try and draw comparisons between the two incidents. Maybe it was mere coincidence, but he could not deny the niggling suspicion he had at the back of his mind as he reached for his cigarettes.

He was on his second cigarette by the time March returned from the adjoining room, trying unsuccessfully to conceal a wry smile as he approached. "What's that?" he said, indicating the dog-eared file.

"Nothin'," replied Gasgoyne, folding it closed. "What did you get?" By way of reply, March produced a freshly printed page from behind his back and slapped it on the desktop in front of his partner.

"Well I'll be blowed," Gasgoyne remarked, regarding a licence photo of a young woman with amber coloured hair. "You should have taken the bet," he sneered.

"Miss Amber Powell," March stated proudly. "Ocean9iew Flats, Port Moreton. Owner of a red Renault, RKO 850."

~

Amber woke suddenly. Upon arriving home she had insisted Daniel take a nap while she prepared dinner, but he had coaxed her into lying down with him and together they had drifted off to sleep. Something disquieting had entered her sleep; something amorphous and creeping which caused her to awaken feeling vaguely disturbed, even frightened. While she lay watching Daniel's peaceful face seeking comfort by reflecting on their wonderful day together, his eyelids fluttered open and he looked directly into her eyes.

"Hello beautiful," he said, smiling warmly. . . Then after a moment, "I think I could get used to waking up next to you."

For this, she kissed him tenderly, but he thought he detected sadness in her face.

"Is anything wrong?"

With a ghost of a smile, she replied, "No, nothing," but under his continued gaze she amended, "I sometimes wake up feeling a bit low. It'll pass."

"Remember to tell the doctor that, when I take you tomorrow." He noted her lack of response. "You are going to let me take you, aren't you? We'll soon have you as chirpy as a canary," he grinned. Amber shrugged listlessly. "If you want to. Okay."

"Come over here," he said, opening his arms in invitation, and using her elbows she wriggled over to him, laying across his chest with her head resting on his shoulder. "I'm sorry you're not feeling well," he said, hugging her sympathetically. "Can I do something for you?"

She lifted her head so he could see the sly smile on her face. "It's a tempting offer, but I don't have the energy," she said, rolling her eyes and collapsing against him."

"Yeah," he chuckled. "It has been quite a day."

"Dan?" Amber asked, after they had lain silent for a minute.

"Mmm?"

"That story you told me. I really liked it."

"Which one? I've been raving like a lunatic all day."

"The Aboriginal one. It was so vivid. Lying there by the river I could see it in my mind while you were talking. It was wonderful. . .the sun and the water and the sky. I think it's very special, the way you can talk about things and tell stories. How do you do it?"

"I don't know. I've never really thought about it. I suppose I just like the sound of my own voice."

"No. Don't say that, even if you are joking. You undervalue yourself, and I'm not going to let you do it."

Her indomitable tone started him chuckling, which had the effect of bouncing them on the mattress. It delighted him to hear her defending him, even if it was against himself.

"Okay," he ceded, revising his answer. "I'm just an observer, that's all. While other people are getting on with their lives, I sit and watch. It's almost a vocation with me. And watching the myriad things twirl like so many fascinating objects, I got to studying what I saw. I began to see a pattern emerge, a link between one thing and another, then another and another, until it appeared all things were connected, interactive in some way. Hell, I've worked out a theory for damn near everything. And when someone asks me to talk, well, I just can't resist the urge to let them listen and see what they think."

There, that wasn't so hard, was it," Amber jibed. "And what about that story you told me by the river? What was that, a fable or something?"

"Yeah, it is, apart from being an interesting way of explaining the creation of the river valley and the reef. We humans must always know why something is. On a particular bend of the river, where the town of Horseshoe Bend is, is where the women used to camp with the children while the men travelled further south to hunt for game, and to collect the coloured clays from Ochre Beach for ceremonies and to trade with other tribes. And that was one of the stories the women used to tell the children. I guess it had the advantage of persuading them from straying too far from the safety of the campsite."

"And I like the way it gives the land personality," Amber added. "The earth, tree and air spirits who tried to console him, and the tricky old sea who drowned him. Wasn't that cruel."

"He was tired though. Tired and defeated, remember. The sea did him a kindness, I think. He couldn't have gone on with such misery." Amber was silent for a while.

"I suppose that's true," she said at last. "He went to sleep and didn't have to wake up again. But it's so sad how his mother's tears came down to make the river. It nearly made me cry." She lifted her head from his shoulder so he could see her face. "I can see you sitting with our children, telling them stories in front of a big log fire. You'll be a great dad," she beamed. "It'll be cold and windy outsideand we'll be all snug and warm, and I'll be in the kitchen making hot soup and buttered bread for supper. Can you see us?"

"Yes, I can. And maybe I could build a stable and we could keep a few horses."

"I could get a manager in to watch my business while I make our home even more lovely. You could teach classes at that little school. I bet you could teach them some important things."

"You could teach them about running a business."

"We could have chooks and goats and pigs," Amber laughed. "We could grow our own vegies and drive a ute into town like real country bumpkins and sell what we can't use ourselves." "Ducks and turkeys" Amber added.

"A dog," said Daniel.

"A cow," she wailed. "Mooo!" And she fell against him laughing joyously. Their laughter rang around the walls, and as Amber exalted in her happinessshe thought of how her lonely flat had never known such a sound before. While their laughter gradually subsided they embraced one another more tightly, until everything was still, and in the silence that ensued they clung to each other needfully, gently rocking and, for a time, immersed in their private thoughts.

After what seemed a long time, Daniel said, "But first, I suppose we ought to get married."

Amber startled him with the quickness of her movement. In an instant her mouth covered his, with a kiss so warm and heartfelt that he felt his mind begin to reel.

She released him, making their lips part with an exaggerated smacking sound, and looked down at him with glistening eyes.

"Gadzooks!" Daniel expressed in astonishment. "Those lips are dangerous. I damn near blacked out."

Amber regarded him with unbridled affection. "That's how much I love you, and there's a lot more where that comes from." "I take it that means you agree with my proposal?"

"Oh no you don't," she admonished. "That means I accept your proposal. You proposed to me and I condescended to accept. I suppose I might make a half-way decent husband out of you, with a little work."

" You've got hopes," he countered. "Us ornery criminal types don't take too well to domestication."

"Ooo, that's right'. I forgot you're a big bad bank robber. How will I ever sleep at night, knowing you're under the same roof?"

"What makes you think you'd get any sleep?" he grinned mischievously and twisted quickly to reverse their positions, pinning her, laughing and struggling under him as he sat upULJKW and began unfastening her blouse.

"What do you think you're doing, you naughty bank robber?" she grinned, her efforts to resist.

"Don't you know when you're being ravished, woman? I'm ravishing you."

"Oh. But can't you ravish me later?"

After opening her blouse, he unfastened the bra to begin fondling her breasts. "State your case quickly, woman, I'm getting warmed up." Amber groaned with pleasure, then clamped her hands over his. "The movie. We're going to. . . ah, cuddle with a movie. You'll spoil it. Aaaa-ooh." She reached up behind his neck and pulled him to her. "Don't, Dan. I want it to be a romantic evening. You'll have to wait. Ooo, now you've made me all tingly," she said with a wriggle, and hugged Daniel's face against her breast.

"If this is meant to cool me down, hon, I've got news for you." Amber giggled and lifted his head. "Can you wait, my love? It'll be more fun after we've eaten and cleaned up and settled in for the night."

"I have a will of iron," he replied, rolling his eyes to suggest the opposite. "Can't say I'm particularly hungry, though."

"Me neither," Amber agreed. "But how about some of mum's yummy pie with cream?

"Perfect!"

"And I'm in need of a shower," she smirked. "Being a nature girl can get kind of messy. Come and have a shower with me?"

"Now there's a good idea," he enthused, and he moved quickly to scoop her up in his arms and carried her off, laughing, towards the bathroom.

Amber suggested they set up the television and video-player in her bedroom, pointing out how much cosier that would be, and Daniel had agreed, cheerfully taking care of the lifting and carrying part while Amber made a game of supervising him. He sat at the end of the bed, searching through the collection of tapes, trying to make a selection he thought they might both enjoy.

"Macbeth?"

"It's a bit heavy, isn't it?" Amber called from the kitchen, where she stood in a short, satin robe, slicing a large portion of pie for Daniel. She smiled to herself. "We could drive to a video store and get you a Rocky movie?"

"Ha-ha, very funny. Perhaps Bambi or Thelma and Louise for you.

Hey! You've got Blade Runner. You want to watch Blade Runner?" "Okay. It's kind of moody, don't you think so?"

"Yeah, in a bleak, sombre, oppressive sort of way. Do androids dream of electric sheep?"

"Philip K. Dick," Amber called back. "Brilliant. I've got the book on my shelf. That's why I bought the movie."

"The extended version is the best."

"That is the director's cut," Amber countered, entering the bed-room, carrying two bowls of pie and cream. "You ready for this?" "Am I ever." He loaded the cassette and slide across to the side of the bed to switch on the lamp. "Atmosphere," he grinned.

Amber used her elbow to switch off the main light. "That's nice." She sat at the edge of the bed. "Here, take this." Offering him his bowl she climbed backwards onto the bed and made herself comfortable. "Hit it, maestro."

Daniel picked up the remote and started the tape running, leaned back into the pillows and chopped off a piece of pie with his spoon.

"This is the life, ain't it? And we've got the whole night and all of tomorrow to ourselves."

"Yeah, this is great," Amber agreed, sidling up close to him."

~

Beyond the bedroom window the evanescent glow of twilight gave way to the fall of night, and the last of the day's beach-goers collected up their possessions in preparation of returning, sun wearied and satisfied, to their homes.

The lights along the now deserted jetty lit the structure in a way that made it appear a strangely anomalous form a skeleton of some great prehistoric lizard, lying supine, its spined vertebrae driven into the bay floor to hold it raised above a dark, lustrous surface. And above the hills, to the east, the waning moon lifted above the silhouetted ridge-top, shining like an ancient golden talisman before a flame, broken at one edge, it's arcane symbols impressed across the ages-old terrain, foreboding behind the wisps of cloud which chased across its path to flush its face incarnadine.

All but one had departed from the beach. A lone figure moving easily over the sand beside the water's edge. Jack emerged from under the skeletal form and halted to observe the ascending, ruddy moon. After a short pause he pushed his hands into the pockets of his sweater and continued on, his eyes wide and searching, probing the night as if for some lurking presence, something demanding vigilance lest it pounce from the surrounding darkness upon an unwary soul.

The warm breeze moved off the land and out across the water. He could smell the sickly odours coming from the kitchens of the hotel and restaurant, the smell of warm bitumen too, and he thought of how it must have been in the time of his ancestors, imagining the cheerful glow of campfires along the beach, the aroma of baking fish, abalone, cockles and quiet conversations spoken in a tongue now forever lost to the region.

It was only a vague sense of resentment which unsettled him, but even that he quickly dispelled with a deep-drawn breath and exhalation, freeing himself of what he knew to be a troublesome affliction. After all, the white fellah's culture and the modern world were not all-pervasive. He even felt sad for those lives which were deprived of communion with the earth on which they walked. A snake without a tongue, he compared; a bat without its chirp. Was it any wonder they were such a crazy lot?

Drawing level with Ocean9iew Flats he looked across to notice a single, low-lit room at one end of Amber's unit the flicker of a television screen behind the curtains of her bedroom window. Them two okay tonight, he observed with a chuckle.

His attention was drawn to a car along the esplanade. It slowed as it neared the flats, stopped for a moment, then pulled purposefully into the driveway to park behind Amber's red Renault. Two men in suits got out of the car and walked towards the front door. He knew coppers when he saw them.

~

"Oh, darn," Amber groaned as the headlights reflected behind her curtains. "That'll be mum again, I bet."

She rolled out of Daniel's arms to the edge of the bed, and stood to adjust her short robe, pulling the belt tight around her waist. "I hope nothing's wrong."

"No. Probably just bringing us more food," Daniel grinned. "I'll pause the movie and wait here, okay?"

"Sure. Let me answer the door dressed like this," she chided, pulling down at the hem to try effect greater coverage. There was a rap at the door. "All right, I'm coming!" she called, sounding annoyed.

She hurried down the passage and up to the door, opened it and found herself smiling at two complete strangers.

"Oh!" she let out in surprise, and quickly positioned herself behind the door.

"Miss Amber Powell?" said Gasgoyne. He produced his badge from his breast pocket. "Detective Gasgoyne, CID, and this is detective March. We'd like to talk to you."

While the two detectives watched, Amber's face drained of colour. Gasgoyne sneered in pleasure, recognising at once the he had seen through his career. Before her disconcertion wore off he took the opportunity to push past her, with March close at his heels. At the centre of the roomhe turned and faced Amber as she reluctantly closed the door. The fear in her face filled him with confidence.

"You know what this is about then," March intoned Amber shook her head, holding closed the collar of her robe. "No." "I think you would be more comfortable if you came and sat down," Gasgoyne instructed, indicating the armchair furtherest from the door.

She moved slowly, unwillingly across the room to sit in the chair. Now Gasgoyne stood regarding her in her disadvantaged position. He sneered at the way she modestly tugged at the hem of her short vestment. This was going to be easy, he knew.

"Three o'clock, Monday morning," he said, and paused for effect.

"I wonder if you could tell us what you were doing at that time?"

Amber attempted to meet his eyes. "Why would you want to know that?" she replied, her voice almost failing.

"If you could just answer the question, Miss, perhaps we won't need to take up much more of your time."

"I was asleep in my bed," she replied quickly, looking from one face to the other.

"You didn't decide to take a stroll at that time, or maybe a drive in your car?"

"I told you already. I was asleep."

Gasgoyne nodded imperiously. "So you did. I just wanted to give you a chance to think it over, that's all."

"Look," Amber rallied. "I don't know what this is about, but I don't appreciate you coming into my home asking impertinent questions. I'd like you to leave."

Gasgoyne chuckled contemptuously. "Yes, I bet you would." "Hey, check these out!" March stood over by the front window, beside the set of Japanese swords. He bent and lifted the short sword from the rack. "Nifty," he said appreciatively, as he slid the blade partially from its sheath to inspect the finely honed edge. "Gosh, it's very sharp. Is this what you used?"

Amber remained silent. Increasing distress was evident in her face. "All right," said Gasgoyne, becoming stern. "Let's cut the bullshit, shall we? We know you were out in your carearly Monday morning.

Where did you go?"

Amber was too afraid to speak and could only shake her head. "Last chance, lady," Gasgoyne stated flatly. "I can arrest you right now on suspicion, then we can do all this back at the station. Would you rather do it that way?"

"I don't know what you're talking about," she responded desperately. "Arrest me for what? What do you think I've done?"

"You're not helping yourself," March chimed in, approaching her with the sword still in his hand. "It doesn't help to lie. You'll feel much better if you share you're terrible secret with someone. It has been a great burden, hasn't it? You can tell us, we understand these things. Was it a jealousy thing?"

Amber stared at him, aghast, while her world seemed to crumble and fall around her. Amid her devastationonly one thought seemed to preserve her tenuous hold on reality, and that thought was the most terrible of all. She was on the very brink of being torn away from the man she loved, her one precious love, to be locked away in a prison cell, alone in her own private hell.

Gasgoyne could restrain himself no longer. He took the sword from March and withdrew the blade, turned it slowly, making the light reflect in Amber's face. She didn't blink, merely watched it as though she were fascinated.

"You cut Lester Bishop with this, didn't you," he said just loud enough to be heard.

Amber stiffened at the mention of the name, there was a startled look in her eyes which was met with dispassionate certainty in Gasgoyne's eyes. She knew he knew. It was over. She slumped in the chair and stared blankly at the feet of the two policemen.

"He raped me," she said quietly.

A grin of victory twisted Gasgoyne's features. "Amber Powell, I am placing you under arrest for the murder of Barry Ivan Curino and for the murder of Lester Bishop. I'm required to tell you-"

"Not another word, and not a move," Daniel enunciated clearly and threateningly from the end of the passage where he stood with a gun levelled at the pair.

For a moment there was no sound or movement from anyone. Gasgoyne's jaw had dropped in surprise. Amber got quickly out of the chair and rushed to Daniel's side.

"Don't even think about it," Daniel warned, presuming his captives would be entertaining ideas of making some sort of move. "Give me an excuse and I'll drop you in your tracks. You," he said to March. "Hands on your head. And you, slowly, open up your coat." Gasgoyne complied, exposing a holstered revolver under his left arm.

"Remove it, left-handed, and slowly," Daniel ordered. "Toss it on the chair." He watched closely as Gasgoyne did as instructed. "Now make like your pal and get your hands up on your head. Now it's your turn," he said, addressing March. "Don't go risking your life by being stupid. Gun on the chair."

"You're making a mistake, fellah," Gasgoyne said anxiously. "Yeah? Well, just make sure you don't make any, all right? Now, both of you, over here and sit on the couch."

As they obeyed, he circled around to stand before them. "Good. Now get your hands in your pockets, and the first one to pull a hand out is going to be a very unhappy chappy, understand?"

He looked up to Amber who still stood by the passage. Her eyes were wide and fixed on the gun in his hand. "I didn't know what else to do," he shrugged.

"What do we do now?" she replied.

"You get smart and give this away before it goes any further," Gasgoyne growled.

"Shut it," Daniel snapped. He looked back to Amber, feeling as uncertain as she looked helpless. "Damn," he cursed fiercely.

"Oh, Dan. What are we going to do?"

"This is all new to me, too. I think we're supposed to tie them up. Got any rope?"

She thought for a moment. "I've got a ball of string?"
"That ought to do the trick."

Gasgoyne turned his head to talk over his shoulder to Amber. "You going to let your boyfriend put himself in prison because of you? Is that what you want?"

The question stopped her. Ambivalence flickered in her face as she clenched her hands against her chest. "No," she appealed to Daniel.

"That's not what I want. I can't think straight."

"It's okay, hon. This is my decision and you couldn't change my mind even if you wanted to. Get me the string and we'll work something out after we get these clods stowed away."

Turning back to the policemen, he said, "Don't get the idea I won't put a slug in either of you, because you'd be dead wrong. But if you behave yourselves, you'll have an interesting anecdote to tell your friends and families. Got it?"

March nodded agreeably while Gasgoyne merely glowered.

Amber brought the ball of string from the kitchenand he handed her the gun to keep trained on them while he began binding their feet. Gasgoyne looked more un-comfortable to see the gun in Amber's hands. "You're not thinking very clearly, are you. If you were, you'd realize you don't stand a chance. Where are you going to run to? You won't last three days. And Dan here has just earned himself ten years jail, unless you start making the right choices. It's up to you."

Amber stood chewing her bottom lip, afraid that any moment her knees were going to buckle under her.

"I'm sure we appreciate your concern," Daniel remarked, tying off around Gasgoyne's ankles and moving to March. "You'll have to do better than that."

"He's right though," March chipped in. "You'll be hunted from one end of the country to the other. You'll be looking over your shoulder every minute, never quite sure if someone hasn't recognised you. I wouldn't want to live like that."

"You've been watching too much television. Australia's Most Wanted," he expressed disdainfully, twisting March around to begin binding his wrists behind his back. "There must be a thousand people in this country, right now, who have been on the run for years. The only way to get caught is to run foul of the law again. I'm not that dumb."

"You have a record," Gasgoyne probed. "That'll make our job easier."

"It might, if I had a record," Daniel grinned.

"A man and a woman travelling together are much easier to trace," March tried. "I'd say forty-eight hours, tops."

"I'd say you're both full of shit," Daniel replied, pushing Gasgoyne forward to start on his wrists. "If you're so damned efficient, what are you doing tied up on this couch?"

No reply was offered, and Daniel finished binding Gasgoyne's wrists and pushed him back in his seat. He looked at them thoughtfully for a moment, and Amber stepped over beside him to hug his arm, the gun now lowered beside her leg.

"Everything was just coming right," Daniel mused.

"She killed two men," Gasgoyne countered. "And you could be next, she's obviously psycho."

"I'm not psycho!" Amber erupted, lifting the gun. "They were cruel to me."

"But you butchered them, for Christ's sake. Don't you understand what you've done? Look," he said appeasingly. "If those men mistreated you, it'll go some way in remitting your sentence. And with a good psychiatrist on your side–"

"No. You're lying," Amber protested. "I could never prove my side of it. I've always known that. You're just saying that so you can lock me away in some horrid prison and let me rot."

"But–"

"Knock it off," Daniel cut in. "We both know she's right. This thing is going to have to run its course, that's all." He turned to Amber. "You got anything more you want to say to them?"

She shook her head, then stopped, realising there was something. "How did you know?"

Gasgoyne looked smug. "You parked right outside Curino's house. That was stupid. Someone remembered the licence plate and we found a strand of your hair inside. If you hadn't denied being there, you might have squeezed out of it with a good enough story. Bishop was just an educated guess. You're not a very good liar, girlie."

"Okay boys, the discussion is over," Daniel announced, and grabbing Gasgoyne by his lapels and pulling him out of the couch, he dragged him down the passage and propped him against the toilet bowl. After repeating the procedure with March, he removed the inside door handle while Amber brought him a roll of masking tape. "I hope neither of you has sinus trouble?" he inquired, and when neither responded, he taped their mouths and closed the door on them.

Returning to the living room, he found Amber sitting in the middle of the couch, bent forwards with her head resting on her knees and hugging her legs. He rounded the couch and sat down beside her, put his arm around her shoulders to lend support.

"They tell me Cairns is nice this time of year."

Amber turned her head to look at him. "I can't let you do this. I can't let you ruin your life, too."

"My life was already ruined, Amber. I told you that. You had better pack yourself a bag and put on some clothes. We're going to be travelling all night."

She sat up. "You take the car, Dan. You'll stand a better chance without me."

He understood immediately. "Oh," he said calmly. "And what will you do?"

"I'll stay here with them, give you enough time to go somewhere. They might not think it's so important to catch you if they've got me. It's me they're after."

Daniel sighed and leaned back into the couch. "Do you know what you're saying?"

Amber nodded, her face beginning to contort with the effort of containing her distress.

"Amber, I can't leave without you. How can you think that I could?" "But they'll put you in jail," she whimpered.

He sat forward again, gripped her arms firmly and gave her a gentle shake, urg-ing her to maintain her control. "To hell with that, that's not the point. Christ, they'll throw the god-damn key away on you! I can't bear the thought of that, can you?"

Amber shook her head dolefully. "No, I can't go to jail. It would be too dreadful being away from you."

"Well thanks for that," he said bitterly. "That's just what I'm trying to say. If you go to jail, what will I do? Start drifting again? Every bloody second I'd be thinking about you, with misery gnawing at my gluts. I can't go on without you."

"Yes," Amber sniffled. "That's just how it would be for me, too." "Then why the hell would you even consider giving yourself up?" "I'm sorry, my love. I was being selfish again. I thought if you got away," she nodded towards Daniel's gun resting on the coffee table.

"I can't take the hurt any more."

"No, honey, don't do that to me." He took her hands and held them together between his. "Don't ever go where I can't follow, remember?"

She smiled sadly, nodded. Tears were beginning to spill down her cheeks.

"There's nowhere else to go," she said miserably.

"Hobart, Bunbury, Gunda-bloody-gai," he replied, imparting an affectionate smile. "We can still be together."

To thisAmber lowered her head and began to sob quietly. Daniel leaned her towards him and hugged her tightly. "It's okay, hon, you don't have to go anywhere you don't want to."

"When I was a little girl," she said, her voice muffled against his chest. "I used to dream that some day I would meet someone like you and we'd be married and live in a big house on top of a hill. You can't know what it meant to me when you asked me to marry you. It was a dream come true. I love you, Dan. Thank-you for making me feel like that happy little girl again."

He responded by tightening his arms around her. "I never thought it was possible to love anyone the way I love you. One thing is certain.

Whatever we do, we do together. I'm not going to be left alone in this world again."

Tears streamed from Amber's eyes as she raised her head. "We'll never part," she vowed, looking pleadingly into his eyes.

"Never," he answered solemnly, and bent to kiss her.

Only after a long time did they separate, and while Amber strengthened her embrace and rested her head on his shoulder, Daniel stared at his gun on the coffee table.

Amber groaned, long and wearily, an expression of frustration and futility. "Oh, Dan, it's all over. There's no future any more. I just want to be here in your arms forever, where I feel safe and loved. I wish I could fall asleep here with you, and wake up in the morning and find it was all just a bad dream. It was only this morning we woke up together, such a short time. It seems so cruel. I woke up knowing I was in love with you, and it was like being in heaven. Do you believe in heaven, Dan?"

"Yes, I do," he answered as confidently as he could manage. "And we're meant to be together, aren't we? That's how it feels to me."

"Yes, honey. We're meant to be together. Nothing can separate us now."

She nestled against him, and for a time there was a deep silence while each delved among their private thoughts. Time felt to take pause, as if the moment had been somehow isolated from the natural world, dislocated from the temporal flow upon which the rest of creation was carried inexorably on, traversing the countless tomorrows.

Amber lifted her head and stretched to kiss his temple, and stroked his face as she studied his features. "Your eye has gone down," she observed. "You're healing very quickly."

"I didn't tell you, did I? The barman said I broke that big galoot's nose."

Hooray for you," Amber cheered. "That'll teach him to mess with my man."

Daniel smiled affectedly, unable to manufacture a reply.

"My adorable man," Amber followed up, and watched as sundry emotions passed fleetingly over his face. "It hurts me to see you so troubled," she said at last. "If you don't want to come with me, it's all right. I understand. I'm sorry, Dan, but I have to."

"I think this is the way it was meant to be for us," he replied earnestly. "Are you frightened?"

"No, I'm not frightened while you're with me. I'm okay. I think I might even be happy, but that must sound terribly stupid."

"Not so stupid. Not stupid at all, in fact. I don't know why, but it feels perfectly right to me. I think I've been walking this knife-edge for years, and I'm tired of fighting for balance."

"Yes, that's a good way of saying it. That's how I feel, too.

I'm sorry for mum and dad, though. How will they ever be able to understand?"

Daniel suddenly straightened. "Bloody hell. I'm sorry, honey. I hadn't thought. . ."

"I'll have to write them a letter," she said, placing a hand against his chest. "I'll explain everything so they can see it was for the best. I'd like to do that now, Dan. While there's still plenty of time."

"Of course," he agreed, then winced. "Christ, they'll blame me!" "No, my love. I'll explain everything, the way it is. It'll be all right, I promise. Trust me."

He nodded, knowing that he had to accept this. Even so, it was a great burden. "Do you mind if I go outside while you do that? I need some air."

"Go ahead," she answered caressing his cheek. "I'll come out when I've finished."

Daniel stepped out into the night and looked around, waiting for his eyes to ad-just to the darkness. When the white sand of the beach grew more distinct, he followed the driveway down and crossed the road, coming up to lean against the timber railing by the foreshore.

Far out on the water, navigation beacons flashed pin-points of bright light in a randomly changing sequence, creating a stroboscopic effect which fascinated the eye. His mind, he noted, was being merciful. There were no uncertainties now, no accusations of failure or stinging self-recriminations as might have been expected; only a calm reali-sation, an acceptance that the struggle would soon cease, and in that there was undeniable relief.

The irony of his and Amber's circumstance was no longer a bitter irony. It was only a seeming irony, born of an unaccountable quirk of fortune which, along the tangled threads of action and interaction, had conspired to hurriedly weave their damaged lives together in time for this unforeseen resolution.

There was a subtle elegance in it, he saw. It was the right and only direction left open to them. Alone, there was little doubt, their lives would have become an unbear-able torment. Together they had combined to fill the void which dwelt in each of them. This was the way it had to be. He had never been more sure of anything in his life; and, he suddenly realised, smiling sardoni-cally to himself as he recognised the twist, seldom had he ever felt the thrill of life more acutely than he did now, as every passing moment brimmed with a thousand piquant subtleties.

Movement in the darkness caught his attention. He turned to look along the road where it terminated against a large sand dune. Someone moving quickly down its slope, then hopping the rail and walking towards him. He watched for a while before turning again to the winking beacons, inhaled the sea air.

"G'day, Daniel."

He turned again to peer towards the approaching figure. "It's me, Jack."

Jack had almost reached him before he recognised the smiling face beneath the shaggy hair.

"Hi. Perfect night for a stroll."

"Yeah, too good a night for being indoors." Jack nodded towards the flat as he came to a halt. "Coppers, eh?"

Discomfort registered on Daniel's face. "How did you know?" "I seen 'em drive in. Soon as they got out and I saw them suits, I knew. I guess it ain't my business but coppers always mean trouble," he said, trying to be tactful and looking across the way to where their car was parked.

"Yeah, ain't that the truth," Daniel replied feigning amusement. "It's about the store window being busted. A goodwill visit, I suppose you could call it. Discussing security measures and the like."

Jack cast him a curious glance before commenting genially. "Looked more like a bust, the way they pushed through the door. They been in there a long time. I been waitin' to see." When Daniel's face reflected displeasure, Jack added. "Me and Amber been friends a long time. We look out for each other."

"Hey, I've been wondering," said Daniel, manoeuvring away from the subject. "The other night when we met, you wished me good luck. Why?"

Jack shrugged and looked to the sea. "Don't you know by now?" "Perhaps, but I'd like to hear it from you."

Jack turned back to Daniel and scanned his face. "Amber's got troubles. She's taken some pretty bad things, you know? I knew you were someone who could help. I seen it straight away."

"Help? How?"

"If you don't know, Daniel, I can't say. Hey, they're beauty scars you've got," he evaded, and imparted an enigmatic glance. "If I was there, I reckon it would have about evened the odds. You need someone to watch your back in a pub fight, you must know that."

Had there been an intentional double meaning there, or was it purely his imagination. . . perhaps even paranoia? Putting aside the assumption that Jack couldn't possibly know the situation, he could almost swear he had just offered help.

"Jack," he began hesitantly. "I get the feeling we're both circling the same carcass here, but neither of us are game enough to approach it. You might not understand this, but time is running out, so if what I'm about to say doesn't make sense to you, we'll just drop the whole subject. Okay?"

Jack agreed with a barely perceivable nod.

After a brief hesitation, Daniel said, "Barry Curino. . . and a guy named Bishop."

Jack acknowledged the names with an emphatic nod. "Yeah. I thought it was that." He paused awhile, but decided to go on. "I tried to let her tell me, but it was too messed up in her head. That's why I thought you might be the one. It's good she told you. I didn't like to see her with all that bad trouble inside, but I couldn't ask, either, you know?"

"Yeah," Daniel acknowledged, and he was pensively silent for a time. "But as I think you have already gathered, things haven't worked out especially well. We've got two coppers hog-tied in the loo."

Jack subdued a smile. "What you gonna do with 'em?"

"I want them set free in the morning. I was wondering if you could see to it. Maybe call the local station in the morning?"

"Sure. You makin' a run for it?"

Daniel's reply was awhile in coming. Jack noted his difficulty. "Yeah," he said at last. "We're going where no bastard can separate us." Jack cocked his head to one side as he considered this, and Daniel had the disconcerting impression of having just confessed everything, although he had thought his reply obscure enough. Jack's countenance, however, expressed nothing less than total understanding.

Both men turned at the sound of Amber's front door being closed, and they watched as Amber made her way down the driveway and across the road.

"Hello, Jack," she said, coming up to them. "Where are you walking to tonight?"

"I was going down the coast to see some friends, but I saw the coppers pull into your place, so I waited to see if you were okay."

Amber looked to Daniel for any indication of what he might have told Jack.

"Jack is a very perceptive man," he said. "But I'm sure I don't have to tell you that."

Amber's lips tightened, forming a contrite smile. She hugged Daniel's arm. "Jack, I didn't know how to. . ." she faltered. "If there was anybody I could talk to. . ."

"Don't worry," he responded with a shrug, and focussing his attention above Amber's head, he pointed.

Daniel and Amber turned to see the ascending moon, its face obscured by a reddish huewhile around it glowed a silvery nimbus.

"It's so beautiful," Amber said softly. "I've never seen it like that before."

"The serpent swallows its tail. No beginning and no end," Jack told them. "Red is the colour for a safe journey. That moon is for you two. A journey of the spirit."

Amber looked at Daniel in astonishment and tacit rebuke, then turned to Jack.

"He didn't tell me. He didn't have to." "Then how. .?

Jack's face was guileless. "I know where you're going," he said, for the first time exhibiting a trace of emotion. "Daniel calls it the place you can't be separated. I know where that place is."

The trio remained silent. Without a word the covenant was struck, and they turned again to observe the celestial anomalyrising into the night sky like a fabulous jewel.

"Did you write the letter?" Daniel quietly asked Amber.

Amber nodded.

"I was thinking. . . . I'd like your parents to have the money to repair their home, maybe even buy a new one. There's plenty."

"That would be nice," Amber replied, squeezing his arm. "Thank-you, Dan."

He turned to Jack. "I have a bag inside with two hundred and fifteen thousand dollars in it. Amber has written a letter for her parents. Could you deliver the letter and two hundred thousand to Beth and Ted, maybe put it somewhere they'll find it?"

"Sure, but what about the other fifteen thousand?"

"Buy yourself a new pair of runners. Those ones look like they've crossed the Nullarbor six times."

~

Three hours after midnight, Amber and Daniel emerged from her flat and walked down onto the beach. Hand in hand they followed the water's edge towards the mouth of the Wunjunjurra, beneath the stars and the moon with its lambent reflection dancing over the surface of the bay. They walked in silence, not through sorrow but with a shared sense of predestination which set every nerve singing and imbued every perception with exquisite clarity.

Today their world had been rejuvenated, once again becoming the wondrous place remembered from childhood; the ether thrilling their senses, alive and brimming with vital urgencies and undisclosed promises; and from above, the blazing heavens seemed to whisper ancient secrets from across the intervening distance, telling of endurance, abundance, harmony within staggering complexity. . .and the merest suggestion of mind.

End

From The Author

Star-crossed was the last of the first four books I wrote as what I considered my writing apprenticeship. I had written a collection of short stories and found I very much enjoyed writing, and that I might even be okay at it. I had, thus far, written a short story collection, a crime adventure, a pair of novellas combined in one book which covered real life disguised as fiction, and then this, my training in writing romance. I was never a fan of romance novels, in fact I had never read one, but I knew that if I wanted to hone any talent I might have as a writer, I must learn to write stories in different genres.

I was so surprised to discover how much I enjoyed writing this one. It came easily once I had pictured the stage upon which the story was to be set, in this case a small, costal town very similar to one I knew intimately. I populated the town with character types readily identifiable to me. The guesthouse, too, was one I had frequented as a wayward teenager who was more interested in becoming a musician than finishing his education.

The characters of Ted and Beth who own and run the guesthouse are based on the two wonderful people who made me welcome when life was getting on top of me at age seventeen. Gordon, the musician, who, in this story, boards downstairs in a small room, is based on a real character. Ted and Beth's son is based on a real person, a man who passed several years ago, and whom, from the time depicted in this story, became a lifelong friend.

It bothered me some, that I borrowed so heavily from real life in writing this story, but I've since learned that this is what writers do. It was impossible not to. Once I had imagined the protagonist arriving in town on bus during an exceptionally hot summer's day, this story just took off. It wrote itself. All I needed to do was to observe and listen to the characters, recording everything said and done. Once emotions came into play it accelerated and I could scarcely keep up the pace. I stayed at my desk without sleep for a tad over thirty-six hours, recording everything that played out, and it was done. My first crime-romance novel. Although, I never thought of publishing at that time.

The story has received absolutely black and white, polarized feedback from reviewers. Some find it defies credence, stretching suspended disbelief too far. Others adore it, being moved to tears by the situation portrayed and the emotions at play. The odd thing is, the tale correlates extremely closely with real events, much of it from my own, personal experience. I occasionally re-read this story just to remind myself of who I once was, and to see if I am still moved by the powerful memories of my youth. I am.

I hope you find it enjoyable.

www.ingramcontent.com/pod-product-compliance
Lightning Source LLC
Chambersburg PA
CBHW031259120726
47906CB00003B/807